This intruder was not exactly a stranger.

His slow scrutiny of her from head to toe and back again was exactly what Nicola remembered from their first meeting. He pushed himself away from the open doorway, unbuttoning his velvet jerkin. "Try me," Fergus said quietly, describing circles with his rapier point.

Her reply was to put her sword at arm's length and to touch the point of his with hers, locking her deep brown stare with his hard gray one, but knowing in her vitals that this would be no pushover.

The end came well before she could score a hit. She could see the fearlessness in his eyes, which, as a child, she had both admired and found intimidating.

"Well," he said, watching the torrent of dark brown hair fall across her face, "some things have changed for the better, but not the temper, it seems. You'll have to deal with that, my lady, if you want to play men's games."

* * *

His Duty, Her Destiny
Harlequin® Historical #802—May 2006

Praise for Juliet Landon

Juliet Landon

His Duty, Her Destiny

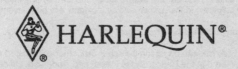

HARLEQUIN®

TORONTO • NEW YORK • LONDON
AMSTERDAM • PARIS • SYDNEY • HAMBURG
STOCKHOLM • ATHENS • TOKYO • MILAN • MADRID
PRAGUE • WARSAW • BUDAPEST • AUCKLAND

ISBN 0-373-29402-6

HIS DUTY, HER DESTINY

Please address questions and book requests to:
Harlequin Reader Service
U.S.: 3010 Walden Ave., P.O. Box 1325, Buffalo, NY 14269
Canadian: P.O. Box 609, Fort Erie, Ont. L2A 5X3

Chapter One

Flinging her thick brown plait over her shoulder, Nicola picked up her rapier and turned to face her opponent with a disarming smile. 'Ready?' she said, sweetly. The young man had put himself on the line by telling her she knew nothing about the Italian style of fencing, not thinking that she could produce a pair of rapiers she'd been using for years. He should have known better.

'What do I do with it?' she asked, innocently.

The young man smiled. 'Your best, my lady,' he said.

'Shall we take these silly guards off the points, then?'

The smile disappeared. 'It's not usual, in practice.'

'Oh, then let's be unusual, for a change.'

'Are you sure, my lady?'

'Quite sure. There, that's better. Now, on guard. Is that what they say?' He had been a nuisance for weeks, this young man: it was time to get rid of him. He could not be more than her own twenty-four years.

Fencing with an unprotected point obviously concerned him, for he was defensive, extremely wary and immediately rattled by her obvious familiarity with the weapon. Only aristocrats took this kind of fencing seriously, and most of them had learned in either France, Germany or Italy; very few in England. But women, never.

Nicola, however, had fenced with her four brothers since she was old enough to stand; she was naturally nimble, graceful, quick-thinking and, most of all, had learned from an early age to hold her own against men. In a house full of them, there had been no place for a faint-hearted woman.

Clearly taken by surprise at her sudden swift attack, his defence came a split second too late and his rapier went flying through the air to slide across the stone-flagged floor of the hall well before he'd had time to settle into a rhythm. It was a very undignified beginning.

'Oh, dear,' said Nicola. 'D'ye want to try again?'

'You've had some practice,' he said, accusingly, picking up his rapier. 'You might have said.'

'I *did* say, last evening. You didn't believe me. On guard.'

He started the next bout with more determination, but with a heavy chip on his shoulder, wondering how this lovely woman, whom men held only in their fantasies, could have learned how to best him at a man's game. His lack of concentration did him no favours, and almost immediately he was being forced backwards again under a charge that for sheer speed left him no time to recover.

Then, for a second time, his rapier took wings, clattering across the almost deserted hall to settle at the feet of a tall man whose powerful shoulders propped up the door-frame and whose expression was less than sympathetic. He looked at the swordsman pityingly and placed a high-booted foot upon the long narrow blade, shaking his head.

Without a word, the young man aimed a snappy bow in Nicola's direction and stalked off to the end of the hall, banging the great door behind him.

The point of Nicola's rapier had touched the floor in slow decline before it dawned on her that this intruder was not exactly a stranger and that his slow arrogant scrutiny of her from head to toe and back again was exactly what she remembered of their first meeting when she had been a mere eleven-year-old and he an uppity sixteen who had made no effort to endear himself to her then, either. On the contrary, she could still recall his frightening incivility, despite the protection of her brothers.

He pushed himself away from the open doorway, unbuttoning his velvet jerkin and sloughing it from his arms like a discarded skin, then dropping it to the floor. Picking up the rapier, he came to stand in a puddle of light from the large bay window, his eyes remaining on Nicola, but giving away nothing of his surprise at the change in her. 'Try me,' he said quietly, describing circles with the point. 'I don't use a guard either. Not even in practice.'

In the intervening years his voice had changed from that of a wobbling Scots-accented baritone to a rich bass, though he made the invitation sound more like a command, which, Nicola remembered, had always been his style. No matter that her family could boast an ancestry to rival any in England, this man's family had exceeding wealth, which, he had been led to believe, gave him the edge. She would show him how wrong he could be.

Her reply was to put up her rapier at arm's length and to touch the point of his with hers, locking her deep brown stare with his hard grey one, but knowing in her vitals that this would be no push-over like the last. This man was five years older than her, for a start. She was tall for a woman, but Sir Fergus Melrose was taller, with the physique of an athlete and the healthy tan of one who had caught the sea breeze and seen the world. She was slender, too, but her opponent's wrists were twice as thick as hers, and his lithe, tautly muscled body was better practiced in the arts of warfare, even the less usual ones.

She had dressed in men's doeskin breeches, a shirt and short padded jerkin in order to do justice to the young man's challenge issued last night at supper, and though she had given no thought to the indisputable fact that she was just as fascinating in this garb as in her finest gown, neither did she realise that now there was an androgynous element about her that any man would find unsettling. As had been proved. Her abundant dark hair was still contained within one plait, but no one would have been fooled into mistaking her body for that of a lad when her unbelted jerkin swung open at each move and the roundness of her hips filled the breeches as no man's ever could.

The sleeves of Sir Fergus's linen shirt were rolled up to reveal his wrists, and now he pulled at the cord of his neck to open the front, a trick her brothers had tried in the past to deflect her attention. She was not caught off guard as he had intended, and although she made no headway at all in the first few moments, nor did she allow him through her defence.

As she had done, he held back, hoping to lure her into a false confidence, though she knew this to be a ploy too, and would not be drawn. But soon she began to tire as the bout continued and, as his pressure became more intense, perspiration began to run into her eyes and stick her soft linen shirt to her chest. She found his style intimidating, his skill with a sword far superior to hers, his energy phenomenal, for he was not even perspiring, and instead of anticipating his next move as she should have been doing, she could not help but wonder how much longer she could continue before her rapier would go the same way as her previous opponent's.

After a vigorous exchange, she allowed her point to lower and saw to her surprise that he was changing his rapier over to his left hand, tapping the point of it under hers to make her lift it again, goading her, telling her that he could beat her left-handed. It was a disconcerting move, and the end came well before she could score a hit or even remove the patronising smile from his face.

Panting, and aching with fatigue, she made a mistake at last and felt the fierce sting of his point catch beneath her jerkin and slash like a razor through the thin stuff of her shirt. She leapt backwards, dropping her rapier and holding her breast with one hand, fending him off with the other as he closed in too quickly for her to evade him. Backing her against the panelled wall, he held her there with his body, his face so close that she could see the steel-grey fearlessness through his eyes which, as a child, she had both admired and found intimidating.

'Well,' he said, watching the torrent of dark brown hair fall across her face, 'some things have changed for the better, but not the temper, it seems. You'll have to deal with that, my lady, if you want to play men's games.'

Her eyes blazed fiercely into his while she chafed at the shameful closeness of him and at her own stupid helplessness, her voice betraying her agitation. 'What right have you to walk unannounced and uninvited into my house? And how would *you* know what's changed?' she panted through a curtain of silky hair. 'My temper is none of your business either. Get *off* me!' She heaved at him, but he was as solid as a wall and, instead of moving, he prised the hand away from her breast, turning her palm over to reveal a sticky patch of blood upon it.

He moved back quickly to inspect the vertical slash on her shirt and the red stain that oozed through the fabric, and it was clear to her then that he had not known of this, not perhaps intended it. It had been the same when she was younger, getting hurt while trying to keep up with her brothers and him not caring of her damage, nor of the silence she had kept about her injuries, particularly to her pride.

Their fathers, close friends for years, had promised the two of them as future man and wife, but who could expect an eleven-year-old tomboy to understand or accept the implications of that? And what brash sixteen-year-old would not be more interested in the child's brothers than in her? Fergus had felt no need to pretend, having more pressing things on his mind than parents' promises.

Clutching at herself, Nicola tried to turn away, but already her legs had begun to shake with fatigue, making her stumble as he caught her quickly under her knees, tilting her body into his arms. She saw the bright window swing away over her head, then felt the sudden sting of her wound and another rush of anger that forced a strength into her arms. 'Put me down! Let me *go*, you great clod! I can manage without you. My steward will…'

But his hands and arms tightened and there was nothing she could do but suffer him to carry her, writhing and fuming with humiliation and her undone plait hanging over his arm, down the length of the hall, up a narrow staircase and through two doors. Finally, he lowered her on to her own tester bed with his arms on each side of her to prevent her from rolling away, ignoring her protests that she could manage well enough without him after all these years.

His face was at first in shadow, so she was only able to guess at the degree of concern in his eyes, or otherwise. But there was little doubt in her mind about his intentions when he caught both her wrists and, transferring them to one large strong hand, held them easily above her head and pressed them down into the soft brocade coverlet. His grip held her tight, and her breast had begun to sting like a burn.

This was as bad as anything she had suffered as a child. 'No!' she gasped, almost voiceless with fear. 'Please...no!'

'Hush, lass,' said Sir Fergus. 'I've a right to see what damage I've done, and I doubt ye're going to show me willingly, are you?'

'You have *no* right. You are not welcome here. Who asked you?'

'Your brother George invited me. I came early, that's all, and as your intended husband I claim the right to inspect the goods beforehand. Hold still.'

As he spoke, his hand was moving her jerkin aside, then the bloodstained slash of her shirt so that the whole of her right breast was revealed, scored lightly across the surface by a bright red line on the inner curve. The blood had already begun to congeal as if a string of rubies had been laid around it.

Speechless, mortified, Nicola watched his eyes in the vain hope of seeing him shamed, but what she saw was not the obnoxious young stripling of her earlier memories. Instead, here was a grown man impervious to shame whose arrogance was beyond anything she had encountered from any of her suitors. Not one of them, she thought, would have dared do such a thing to her.

He had grown even better looking in the last twelve years, his contours more chiselled, his bone structure more sculpted under the bronzed skin, the cheeks lean and blue-shadowed around his square jaw. His cap of short, almost black hair made a peak on his forehead, and a pale scar line ran beneath it, almost touching one angled eyebrow. He wore a gold ring in one ear, and he smelled of the outdoors and a hint of woodsmoke. And he had better say no more of intended husbands. Or intended wives.

'Tch!' she heard him say. 'Not too badly marked. I expect I'll still have ye, scar and all.'

'That you'll not, sir!' she snarled. 'Not if you were the last man alive in England. Now get out. This is *my* house. Get *out*!'

He did nothing to cover her up again. 'Then 'tis just as well I'm of Scotland, lass. Isn't it?' As if knowing that she would bound up like a spring to attack him, his release of her was cautious, his move backwards cat-like, taking him well out of range and halfway to the door just as her two maids entered, alerted by the sound of voices.

Fortunately, they were too late to see her roll off the bed and pull her shirt across herself, but further investigations showed that there were unusual drops of moisture hanging along the lower lids of their mistress's eyes, prevented from falling only by the thick fringe of black lashes. And then they saw the blood, and Nicola had to do some very quick thinking, in spite of feeling faint.

But the two maids could recognise a sword wound when they saw one. And so it was that only a very few people ever knew exactly what had transpired on that early morning in mid-June in the year 1473 at Lady Nicola Coldyngham's London home on Bishops-gate.

After a twelve-year absence, this was perhaps not the best way for Sir Fergus Melrose to reintroduce himself to Lady Nicola, though it typified their brief encounters in the past when invariably she had been the one to come limping home. She had been a nuisance then, a scruffy little hoyden with a too-large mouth and eyes that tilted upwards at the corners, like an imp. Now, her face had grown to accommodate the mouth more comfortably, and the pointed impish chin was the neatest he'd ever seen. But the eyes…ah, those eyes. He'd had a hard time concentrating on the sword-play with those great dark-lashed orbs sending out beams of hostility and rivalry at him, which he had purposely called temper, just to rile her more. They were eyes he could have drowned in.

It was not temper, of course, but passion and some fear, commodities he'd seen plenty of during those early days when keeping up with her adored brothers meant everything to her. Even at sixteen he'd been aware of problems, for Nicola was the product of Lord Coldyngham's third wife who had found the demands of mothering too great for her after Patrick's birth. The following years of being motherless from the age of three had had an effect on the daughter, which she had handled in the only way she understood, by being one of the sons. Fergus was both astonished and relieved to see that the strategy had done no obvious damage, though some traits still lingered, apparently.

He retraced his steps down to the great hall, though not nearly as great as the one at her family home in Wiltshire where big windows held stained glass coats of arms and heraldic crests that the Coldyngham brothers knew by heart. Though well known and respected, his own family could boast only four Scottish generations that had acquired wealth by the usual dubious means and by the shrewd business flair common to all the Melrose elders. And now he had come, at last, to make good the promise to his father last year, just before his untimely death. Nicola's eldest brother, the new Lord Coldyngham, had said he would meet him here, and Fergus felt certain Nicola would never tell her brother how she had just lost a contest. She had never been one to cry for sympathy.

I can manage without you, she had said to him. *And how would* you *know what's changed?* Again, he felt the soft weight of her in his arms and saw the forbidden fruit of her breast with its shocking stripe of red, the most beautiful and strangely moving sight he could ever remember. In twelve years it was to be expected that changes would have occurred, but never in his life would he have believed how such an unkempt and boyish lass could turn into the ravishing and fiery woman able to accept his challenge to a bout of fencing.

Her unusually physical and competitive childhood had kept her sharp and trim, yet there was now a heart-stopping vulnerability to go with the luscious curves of her body that, as a brash lad of sixteen, he had not had the wit to expect. The hardest part of the contest had been to ignore the element of sheer feminine loveliness, the slender sway and graceful dancing steps, the pull of the linen shirt across her breasts, but it was also why he had prolonged the contest when he could have ended it in seconds. Perhaps that vision of the captivating Nicola, the swanlike, pristine, unknown Nicola, was the reason for his stupid mistake at the end.

She was, naturally, still as angry and contrary as she'd been as a young lass when she had refused to conform to anyone's ideals of ladylike behaviour. Not even at eleven and twelve years old had she made the slightest effort to show him the docile good manners and obedience of a wife-in-the-making. He had never intended to oblige his father on that score, but she had done nothing to make him change his mind. Not then. Nor had he commended himself to her as he'd been instructed to do.

But if he had known how she would blossom like an exotic flower, would he have felt differently about his father's wishes? Would he have anticipated taking her to bed as he did now? Would he have looked forward to contests of fighting and loving, subduing her, making her yelp with pleasure instead of anger? God, how he wanted her. How he was intrigued by the tangled facets of her womanliness. Come what may, he would have to show her that he was not the unkind, unlikeable lout he had been all those years ago. And he had better make out a good case, here and now while he still had a chance, or she'd do something desperate rather than accept him.

Picking up his patterned velvet jerkin with the fur-trimmed sleeves, he slipped it on, pulling its lower edge down over his hips. His feathered felt hat lay upon the cushion of the window-seat where he had left it earlier, so he sat down beside it to wait for George, knowing that he'd not be long. He would want to settle this business once and for all. They had promises to keep to their fathers, George's being to see his sister taken well care of. But Fergus had been away on the high seas for some time, then up in Scotland to see to his own family affairs, and only recently had he been able to return to his house in London where his late father's ships were docked. It would have been useful, he mused, if her father had been here to help persuade her, for she would take some persuading now.

Behind him, a clatter of hooves in the courtyard announced someone's arrival, and Fergus leapt to his feet, his face beaming for the first time that morning. The door swung open. 'George...no, Lord Coldyngham now, isn't it? Well met at last, old friend,' he said.

'Fergus! No, *Sir* Fergus now, eh? Well met indeed, man. You're looking disgustingly fit. Were you not even wounded?'

They hugged and back-slapped, sizing each other up as they had done since they were lads with more rivalry than friendship in mind. 'Yes, I was,' said Fergus, tapping the tawny velvet sleeve. 'My left arm.' She had not liked it when he had changed hands, for it was less than courteous. 'I try to exercise it as much as I can. It's mending nicely.'

'Good. And the steward let you in, did he? Nicola not down yet? That's unusual. She likes being her own mistress now, Ferg.' Whether he intended it or not, there was the hint of a warning in his remark. 'Sorry to hear about your father,' he added. 'Buried at sea, was he?'

'Yes. Pirates. Last October. My lady mother sends her regards. And our condolences to you too, George. I see your father left his town house to Nicola.'

'This place?' George looked around him at the small but elegant panelled hall with a large tapestry at one end and two bay windows along one side. Above them, timber beams were painted in multi-coloured patterns, and underfoot a drop of red blood showed brightly on the stone-tiled floor. Quickly, Fergus placed his foot over it. At one end of the hall, a long table had been laid with pewter, silver, polished wood and a set of bone-handled knives. As they spoke, servants entered bearing jugs of ale, bread rolls and a dish of scrambled eggs, butter, cheese and a side of ham.

'Yes,' George said. 'Father always used it when he came to sit in parliament. He left it to Nicola for her use instead of a dowry. I suppose he thought it would give her the independence she likes, but we really didn't think she'd come to live in it full time, as she does. Oh, she has a complete household to look after all her needs,' he went on, catching Fergus's glance of mild surprise at this unusual arrangement, 'and living next door to a priory gives the place an air of respectability but…well…you know the impression people get when a young woman lives independently. Especially in this kind of style.' He looked across the table at the gleaming dishes reflected on the shining surface. 'For all her ways, Nicola certainly knows how to manage a household, but neither Lotti nor I are too happy about the way she keeps open house as Father did. She doesn't appear to see the dangers, and I can't even get her to think about finding a mate. I suppose she's enjoying herself too much the way things are.'

Fergus cleared his throat, hearing a kind of warning in George's words. 'And Daniel?' he said. 'And Ramond?'

'Daniel is running the Wiltshire estate for me while I'm in London, and Ramond is studying law at Gray's Inn. I expect he'll be a diplomat in a few more years.'

'And Patrick?'

'Ah…Patrick.' George led the way to the table, taking the bench opposite Fergus and settling himself with the air of a prosperous London merchant about to negotiate a deal. Which was not far from the truth. As the eldest of the Coldyngham family, he was but one year older than Fergus, and whether his inherited haughty Roman nose had helped or not, he had become both noble and successful. With a large house and business here in the city, a lovely wife and two children, George had been his father's pride, honest, sober, well liked and respected, wealthy and as darkly handsome as Fergus. Indeed, the two had occasionally been taken for brothers during their student days at Cambridge. 'Young Patrick's still at Oxford, but heaven knows why,' he said. 'I doubt he attends more than one lecture a week, and he's spending money like water. He won't come into his inheritance until he's twenty-one late this year, so until then I'm having to advance it in bite-sized pieces.'

'What kind of debts?'

'Oh…' George grinned '…he's doing all the things that we did, only more so. But I don't remember costing my father as much as Patrick does. As for Nicola— well, that's why you're here, isn't it?' He poured ale into two wooden beakers and passed one to Fergus. 'I have to tell you, Ferg, that she prefers not to recall the agreement your father and mine made all those years ago, so I thought it was about time we made a decision one way or the other. I don't really understand the reasons behind this promise of theirs. I suppose there must have been one. Wealth. Connections. Perhaps just friendship. I don't know. But none of us can expect an old arrangement like that to stand unless you both want it. It's not legally binding, after all.' He looked at his friend over the top of his beaker before taking a long swig. 'Well?' he said, wiping his mouth and reaching for the ham. 'Want some of this? Pass your plate.' Deftly, he carved, trying not to notice Fergus's lack of response.

Absently, Fergus held out his plate and watched each pink layer pile up before he remembered to say stop.

These were questions he could have answered, but chose not to. 'Is there anyone else?' he said. 'Suitors?'

'Oh, good lord, man, dozens,' said George. 'They're here first thing in the morning till last thing at night. She has…' he laughed '…her own way of getting rid of them. You know Nicola.'

Yes, he had known how, as a child, she had been well able to deal with the local lads, beating them at most things. 'What?' he said.

George took a bite of food and answered with his mouth full, which he would not have been allowed to do at home. 'Trials and tests,' he said, munching. 'If they don't come up to scratch, they're out. Not much change there, Ferg.'

So that was what the contest had been about earlier Fergus could not help a flutter of concern that, although he had passed the first test with flying colours, it might have cost him too dearly. 'But no one in particular?' he insisted.

'Not that I know of. Why?' George stopped eating and looked at his friend intently. 'You really interested, after all this time?'

'I promised my father before he died.'

To George, this pronouncement lacked conviction. 'Ferg,' he said slowly, 'putting promises aside, for a moment. With your wealth you could get any woman. This agreement… promise…call it what you will, was conditional upon a contract when you both reached the age of consent, and while I've done my best to get Nicola to commit herself to my father's wishes, she's never been one to have her mind made up for her. You remember what she was like as a little 'un. As stubborn as hell and kicking over the traces even then.'

'Vaguely. I must admit my contact with her over the years hasn't been good.'

'No, it hasn't. And she's grown up. She's made an impression.'

'Then there *is* someone else, isn't there?'

'No one that matters, no.'

'Then I have first call. And I'm calling, George. I intend to honour the agreement. It was my father's last wish, and I promised him.' Not for a moment did he expect George to be taken in by that, knowing what he did of Fergus's resistance to his father's control. They had not seen eye to eye until recently.

As he suspected, George was not easily duped. He put down his knife and leaned forward. 'You've seen her, haven't you?' he said in a low voice. 'Why else would you be so insistent, eh?'

Fergus's stillness was all the answer he needed.

There was a silence between them as George, ever the merchant, assessed the balance of trade. 'I suppose you know,' he said at last, 'that you'll be starting at a disadvantage?' When Fergus merely looked straight ahead, George felt it his duty to remind him. 'For one thing you've left all this a mite too late. If you'd come when she was fifteen, Ferg, you might have found her easier to deal with. As it is…'

'She's been courted. Yes, but she'll have to forget them, won't she?'

George leaned back and took a deep breath. 'I think, my friend, that *you* are forgetting something. Nicola is not your average young miss with stars in her eyes, waiting for the masterful swain to sweep her off her little feet. Far from it. She's quite capable of keeping herself on ice until she sees *exactly* what she wants. And considering how she used to hate your guts when you took us all away from her on your wild goose chases whenever you came to stay, I'd say you have as much chance of winning her as you have of flying. I know she's a beauty, Ferg, but you'll have to do more than pull her hair and hide her pet rabbit if you want to get her into your bed. She has a long memory you know.'

Though his jaw tightened, still Fergus said nothing.

'Did you think it was all cut and dried?' said George.

'No, I know I have my work cut out for me, but I have to try. I realise I want her, George. Will you help me?' He dared not trust himself to say more, and for a moment, Fergus thought his old friend was going to refuse, so long was the pause before he replied.

'I shall not see her hurt, Ferg. She may occasionally adopt the lad's role when it pleases her, but that's for a reason that's gradually losing its validity. It doesn't mean she's tough or insensitive to pain. She's not. She's a woman now, with all a woman's needs, and she'll not be easily won over. The decision will be hers, believe me.'

'I do believe you.'

'So, you still think you have a chance?'

'As I said, I have to try. You know my ways, George.'

George, Lord Coldyngham, leaned forward intently, placing his hands palm-down on the table. 'Yes, I know your ways well enough, Ferg,' he said. 'And they may have worked on Scottish lassies or even on Cambridge whores, but they'll not do for Nicola. She's different.'

'I *want* her, George,' Fergus insisted. 'I have to find a way forward. I think she'll respond to my way, eventually.' She *was* different, he knew. In every way she was rare and priceless, and the sight of her half-naked on the bed, below him, wounded, was something that would stay in his mind for ever. Heaven knows what might have happened if the maids had not returned at that moment.

'Oh? You've spoken, then?'

'Briefly.'

'She's still afraid of you?'

'She'd not admit it, even if it were true. She still dislikes me, yes, but I cannot blame her for that. I gave her no reason to do otherwise, did I?'

'Then, yes, you *will* have your work cut out. But I'll help.'

'Thank you. It's the most I can expect after all this time. The rest is up to me.'

'Er…no, Ferg. The rest is up to Nicola, wouldn't you agree?'

Wincing at his own clumsiness, Fergus nodded. 'Yes, I do agree. But never fear, George, I shall win her even if it takes for ever.'

George leaned back to watch his friend pour two more beakers of ale from a large jug with a smirking face modelled on its side. Fergus's expression, he noted, was anything but amused, but held that grim determination he had shown as a youth when it was woe betide anyone who got in his way. Then, he had habitually won whatever he set out to win; now, George was not so sure. Nicola, he thought, might be in for a rough ride. And Fergus too.

Fergus's thoughts went along much the same lines, though it also crossed his mind that he would be expected to pay very dearly for that string of shining rubies he had placed upon Nicola's beautiful breast only an hour ago.

Chapter Two

In the cosily panelled solar hung with tapestries and filled with morning light from a large pointed window, the sound of bells from St Helen's Priory next door drowned out the constant thudding of Nicola's heart as the two young maids went about the task of tending her wound. The thick oaken door had been locked and bolted since the departure of the unwelcome guest more as a gesture of defiance than necessity, for none of the three expected him to return, though the locks and bolts of Nicola's heart could tell a different story.

For many years, the thought of marriage into the house of Melrose had seemed too remote to be real, especially during her father's long absences from home when, motherless, Nicola had been left to run wild with her brothers, cared for by a large household and one aged nurse. Eventually, he had sent her to York to join the household of another noble family, there to learn the manners and graces required of all such women aspiring to good marriages. Nicola's aspirations, however, were to avoid one marriage at all costs, the one to Fergus Melrose that her father was set on. When her father had died fourteen months ago, leaving her a sizeable income from property and his comfortable house in London, she believed that at last she would be allowed to manage her own affairs.

Stripped of the lad's clothes and sitting almost naked on her bed, she gritted her teeth at the next application of the maid's special salve, letting her breath out slowly. 'Mannerless churl!' she hissed. 'Still as full of himself as ever. I should have worn my dirk and stabbed him with it. That would've wiped the smug look off his face. Ouch!' She grabbed at Rosemary's hand. 'Stop now.'

'And didn't ye notice his fine figure, then?' said Lavender, rinsing out a pink-stained cloth in a bowl of rosewater. 'There's many a maid would like a wee while in the dark with such a one, mistress. I didn't see any in York with a face as comely as that. Nowhere near.'

'Nor in London, either,' said Rosemary.

'Handsome is as handsome does,' said Nicola, pulling the fine linen chemise over her head and sucking in her breath at the touch of it upon her skin. 'There's nobody you've seen who'd have done this to me, either, and then walked away.' The part in between was too shameful to speak of.

Yet she remembered only too well his eyes and the flood of excitement and heat that had suffused her face and neck at his shameful scrutiny, and that almost imperceptible moment when she saw him struggling to stop himself from touching, when his voice had thickened like deep velvet even while saying something stupid about a scar. It was not only her wound his eyes had examined. She knew. She had been watching them. She had seen them widen, and his lips part.

Slowly, carefully, she eased her chemise into place and then sat so still and quiet that Rosemary had to look hard to see if there were tears again. She was not weeping, but in answer to the gentle enquiry, Nicola kept her hands close against her breast while a frown deepened in the centre of her lovely brow. 'He meant it,' she whispered. 'He meant to hurt me. Again. Nothing's changed, has it? Except that now he's bigger and stronger than ever.'

Lavender and Rosemary, their partnership being one of life's coincidences, had been with Nicola for ten years since they were fifteen and eighteen respectively. Now they came to sit upon the soft coverlet at the end of her large curtained bed to offer their mistress some advice.

'Of course things have changed,' said Lavender, settling her large open blue eyes solemnly upon Nicola's hands. 'You're obviously not the scruffy little lass you were when he last saw you, eleven…twelve years ago, are you?' She reached behind her for the burnished steel mirror and passed it to Nicola. 'Take a look. That's a woman *he'll* not have seen the like of in all his… what…thirty years, is it?' It was twenty-nine, but addition was not Lavender's strongest subject.

Nicola grimaced, pushing the mirror away. 'Oh,

you're prejudiced,' she said. 'But it's made no difference, has it? And if my brother has invited him here to
revive all that marriage nonsense, he can think again.
He knows perfectly well what I feel about it. There was
no formal betrothal and I'll not be bound to him. Nor
will I ever be. Not for his father's sake, or mine.'

'So now,' said Rosemary, smoothing her white apron
seductively over her thighs, 'you have to show him how
you've changed, even if he hasn't.' Privately, she
doubted that Sir Fergus had cut such a dash at the age
of sixteen, but there was no way of knowing. 'You have
fine manners now, and you know how to give a man the
cold shoulder when he doesn't please you. And if you
were to wear your finest kirtle when you go down to
meet them, he's going to get the message, isn't he? Perhaps it was the lad's clothing that made him behave so
badly. So what will it be, the grey satin? The red? The
green silk with ribbons?'

'Not green. That's the colour of hope. Sanguine, I
think.'

Lavender's wide blue eyes met Rosemary's hazel
ones long enough to transmit a shadow of alarm. Blood-
red might be appropriate, but it was hardly the colour
of compromise, was it? 'Sanguine it is, then,' she said.

'And may the best man win,' murmured Rosemary
to herself.

As both Nicola and her two maids had intended, the
preparations of the last hour stopped the two men's
conversation in mid-sentence, though George might

have predicted the sheer amazement that Fergus betrayed before managing to marshall his features once more into the customary inscrutable mask.

The plaited hair was now quite hidden beneath an extravagant confection of floating veils that fluttered like a massive butterfly around Nicola's head, kept in place by dagger-long pins and scattered with seed-pearls. The tomboy clothes had been replaced by a blood-red damask gown with wide floor-length sleeves and fur linings that touched the hem, sweeping the ground behind her. Beneath her breasts, a wide velvet sash revealed the contours of her lovely body and, because she had something to conceal, a richly jewelled collar covered her bosom, winking with diamonds and rubies. And for the second time, Nicola could feel Fergus Melrose looking at her without the usual disdain.

She smiled at George, holding out her arms for his greeting. 'Lovely to see you,' she said. 'How are Lotti and the children?' With a graceful arc of her body she put up her face to be kissed, touching her brother's mulberry-brocaded arm and approving his cote-hardie with an up-and-down glance. 'This is nice. Is it new?'

George understood the snub to their guest, exerting a gentle reproof. 'Nick,' he said, 'you know why Sir Fergus has come today at my invitation. I believe you've already met this morning.'

She had not greeted him then, and she would not do so now. 'Oh, I know what this is all about, George dear,' she said, 'though you should have given me some warning. I could have been out.' Purposely ambiguous, she left it to them to decide on her meaning. 'As it is, I have no intention of discussing plans for my betrothal before strangers. I'm sorry you've spent your valuable time for so little reward, Sir Fergus, but perhaps you'll take a glass of malmsey before you go, and tell us all about your adventures. You must find London so very dull.'

'Nicola,' said George, firmly, 'Sir Fergus is hardly a stranger to either of us and I think he deserves your consideration, now he's taken the trouble to appear. Surely we can discuss this like adults?'

Until then, she had avoided looking at Sir Fergus, though she could have described his fashionable attire from the peacock-feathered hat down to the soft kid boots decorated with bone toggles, the jewelled dagger and the tasselled pouch at his belt. He disturbed her now as much as he had ever done, and though she had been rehearsing what to say for the past hour, the tightness in her lungs robbed them of the power she had intended. Now, she was aware that she had provoked him, for he pulled back his shoulders, frowning.

'I can reply to that,' he said, ignoring Nicola's expression of bored resignation. 'You have every right to be vexed by my long absence, my lady, but the reasons are simple enough. My life has not been exactly to do with as I pleased these last few years. I was at sea with my father until recently, putting me out of touch with almost everyone, then attending to my family since my return. You've not been in London long either, so I understand, and before that you were some years in York. Hardly the best circumstances to pursue that duty to our fathers, was it? No one regrets more than I that I was not able to visit my friends in the last few years, believe me.'

'I am not in the least vexed by your lengthy absence, Sir Fergus. I only wish it could have been longer still. And it makes little difference whether I believe you or not.' Nicola raised her eyes no further than the pea-sized buttons on his doublet. 'The plain truth is that after years of total silence, during which you could presumably have married several times over, your sudden appearance here suggests desperation rather than commitment. You can hardly expect me to be flattered that you have been struck by a sudden call to duty. Were there no other ancient families to whom you could attach yourself, or did your so-called duty to your father suddenly acquire a deeper meaning for you? Do tell me what I've done to deserve this unexpected burst of attention.'

'Nicola!' warned George.

But now she had the man's full heed and, while it lasted, there was yet more she could say on the subject. 'Let us not waste any more time on such a lovely day,' she said, bunching her long skirts into a pregnant pile before her. 'We all have more interesting things to do than talk about duty. When I choose a man to marry, he will be a nobleman with blood the same colour as my own, not a newly knighted provincial nobody with equally new coins in his pouch.'

She had a hand on the door-latch as she delivered this last appalling insult, and it was the horrified look on her brother's face that made her hesitate. 'Don't worry, George dear. Our guest won't be demanding rapiers at dawn on this occasion. Will you, Sir Fergus?' Her huge dark eyes blazed with scorn into the hard grey steel of her adversary, and she knew that her hit had damaged him as much as his earlier one upon her, perhaps more so, and that he would do nothing to counter it. Not then, anyway.

The sharp clack of the latch hung heavily in the ensuing silence like the distant sound of lances shattering upon armour. No man would have escaped such a volley of insults with his life, and no woman would have walked from a room without leaving behind some kind of awareness that there was more to this than mere dislike of a man's pedigree, however deeply embedded that had become.

'I'm sorry, Ferg,' said George. 'I must have forgotten to tell her about your father. But still, she had no right to…tch! This is dreadful. I wish I'd asked Charlotte to be with us.'

Sir Fergus placed a hand over his friend's arm. 'I think we both expected that kind of reaction,' he said. 'If we didn't, then we should have done. Don't take it too personally.'

'Even so, it looks as if her line-up of suitors has given her big ideas. She may well prefer a title, but, if so, that's not the Nick I know. Give her another year, Ferg, and then see. Eh?'

Walking over to the window, Sir Fergus collected the

two abandoned rapiers and leaned them against the wall. 'No, I shall not wait,' he said.

'Oh…well…no, I can't blame you, of course.'

'I shall press on with it. I'm a fighting man and she's a courageous woman to fight me back. We shall come to terms by and by, you'll see.'

'Well, I'm relieved to hear it. You were never one to give up easily, were you? Nevertheless, I shall go and speak to her. I'm determined you shall have a full apology before you leave.'

'Not necessary, George.'

'Of course it is, man. Help yourself to Nicola's malmsey. I'll be with you in a few moments.'

'Nicola! Wait!' George, Lord Coldyngham, called to the white butterfly disappearing round the bend of the passageway, striding over the stone-flagged floor towards her, though his request was ignored.

'Oh, George,' she called over her shoulder, 'not again, please. I've heard enough on the subject to last me a year.'

Catching up with her before she reached the door to the garden, he ushered her sideways along the gravel path and into the bright greenness of new growth and vine-clad arbours. A circular fountain held centre stage, its jet of water cutting across the sun and scattering its light into sparkling droplets that pattered down upon the darting silver shapes beneath. Yellow king-cups clustered around the edge. 'Nicola, you've gone too far,' he said, severely.

She stopped and sat upon the wide stone edge of the fountain, trailing one hand in the water and looking up at him with feigned innocence. 'And in future, George, would you mind allowing me to issue my own invitations? Would you and Lotti expect me to invite my friends to your home without telling you?'

'I'm sorry. I sent him a message to meet me here. He came early, that's all. Was he so discourteous to you that you had to insult him, a guest in your own home? That was not well done, Nick. Did you not know that his father was killed at sea scarce eight months ago?'

Nicola's eyes clouded as she took her bottom lip between her teeth, halting the prepared riposte. 'No,' she whispered. 'Why didn't you tell me?'

'When was I supposed to tell you?' he said, crossly. 'I thought you'd have heard it from your noble friends. They seem to have plenty of gossip about births, marriages, deaths and—' He stopped, abruptly.

'Yes? And affairs, you were about to say? Don't try to wrong-foot me, George. You forgot. Admit it. At least he now knows, as you do too, that I've just given him no more or less than he damn well deserves. It would hardly have penetrated his thick skull, anyway.' She turned her face away angrily, recalling that morning's shameful episode. 'He's done far more than that to me and nobody ever demanded an apology from him. Monster!'

There was a quick unseen movement of her brother's handsome eyebrows and a tightening of the lips to prevent a smile. He reached out a hand to clasp hers, well aware that there was much more to her hostility than she was saying.

'George,' she said, suspecting some imminent persuasion, 'there's really no more to be said.' Sideways, she observed the long mulberry brocade cote-hardie with its precise pleats beneath the red leather belt. Everything about him proclaimed wealth and good breeding with never a trace of ostentation.

'Yes, there is.' He kept hold of her hand, and she knew that there was indeed more to be said and that she was not nearly so dismissive as she pretended to be. 'In spite of the insults just now, Nick, Fergus is still willing to offer for you. He made a promise to his father when he was dying. Ferg was wounded in the same skirmish. They were fighting off pirates.'

'Promise, fiddlesticks!' she scoffed. 'George, what *nonsense*.' Her laughter did not last long, for she felt again the hard intimate pressure of Fergus's body upon hers and knew instinctively that it could not have been the first time he had held a woman like that. Or exposed her breast, for that matter. 'You've got it wrong. Whatever he's told you, you've misunderstood. He no more wants to marry me than I do him, and if he's told you different then he's lying. There was never a moment when he could find a civil word to say to me, and most of the time I might not have been there at all. Why would he suddenly come and offer for my hand if not for links with the Coldynghams?'

It took little effort for her to remember the time she had placed her eleven-year-old hand in Fergus's while he was looking the other way. Without a word or a smile, he had pulled his hand away as if it had been scalded, leaving her close to tears at an insensitivity she could not begin to understand. She had never forgotten the snub, nor had she ever repeated the attempt. Even now, when she might have been expected to know how an age difference of five years will eventually close and disappear, the recurring humiliation of being a female child trying to hold her own against older lads in their own peer group had stayed in her tender young psyche and refused to fade with time. She had not nurtured it, just not forgotten the pain of rejection that accompanied each of his visits when only blind hero-worship forbade her to stop trying for his approval.

Consequently, she had made a fool of herself time and again to the embarrassed amusement of all her brothers except Ramond. He had been the one to go back for her, the one who would pick dock leaves to salve her nettle-stings, the one to help her down a tree when the others had deserted her to follow Fergus. Dear Ramond. He was the offspring of the second Lady Coldyngham; George and Daniel shared the first. Nicola and Patrick shared the third, though she had died at Patrick's birth. When an unexpected girl had arrived to interrupt the flow of lads, the chosen name had only needed to be docked by one letter to make it suitable. Similarly with the middle names: Leonie for Leo, Phillipa for Phillip.

'It's not nonsense,' said George, 'nor do I believe for one moment that Fergus is merely seeking a connection. I'm telling you, he wants to marry you. He's changed, Nick.'

Nicola jumped to her feet, snatching her hand away in annoyance. 'He has *not*, George. He's not changed one whit. And I'll be damned if I'll give myself to that…that churl just because of his father's promises. He can go and look elsewhere for his breeding stock. I can have my pick of lords and earls any time I choose. Tell him he's too late. Tell him I'd rather stay unmarried for the rest of my life than accept his patronising offer. Condescending…overbearing…superior…highhanded…' Slowly, very slowly, her salvo fizzled out as she shook her head, her eyes filling with sudden tears. 'Isn't it ironic?' she whispered.

Surprised, George watched the transformation from indignant woman to rueful child. 'Come here, love,' he said, holding out a hand. 'Tell me what's ironic. That Fergus should want you, after all?'

She allowed him to pull her back to sit by his side again, reluctant to complete an admission she had never voiced, even to herself. 'That when we were children, I would have done anything for him. Anything. I thought he was… Oh, this is ridiculous, George.'

'You admired him so much?'

'Worshipped him, more like. I would have been happy for him just to smile at me, speak kindly to me, but he rarely looked my way. All he came to Coldyngham Park for was to be with you and the others. I suppose I should have had a sister, then I wouldn't have pretended to be one of you, would I?' She sniffed and wiped her eyes with her knuckles, trying to laugh it off. 'But then, I was a silly child. I knew no better. Now, I don't care for anyone's approval. I don't need anything he has to offer.'

'Still hurting after all these years, love?'

Unconsciously, one hand moved upwards to press a palm upon her breast where a nagging sting lay just beneath her chemise. 'No,' she said, so softly that George had to look to see the word. 'No, I don't care a fig who he marries as long as it's not me. I know what he's like, George. I can do better than that.'

'You know that you insulted him.'

'Yes. And he'll not expect me to apologise.'

'Oh? Why do you say that?'

'Just take my word for it.'

George's silence did not mean that he had nothing to say. This time, he was thinking that for both Fergus and Nicola to deny the need for an apology, Fergus must have done some insulting of his own. And the only thing George could add to the picture was a stolen kiss. That might explain their very obvious silence regarding that earlier meeting. 'You'll be with us for supper later on?' he said. 'Charlotte's birthday. A few friends, that's all.'

'Yes, I'd not forgotten. You'll allow the children to be there?'

He smiled. 'I shall get into the gravest trouble if they miss you.'

Whether Nicola suspected that one of the 'few friends' might include Sir Fergus, she made no further mention of him until George asked if she would come and say farewell. 'Excuse me this once,' she said, placing her hand over his. 'You invited him here, you show him the way home.'

He picked up her hand and kissed the knuckles, levering himself up from the fountain wall. 'Until this evening then, love.'

'George…' she said, holding him back by a finger.

He stopped and waited.

'George, you're not going to insist on this…this promise thing, are you? I know it's what Father wanted and I suppose he must have had a good reason, but I don't think he'd have insisted, would he?'

Gently, he shook her hand, though there was no smile to make light of it. 'Of course I shall not insist. Whatever gave you that idea and, in any case, what good would it do? I don't have any power to hold back your inheritance because you've got it already. Anyway, you know what my thoughts are about women being allowed to choose their own husbands.' He came to sit by her side again, closer this time. 'Nobody's going to insist,' he said, looking into her darkly troubled eyes. 'But…'

'But what?'

'Well, all Father ever wanted was for you to be safely married. For your own protection, you know. You have a large income, property, a house here in London with a large household…you know…plenty of fortune-hunters on the lookout for more. You can't call Fergus a fortune-hunter, whatever else you might call him. Perhaps that's what Father had in mind. Some men have ways of making themselves very agreeable until they've got what they want. I'd hate to see you taken along that road.'

'Well, no one could accuse Fergus Melrose of making himself too agreeable, could they? Far from it. But the road up to Scotland is a very long one, George, and I don't see my future up there as a breeder of Melroses while he careers off round the world. He may have stallions and mares in mind, but I want more from life than ritual mating once a year.'

Making no attempt this time to hide his amusement at her picturesque speech, George shook his head, laughing. 'Nick,' he said at last, 'all I ask is that you don't dismiss him quite so soon. People do change. You have. Give him a chance, love. Why not talk to Charlotte about it? She's quite anxious about you.'

'George, I'm twenty-four, not twelve. Why should she be anxious?'

'Vultures, love,' he said, rising again. 'Too many vultures.'

'What are they…something legal, is it?'

'No, vultures are nasty big birds that the king keeps in his menagerie at the tower. They tear juicy bodies to pieces with their greedy beaks, bone, fur and all. Some men are like that, and some will protect you from vultures. Fergus is one of those. I know him better than you, and if he says he wants you it's not because he wants your wealth or ancestral links. Why else d'ye think he came round here early if not for a sneak preview after all these years? Eh?'

'Curiosity, I expect.'

'Yes, and now he's seen you, not even your insults have put him off. He still wants you, love. I told you.'

She stared at him, stuck for words. 'I…I thought… he…'

'He'd go off with his tail between his legs? Hah! You should know him better than that, lass. He's got more between his legs than a tail.'

'George!' Her heart lurched uncomfortably, making her aware of the sharp pain of her wound.

'Sorry. I'll go before I say any more. See you this evening.' He grinned. 'Don't look like that. You've got four brothers, remember. You must have seen.'

'I didn't look,' she called after him.

'Little liar.' He laughed. 'Swimming in the river? You too?'

Yes, she remembered that, and the time she'd followed them and got out of her depth and was rescued by Ramond long before the others even noticed, so intent were they on watching Fergus. He had always been graceful and strong, excelling at everything, leading them into risky situations, yet always emerging first, triumphant. She recalled how he had ridden bareback the stallion that none of them would go near, how the maids would giggle and ogle him, how shamefully excited and angry she had felt when she discovered he had kissed one of them. How she had longed to be the one instead of a nobleman's chit for whom he had no time. Whatever she had done, there had always been time to dream and then to weep with forlorn childish tears. How she had hated and adored him.

* * *

Nicola had known that Fergus Melrose would be there—*Sir* Fergus, as she was now supposed to call him—and while she tried to convince herself that she didn't care, that she would not dress to impress anyone, least of all him, the end result would have done justice to a Botticelli goddess floating in from the sea. Blue silk, very full, very sheer and diaphanous, very low-cut and high-waisted, very suitable for the kind of open-air feast that Charlotte enjoyed most.

Her hair, severely pulled back into a long sleek plait that reached her waist, was crowned with a garland of blue flowers echoed by a tiny nosegay tucked into the vee of her bodice to hide the top edge of an unsightly red line. Pendant pearls from her ears were the only other adornment and, if she did not quite believe the mirror that told her she looked ravishing, then she had to take account of her maids and the stares of the guests. Especially from two of them.

'Since no one has yet offered to introduce us, my lady,' said a personable young man to Nicola, 'then I must needs do it myself. I asked my brother to, but he has declined.'

'And who is your brother, sir?' As if she couldn't have guessed.

'Over there,' he said, glancing with a certain relish across to where his elder brother lounged against a marble table laden with food. 'Sir Fergus Melrose.'

Nicola followed his glance, relieved to have a genuine excuse to look at him so soon after her arrival.

Then, seeing the message that awaited her, she wished she had not done. *The business of the day is not yet over,* he was telling her. *You'll not get rid of me so easily.*

'My name,' the young man was saying, 'is Muir. I expect he's mentioned me.' His merry brown eyes were revealing far more than his name—his admiration, for example, his interest in every detail of her appearance as well as in some that were hidden. In that respect, he was easier to read than his brother, more affable, more extrovert in his much-padded pink satin doublet that made her wonder how he managed to squeeze through doorways. The pleated frill below his belt was skimpy enough to reveal what older men kept politely concealed.

'Master Melrose,' said Nicola, averting her eyes from the pronounced bulge, 'why did your brother refuse to introduce us? Would he not approve of us being acquainted?'

'Apparently not. In fact, he was quite specific about the problem. He said I'd get under his feet. Wasn't that discourteous of him?' Like a watered-down version of the original, he was almost as tall, almost as dark, but not nearly as imposing as the brother he criticised; even without the gathers, Fergus's shoulders were wide and robust, his chest deeper, his neck more muscled, his manner more dangerously mature, less boyish.

'Extremely discourteous,' Nicola agreed, bestowing on Muir her most charming smile as long as the two grey eyes glared at them from across the garden. 'Surely he must have known we'd meet, somewhere?'

'Not if he could help it, my lady. It was your brother who invited me here. Fergus is trying to persuade me to go back home to Scotland. I came here to the capital for a wee visit, but I didn't think it would be quite so short.'

'And what is the purpose of your short visit? Business?'

'Er...not quite.' His smile was mischievously rueful. 'An affair of the heart, my lady.' Clapping one hand to his heart was too dramatic for it to have been genuine. 'I had to make myself scarce.'

'I see. In some haste, I take it.'

'In *great* haste,' he agreed, grinning.

She felt the hostile glare still upon them both and assumed that the younger Melrose was not averse to queering the pitch of his elder brother by telling her of things that ought to have been private. Also, that in revealing his own penchant for non-serious affairs of the heart, he might in fact be offering her the chance to flirt with him and thereby to annoy the arrogant Fergus. With an air that exposed intentions unashamedly several stages ahead of hers, Muir Melrose wore his virility like one who had just discovered its purpose and was ready to put it to good use.

At once, she knew what she would do, that she would have to be careful, and that between them they could make Fergus Melrose's ambition somewhat more difficult to achieve. It would not be hard to do and must surely be more fun than today's worsening relationships.

'Then you cannot go home soon, can you? Not immediately.'

'It would be a great pity—' he sighed '—now we've been introduced. Would you allow me to call on you, perhaps?' When she purposely kept him waiting for an answer, he pleaded, gently, 'For the summer months?'

'Oh, not *months*,' she said. 'Weeks…days…'

'My Lady Coldheart,' he said, pulling a tragic face, 'you cannot be serious. Are you so very hard to please, then?'

'Alas, I am indeed, Master Melrose. My standards are high, you see, and my interest appallingly short-lived. I'm afraid I send men packing, as your brother may already have told you.' Their laughter rang like a peal of bells across the sunset garden, and this time she refused to meet the grey eyes that watched the start of yet another impediment to the day's plans. Then she told Master Melrose of last night's fencing wager and the way she had dealt with it this morning and together they laughed again and went to look for food with an unspoken agreement already forming between them.

Lord and Lady Coldyngham's grand and spacious home sat securely on the bend of the Thames in one of the most desirable and attractive stretches between the royal palaces of Savoy and Whitehall. Built around a central courtyard with stables and service buildings at one side, the house extended towards the river with large gardens and orchards and a private wharf where barges were moored. For Lady Charlotte's thirtieth birthday, the green expanse of bowers and arbours had been hung with streamers of ivy and coloured ribbons, the lawns scattered with satin and velvet cushions while musicians played and small tables were piled with food, and flagons of wine were placed up to their necks in the stone channel of water that ran from the fountain.

So Nicola allowed Master Melrose to offer her the choicest and most succulent morsels of food that came with every accompaniment and garnish, saffron-dyed and disguised, moulded to look like fish or hedgehogs, even when they were not, decorated with feathers, gilded, pounded, pureed, glazed and spiced. Nothing was meant to look like what it was, or taste like it, come to that. For Lady Charlotte, it was a triumph of a meal; for Nicola, it was utterly tasteless, but not for the world would she have said so, nor would she have said why.

Meanwhile, there were other guests to talk to, most of whom she knew, mummers to watch at their antics, jugglers to admire, a jester to avoid if one could, and musicians to applaud for the way they incorporated the duet of tin whistle and tambourine. Nicola had brought presents for Roberta, whose name had been prepared for another boy in true Coldyngham fashion, and eight-year-old Louis, the elder by two-and-a-half years. She gave the tin whistle to Roberta and the tambourine to Louis, who marched solemnly away to show the guests how it was done, though later it was observed that Roberta was rattling noisily and Louis was tunefully piping.

They played tag and blind-man's buff, and anything else to avoid having to speak to any group of which Sir

Fergus was a part and, at last, Nicola gave her garland of flowers to Roberta to take to bed. Naturally, she had to part with the nosegay from her bodice for Louis, by which time she was sure no one would notice.

It grew dark and the music changed to dance rhythms, the river sparkled with reflections from torches, and the distant sounds of Thames oarsmen echoed on the night air as they took their last customers home by wherry. Mellowed by wine, the guests joined hands to snake their way through the plots and arbours, benches and trellises, singing the two-line refrain while male soloists sang the stanzas as the rest marked time on the spot. Then off they went again, lurching and laughing, unsure whose hand they held in the darkest shadows away from the torches.

Muir Melrose pulled at Nicola and headed purposefully away from the light. 'This way,' he said. 'Come on.'

His flirting, Nicola thought, had gone far enough for one day. 'No,' she called. 'No...er...this way.' She pulled, bumping into someone.

'Come on,' Muir laughed. 'We shall lose them if you—'

She shook off his hand to pick up her long skirts, which were in danger of being trampled, draping them up over one arm. But again her free hand was sought as she was nudged along the line of dancers and, to escape the singing jostling bodies, she went with him, expecting to join up again when she could see what she was doing. His hand tightened insistently over hers, and the noise of the dancers' cries was cut off by a thick screen of darkness.

'Master Melrose,' she said, coldly, 'we should be going the other way. Please…let go.' She tried to free herself, but in the dark tunnel of foliage where only pin-pricks of light filtered, his arms closed quickly around her, bending her hard into his body. Then she knew, foolishly, that all young Melrose's attentions had been directed towards this end, a far from innocent conclusion to his gentle and inoffensive dalliance. Not even to vex Sir Fergus had she wanted it to go this far, and now she was angry beyond words that this gauche young man believed she could have as few scruples as any servant-girl against being bussed and groped in the shadows.

She struggled fiercely, dropping her skirt to beat at him and push him away, but he was remarkably strong, too strong for his size, and there was no chance for her to cry out for help before his mouth silenced her protests with a firmness that belied all his earlier frivolity and playful-ness. After his teasing manner of the evening, this was cer-tainly not what she had expected from him and, although she had understood from the start that he was probably promiscuous, she had not for one moment believed that he had intended to defy his brother so insistently, or so soon. Or without any kind of warning. This was more than flirting—this was a determined, serious and skilled per-formance that from the first touch had the effect of hold-ing her mind into that one place where sensation burst into bloom like the springtime of all her twenty-four years.

Her hands forgot to beat, but clung helplessly to his shoulders, as bewildered as her mind. Obedient to the hard restraint of his arms, lured by the skill of his lips, she had no choice but to surrender to the confusing thoughts circling her mind that this did not match the rather silly, witty, shallow creature she had saddled herself with for the last few hours. It was a complete revelation, and an exciting one, but a high price to pay for a scheme that had so soon got out of hand.

For all her popularity with men since her appearance in London, and indeed before that, she had never allowed more than a chaste kiss upon her cheek. Her inexperience showed, for now anger, outrage, and something quite new and fearful combined to tell her that, however much she had wished for a kiss with someone else, this must be stopped by any means available, whether ladylike or not. With a push of superhuman strength and a twist of her body, she tore her mouth away and bent her head towards the hand that held her wrist in a grip of steel, biting hard into his knuckles and releasing all her fury, not only at his immediate behaviour but at his deception too.

She felt the resistance of bone under her teeth and the taste of his skin on her tongue before his fingers relaxed and pulled away and, though she half-expected a howl of pain from him, there was no protest and no retaliation. It was as if he had been waiting for it, deserving it, accepting it.

In uncharacteristic silence, he put his arm across her shoulders to lead her forward as if he knew the way

back, but she balked at this too-easy dismissal, taking
time to lash him with her tongue before they parted.
'Don't ever…' she panted '…*ever* come near me again.
Do you hear me? Now leave me…let go of my shoulder—' she shook his hand away '—and speak to me no
more of friendship, sir. You are *despicable*! Go away!'

It was too dark for her to witness his departure,
though she felt that he bowed before he left and, in
only a few more hesitant and lonely steps, she was
within sight and sound of the music once again. Most
of the guests had now regrouped around a male soloist
whose low voice, accompanied by his own lute, was
holding them all spellbound. Thankful of the darkness
and their diverted attention, she waited for a moment
to gather her thoughts, to smooth her hair, and to lay a
cooling hand upon her mouth that still tingled from his
kisses. Her pounding heart she could do nothing to
moderate. Like a shadow, she glided round the edge of
the crowd to see who sang and played so sweetly, ex-
periencing such a weight of numbing disappointment
that her first real kisses should have come so insin-
cerely from a man of his small calibre, a virtual stranger
and self-confessed philanderer. It had served her right.
She should have had more sense. He had disappeared
quickly enough afterwards with not a word of explanation or apology, not even an enquiry after her state. The
man was a worm, after all.

Dazed, still furiously angry and disturbed at the vi-
olation of her emotions, she felt the dull thudding in her
chest change to a stifled gasp of horror as she peered

through the crowd, rooted to the spot and unable to believe what she was seeing. His dark head bent over the lute, the soloist was Master Muir Melrose and, by the soaring final chord and the warm applause at the end, it was clear he had been there for some time.

Now, with her heartbeats drowning out all other sounds, her eyes combed frantically through the group to find the one man she had avoided all evening, the one whose message had warned her that his business with her was not over. He was there, alone, standing by the fountain and holding one hand tightly clasped inside the other, not applauding. As she watched, he lifted the hand to his mouth then back to its mate for some kind of comfort, turning his head as he did so as if to seek her out.

Through the dancing shadows and the flare of torches, their eyes linked at last and held, part possession and part solace, and while her eyes communicated shock and disbelief, his message was that he was in charge, that she was not free to follow his brother's lead, and that she would not escape him. A shiver of fear coursed through her again. Fear and excitement.

Slowly, he wound his way through the scattering crowd and came to stand beside her. She, reluctant to be seen so patently avoiding him, remained fixed to the spot, overwhelmed by the urge to flee, but hampered by legs that would not obey. *'Barbarian!'* she growled at him under her breath.

His hand moved over the wounded knuckle, though his eyes remained upon her, searing her with their unaccustomed warmth. 'Wildcat!' he whispered. 'I can tame you.'

The daunting words brought her eyes to his face again, as he knew they would. But if she hoped that the creases around his mobile mouth were formed by pain, she was forced to conclude that there was quite a different emotion on display there and that he had seen how her hand stole of its own volition to comfort a certain sharp pain of her own.

Chapter Three

'What is it, love?' said Lady Charlotte to her sister-in-law. 'I saw you speaking to Sir Fergus before he left. Are you still angered? Or is he angered that you spent more time with his brother than with him?'

'No, Lotti,' said Nicola.

Not quite satisfied, Lady Charlotte drew Nicola's arm through hers and strolled away from the river's edge towards the house. It was still ablaze with light from the torches, the musicians were packing away their instruments and the servants glided through the shadows to gather left-overs into baskets. Ripples from the last of the departing wherries lapped shallowly at the jetty and rocked the one remaining boat that belonged to Lord Coldyngham.

Merchants' wives, collectively envied for their access to the newest styles and finest fabrics from Venetian and Genoese trading galleys, had a reputation for wearing their wealth without the slightest flair. But

Lady Charlotte was an exception; tall, elegant, madonna-like in many respects with soft sea-coloured eyes that changed with the light and a top lip that barely covered her white teeth, she wore her wealth with more sophistication and discretion than most. She and George made a perfect couple and, for Nicola, Lotti was the only woman with whom she could talk intimately. Tonight, however, she did not intend to talk about Fergus Melrose when she suspected that parts of the conversation might accidentally leak back to her brother during the night. George's enthusiasm for the match had not been lost upon Nicola.

They sat together in one of the leafy alcoves on one side of the garden where Nicola watched the full moon's reflection, striving to place those amazing kisses in the context of Fergus instead of Muir, trying hard to reverse her disappointment yet unable to think more positively about such a phenomenon. A few moments ago, she was sure he meant to chasten her, humiliate her. It was what he was best at, after all. He had done it that morning. Now, she was sure of only one thing: that they both intended to do battle.

Lotti's head dipped gracefully. 'George has told me something of the problem,' she said softly, 'but can you hold that against Fergus now, after all these years? It was a long time ago, love. He obviously intends to win you, you know.'

Nicola's resolve not to speak of him instantly dissolved. 'He wants to win because that's the way he is,' she said. 'He's always been like that. Tell him he can't

have something and he'll prove to you that he can.
Imagine being married to a man like that.'

Lotti's sigh finished with a musical, 'Mm…m.'

'I don't mean *that*,' said Nicola, smiling at last.

'Is it someone else? You have a lover?'

The question took Nicola by surprise. 'Not a lover,
exactly. Friends, not lovers. There's Lord John, and…'

'You mean Jonathan Carey, Earl of Rufford?'

'Yes.'

'And you're fond of him?'

'Well…yes…in a way. He's fun to be with.'

'He wants you to marry him?'

Nicola glanced at Lotti's profile, but could see nothing of the concern in her eyes that George had spoken
of. But the question was not easy to answer. 'I don't really know,' she said. 'I think…well…I think so.'

'You mean he's not said as such in so many words,
is that it?' When Nicola hesitated even more, Lotti
began to understand. 'You mean he wants you to go to
bed with him. Yes, well…he would.'

'What d'ye mean, he would? He's nice. Very courteous.'

'Of course he is, but how much do you know about
him?'

'Well, I know that he's experienced. Most men of his
age are if they get half a chance. I expect Fergus Melrose is too. I dare say Lord John would marry me if I
gave him a little more encouragement.'

Experienced was not the word Lady Charlotte would
have chosen to describe the dubious charms of the Earl

of Rufford—Lord John, as he was known to his acquaintances. 'Then for heaven's sake don't give him any encouragement, love. Marry Sir Fergus. You'll be on safer ground there.'

'Thank you, but no. Stuck up in the wilds of Scotland with nothing but a clutch of bairns for company is not my idea of safer ground, Lotti.'

'He's comely,' Lotti replied. 'And wealthy. And intelligent. What more d'ye want?'

Nicola cast a reproachful glance at her sister-in-law before returning to her study of the moon. 'Do you have a spare four hours?' she said. Then, regretting the reply, she tried to put into words the essence of her objections while wondering if Lotti would be able to see what lay beneath them. 'Lotti,' she said, 'I want to keep hold of my new life. That's what I want. I've only just discovered how it feels to take control of my own affairs, to be secure in my own home, be my own mistress. Without a mother I've had to suffer the control of four men in different dosages. Then the strict family in York. Now I've chosen friends who like me for my own company, men who actually seek me and vie for my attention. That's new, Lotti. I'm enjoying it. I could become addicted. Do you understand? I know George thinks they're all after something more interesting than me, but that's what I've always been told, never that I was worth seeking out for myself alone. Now I know different, and I can pick and choose, and I can stop a man's friendship if he doesn't come up to scratch. I'm turning the tables, Lotti.' She laughed with excitement, not noticing how Lotti studied her carefully. 'I shall go too fast for them and leave them behind. For the first time in my life I can call my own tune and have men dance to it, and if Fergus Melrose wants to join in, he'll have to do the same. So it's no use asking me about marriage, Lotti. I don't know. I'm not interested. Ask me again in ten years.'

'So you're still a virgin?'

'Yes, silly. Of course I am. What makes you think I'd give that away so soon?' Furtively, one hand crept up to hitch the vee of her bodice by a notch and to hold it there as the moon smiled knowingly back at her.

As far as it went, the explanation would probably convince Lotti, though Nicola knew only too well how much more personal it was than that. It was to do with the prickly defence she had placed around that tender place deep inside, a place that Fergus Melrose had trampled over and must not be allowed to reach again. It was to do with their old immature relationship where he had been the one to call the tune and she had followed, blinded by the force of adoration.

Yet now there was a new and more disturbing element that made it hard for her to dismiss him as she would like to do, as she would have done to any man guilty of such advantage-taking. Fergus Melrose would not be pushed aside as other young hopefuls had been, and she would have to fight him tooth and nail to maintain her ground and to show him that he could never be a part of her life. Whatever reason he'd had for changing places with his brother and making love to her, Nicola understood that he did not mean to play by the rules.

Her night at her brother's River House was anything but peaceful, despite the ministrations of her maids, the coolness of white linen sheets, the regular call of bells and the nightwatchman's reassuring cry. From the first fierce invasion of his lips, she had been badly shaken, but the question that remained longer than all others was to do with his deceit. Would she have pushed herself away so soon if she had known it was Fergus instead of his fawning brother? 'Damn you!' she whispered to her pillow. 'I'll make you pay dearly for that.'

'George, dearest?' said Lady Charlotte to Lord Coldyngham that same night, slipping a bare arm through his.

He clamped it to his side, possessively. 'The answer's no. I'm too exhausted.' His grin was poorly concealed.

'Stop teasing,' she chided. 'It's not that.' Even now, he was still able to send shivers down her legs. 'It's something else.'

'So if it's not that, it must be money. How much?'

'George, stop it!' Charlotte pulled at her arm, laughing when George held on to it. 'Listen to me seriously. You've *got* to get Nicola and Fergus together somehow. Are you hearing me?'

She had few clothes on; in the light of one candelabra, she glowed like a young girl, alluring and lissome.

It was not likely that George was listening as he turned her in his arms and let his hands wander. 'Well, that's the general idea, my sweet, isn't it?' he murmured in her ear. 'Come to bed. We'll talk about it tomorrow.'

'George, she's getting too friendly with Jonathan Carey. She believes he'll marry her if she encourages him to.'

His hands stopped caressing. 'Is that what she said? Carey doesn't need any encouragement, from what I've heard.'

'Yes, they're close. It's dangerous, love. She *must* marry Fergus. It's the best way for her to be safe. You know how persistent men like Lord John can be. He'll not be the only one, either.' She would not have said as much to Nicola, but the problem was serious, for while it had been acceptable for her father to live alone at the Bishops-gate house whenever he needed to, it was not at all the same thing for Nicola to do so. Widowed, she could have got away with it, but Nicola had neither husband nor father nor family with her, and was therefore living outside a man's rule. For her to entertain a stream of young men on the basis that she was merely exercising her independence was asking for trouble. An ungoverned and unprotected woman could very quickly be saddled with a reputation that would take some living down. Charlotte could not quite understand why Nicola didn't seem to care.

'Well, the trouble is, love,' said George, 'that my sister's dislike goes so far back that Fergus is going to have a real battle on his hands now. They didn't even look at each other this evening.'

'She looked plenty at his brother, though. Was that to annoy Fergus, d'ye think?'

'I'm sure of it. That's been the least of her rudenesses so far.'

'Did you know she has a wound on her breast?'

'A what?' George frowned, turning her to face him.

'I saw the top of it just below her chemise. She's been fencing with the guards off again, I suppose. I do wish she wouldn't. Can you not speak to her about it?'

'Are you *sure*?'

'Yes, positive. Why?' George was used to keeping his thoughts to himself, but his wife knew him too well to be deceived. 'You know something, don't you? Tell me,' she said.

'There were two rapiers in the hall. I wondered what they were doing there at that time of the morning. Fergus picked them up and placed them against the wall. I thought that was a bit odd, too.'

'God in heaven, George, what are you saying? That Fergus…and Nicola…?'

'Fought. Before I got there. She'd not beat him at that. None of us could.'

'Argh!' Charlotte pulled herself out of George's arms with a cry of despair and went to hold the carved post of the bed, leaning her fair head against the knotted curtains. 'That puts *him* out of the running, then.'

'Not at all,' said George. 'I know his ways.'

'What?' She turned angrily. 'To wound a woman first before he…?'

'Well, I don't think he's ever gone quite as far as that

before, but he has his methods, and he'll certainly make her pay attention to him, one way or another.'

'George Coldyngham, you can be so crass when you try, can't you?' Charlotte snapped, trying to push past him to her side of the bed. 'I've never heard anything so ridiculous, and if I were Nicola I'd—'

She was caught up by George's arms and thrown sideways on to the bed like a skittle with him on top of her, and the tussle that ensued was too short to be anything like equal. 'But you're not her, are you?' George whispered, taking a handful of her moonbeam hair. 'You're the woman I've had my eye on all evening, and now I've got you here, all to myself, and I'm not sharing you a moment longer with anyone. Now, do you give yourself, or do I have to take you?'

'Mm…m, a bit of both?' she said, showing him her lovely white teeth.

While Lotti and George saw Fergus as a solution to the problem of Nicola's safety, Nicola herself saw things rather differently. Her brother and sister-in-law had not, after all, experienced what *she* had experienced of the man's youthful callousness and now his grave discourtesy when he had taken advantage of her right under their noses. The memory of the kiss had kept her awake half the night as she alternately ascribed it to a kind of revenge, then to curiosity, then to a manly thing, then to some misguided idea that it might help to persuade her. None of them rang true.

Convinced that she must be the one to hold the reins

in this matter, she set to work as never before to put as much distance between them as it was possible to do in a place the size of London, a device not so very difficult with the help of friends and fair weather. The first day she spent at the Tower of London, where the Yorkist king Edward IV kept his menagerie of lions and an elephant, a camel and a black-and-white striped horse. She went hawking outside the city walls and returned home to discover that Sir Fergus Melrose had called and left her a white rabbit. It was a very satisfying day, and she called the rabbit after him, being unsure of its gender.

The next day she devoted to visiting several of the convents near Bishops-gate. To her delight, she discovered that Sir Fergus had called again while she was out, but no one could tell him exactly where she would be. The gardener grumbled that Melrose had chewed through four of his lettuces.

The next two days were taken up from morn till night with another endless round of activities designed especially to keep her from home; a day spent mostly on the river as far as Richmond, another day shopping on Cheapside, returning home by suppertime to find that Melrose had demolished more lettuces and was imprisoned in an empty coldframe. It was all going very well, for Sir Fergus had called yet again. She had begun to hope that he would soon take the hint, but she had forgotten how Fergus thrived on challenges.

Jonathan Carey, Earl of Rufford, thrived on challenges of a different kind that Nicola, in her innocence, had not fully understood until last night, when Lotti had pointed out with alarming frankness that Lord John had not mentioned matrimony and that it would probably be bedlock he had in mind rather than wedlock. He had never approached George for formal permission to court her and, though Nicola felt that perhaps the handsome earl's thinly veiled suggestions were putting the cart before the horse, so to speak, a hint of marriage would have been more in keeping with her declaration to Lotti that her friends wanted her for her own sake. That had been a monumental piece of wishful thinking, for she had no way of knowing what they wanted her for.

As for Fergus Melrose, he was the exception. He wanted her for the Coldyngham name and for his personal promise to his father. Believing himself to be her favourite, Jonathan Carey wanted her for her companionship, and presumably if George had thought her reputation to be in danger because of it, he would have told her so.

The day was bright and warm as Nicola and Lord John rode side by side through Bishops-gate past the Bethlehem Hospital and the Priory of St Mary's Spital, both of which she had recently visited. Beyond the fine houses and gardens was the Shoreditch, open fields and windmills where they and their friends could freely show off their horses, eagerly placing bets on the outcome of their races.

He was a pleasant companion, one of the first to come a-calling when she had first moved to Bishops-gate; although there were a few little weaknesses in his character, none of them had been serious enough to disturb Nicola. He was apparently wealthy, so George's fears that she would be a target for bounty-hunters was not applicable there. He was pleasantly good-looking rather than striking, graceful and willowy rather than robust, well mannered but sometimes embarrassingly flirtatious, chatty, good fun and ever ready to entertain her, and if she found herself lending him money for expenses while they were out, that was because he forgot to carry any with him. He also forgot, dear man, to pay her back, but no matter.

His trim sandy hair hardly moved in the breeze as he turned to look over his hugely padded shoulder at the troupe of friends riding behind them. A high embroidered collar embraced all but the front of his neck where an ornate tassel held his short cloak together. Nicola liked his style.

'Well, my lady,' he said, turning his twinkling blue eyes towards her. 'There'll be a few bets laid on your new nag, but I think I may well go home with funds in my purse today.' He patted the blue leather pouch that hung from his belt over a blue pourpoint. Everything matched, even his sapphire ring. 'What's the prize for the winner to be?' he whispered, leaning towards her. 'A night with the chaste Nicola?'

Nicola looked straight ahead, ignoring his teasing look. 'The winner may take me back home by all means,' she said lightly, 'but that's all. Anyway, I shall win on my Janus, then I get to choose my own escort.'

'Ah…' he laughed '…then I cannot lose, can I?'

'Don't be too sure, my lord,' she said, patting the smooth neck of her mount. 'My choice will not always fall on you, you know.'

The merry smile left his face, though his eyes watched hers to assure her of his intentions. 'I shall take it very ill, Nicola, if it does not. You know how I feel about you.'

Privately, she wished he would not. She had no objection to mild flirting, but this kind of talk was difficult to handle, coming from him, too restricting, too uncomfortable. What was the matter with men these days? Fortunately, the usually well-mannered Janus threw up his head and danced sideways as a hedgehog scuttled away from the track before them, claiming her attention until he was settled.

She had bought Janus only a few weeks ago, and still only suspected the kind of speed of which he was capable with those long delicate legs and deep chest. He was a three-year-old gelding with dappled-grey shading and charcoal socks, like a silver ghost in a leafy-shadowed forest. He was exquisite and showy, full of energy, and he had cost her forty guineas, and she was sure that none of her friends, including Lord John, knew that she had been used to racing her brothers in the past.

Being unmarried and free, she had chosen to wear her hair in one thick plait braided with ribbons and a gold circlet that sat well on her forehead. A broad green sash supported her breasts, pushing them high beneath a tiny bodice of patterned green brocade, its wide neckline showing off an expanse of peachy skin upon which she felt Lord John's purposeful attention.

Just as purposefully, she laughed and chatted to all the young men in the party with equal gaiety, laying small bets on their challenges and cheering as they jumped the stream, leapt over logs, and raced from one windmill to the next.

'Your turn, Lady Nicola,' called Lord John. 'Let's see the pace of that mule you've bought. I swear two circuits of the common will see him winded or you tumbled in the stream. One or the other.'

'I'll take you all on, then,' she replied.

'What's your prize?' called a man's voice from the crowd.

She had been thinking. 'I get to ride home pillion behind the winner.'

There was laughter at that. That, they said, was *her* prize, surely?

'Take it or leave it,' she called.

'We'll take it!' said the deep voice. 'Ready, lads?'

That voice! 'Ready, lads?' The words he had always used to call her brothers away on the next adventure that had never included her.

'Who's that?' she whispered to the young groom whose cupped hands waited for her foot. 'I don't recognise the voice.' It was untrue. She recognised it well enough, but dare hardly admit to it.

'You'll see better from the saddle, m'lady,' said the groom. 'You're not riding sideways, then? Hup!'

'No,' she said, throwing one leg over and tucking her

skirts beneath her. It was unladylike in the extreme, but she intended to win this race and that could not be done without a secure seat. 'It's all right. My friends have seen my ankles before.'

From the height of Janus's back, she turned to see what she most feared and was caught, well before she could avoid them, by the triumphantly laughing eyes of Sir Fergus Melrose. Supremely confident, he towered a head above most of the others on a bay stallion at least two hands taller than her delicate racy gelding, yet there was no time to exchange more than one forbidding glance before the horses jostled into a prancing snorting line, stamping and tossing with impatience.

'Two circuits!' somebody called, and she knew it was him.

Hostility burned a scowl upon her face, for now her chances of winning had lessened considerably. Worse still, she had hoped for another day free of his presence. Even his complete retreat. Now that possibility had all but disappeared. Clenching her teeth, she gathered the reins and watched the white kerchief fluttering in the breeze, ready to drop.

'Off!' The kerchief descended and Janus leapt forward well ahead of the others as if he knew the signal as well as she. A stampede of hooves threw sods of dry turf high into the air as a sea of colour surged across the common land towards a distant windmill, its arms waving lazily to them in a clear blue sky. It seemed a very long way away, and Nicola was the only woman in a field of determined men.

Sheep and lambs belonging to the commoners had, since the previous contests, herded themselves together well away from the yelling riders who thudded forward, led by the silver-and-green image of Nicola. Just in the lead, she was able to choose the narrowest part of the stream to jump, hardly noticing a change in Janus's stride as he flew over it like a swallow. But the ground was hard and unkind to horses' hooves, and the sound of crashing behind her told a story of spills and worse.

In Nicola's mind, however, a force had taken hold that harked back to her youth when, as an eleven- and twelve-year-old, her main ambition had been to make Fergus Melrose recognise her abilities, to place herself on his exalted level and, dream of dreams, to beat him. That would be triumph indeed. That would show him, especially after that humiliating episode with the swords. So she forgot how uneven the contest was, and how things had always been between them, how he always won and how bitter was the pain not only of losing but of being ignored, too. This time, she would give him a good run for his money, and she would ride pillion behind a man of her own choosing, whose name would not be Fergus Melrose.

Janus was everything she had hoped he would be, fast, sure-footed and agile, and possessed of excellent stamina long after many of the others had dropped back on the second circuit. Passing those friends who had not taken part, she was aware of their cheering for her and of their warning that the stranger on the big bay was close behind her. Indeed, she could hear the pounding of his hooves close by, the steady unbroken rhythm and the untroubled breathing, though she would not turn to look. She placed Janus carefully to clear the stream again, but now the big bay stallion leapt it as if it were not there, then went loping across the ground as if he was fresh out of the stable and his rider taking the morning air.

From then on, no matter how she kept up the pressure on the gallant Janus, Sir Fergus stayed half a length in front as if to tease her into believing that a win was still possible when she could sense that it was not. Hoping for an extra burst of speed at the end, Nicola dug her heels into the horse's heaving sides and dropped her hands, urging him on with her fingers in his mane. But the distance between them increased and, though there were others not far behind her, the race might as well have been between only Nicola and Fergus for all it mattered, for Fergus romped home as he had always done ever since she had known him.

Lathered with sweat, Janus dropped his head as Nicola slid to the ground, ready to hand him over to the waiting groom. She was tired, angry and bitterly disappointed that this man should have spoiled what had begun as fun and games, no more. Now, it was the same as ever, and she had been robbed of her success because he couldn't bear to be beaten by little Nicola Coldyngham.

He turned back to meet her, smacking the sweating neck of the glossy bay, not as smiling in victory as she had expected him to be, though surrounded by admirers. Leaning down, he held out a hand to her. 'Jump up behind me, my lady. Put your foot on top of mine.' It took him barely four seconds to recognise the defiance in her eyes, and his dismounting was a quick roll off the horse's back that brought him very close to her. 'I'm taking you home, Nicola,' he said, grimly.

'I am not ready to go home, sir. I'm staying here with my friends. I know you can claim the prize, but you'll have to wait,' she said, trying to dodge round him.

Fergus was not inclined to argue, for now the other riders were approaching, Lord John amongst them leading his exhausted horse through clouds of steam and shouts of congratulations. Fergus acted. With one sudden dip of his body, he caught Nicola like a puppet and tossed her up on to the wide rump of his bay, behind the saddle. Then, before she could protest or wonder how to get down from that perilous height without breaking an ankle, he was seated in front of her, gathering the reins and moving away, calling to Nicola's groom to lead Janus behind them.

On this rare occasion, Nicola saw the wisdom of holding her tongue. For one thing, much as he deserved it, she did not want Fergus's overbearing behaviour to become an issue or to spark off an incident. For another, this conclusion to her losing and his winning was so unlike the way it used to be when she had been left alone and dismal, that something in her rejoiced, childlike, to be acknowledged as the one who might…just… have won.

Lord John was not so impressed. 'Who are you, sir?' he snapped at Fergus, his coarse skin blotched and sweating profusely, his fair hair dark and sticky and very untidy. He looked suddenly dissolute and old.

'Sir Fergus Melrose, my lord, at your service. The Lady Nicola and I claim our prize. First man. First lady. I'm taking her home now. She's been out long enough.'

From behind his back, Nicola nearly spluttered with indignation at this latest piece of interference, but again she kept her peace. Joining in would gain nothing except, possibly, to be the centrepiece of a brawl.

'And who are you to say when Lady Nicola has been out long enough? Are you related?' Lord John said, coldly eyeing Fergus's expensive saddle and boots.

'Distantly,' said Fergus. 'Lady Nicola and I have an agreement of long standing. We shall soon be betrothed. I give you good day, my lord.'

'What!' Lord John's colour drained away as they watched. 'You are—? Is this true, my lady?' He looked up at Nicola with eyes, usually so merry and teasing, now staring and cold with fury.

Determined not to be drawn into an unseemly discussion before all these sharp ears, Nicola put on what she hoped was a brave smile intended to placate her friend. 'We'll talk about this another day, my lord, if you please, when we have more privacy. This is not the time or place. Sir Fergus is a friend of the family. I've known him since we were children.' By the time she had finished the last sentence, Fergus had put his heels to the bay's flanks and was already moving away through the envious and curious spectators, and Nicola had to snatch at his belt to keep her balance, leaving Lord John truly speechless with rage at being robbed of his prize. He would certainly have been allowed to win if Fergus had not appeared.

The look on Lord John's face as they left made her arms prickle with an icy chill: it was a look she would remember for some time.

She waited until the friends were out of their hearing before launching into a reprimand of the kind she would like to have delivered twelve years ago, if she had had the courage. 'If you think this is the kind of behaviour appropriate from a suitor to a lady, Sir Fergus, you had better take some lessons, it seems to me. Your rudeness was well-nigh unbearable when you were sixteen. It certainly hasn't improved, has it? Is this the best you can do?'

'Move up closer,' he said over his shoulder, 'or you'll slip off. And put your arm around my waist. Come on, lass, hold on to me.'

'There's no reason why I should not ride my own horse,' she snapped, looking back at the tired Janus being led. The groom winked at her, cheekily.

'You might not think so, but I want you where I can get at you, for once. And this is as good a place as any.'

'Well, that much *has* changed, I grant you, but I am not interested in being got at, I thank you. Not by you, anyway. This can do nothing but harm to my good name, which I am most careful of, especially after…' she faltered, not quite sure whether he was giving her all his attention '…after what happened earlier this week.' She was glad he could not see the blush. 'It would be best if you were to look elsewhere for a wife. There must be many eligible women who quite like to be wounded, then groped, then snatched away from her friends like this. It's a pity our fathers didn't consult the relevant parties all those years ago. It would have made these continual refusals unnecessary, wouldn't it?' She clutched at him as the horse checked, then started again, wishing she could see the result of her tirade upon his face, to judge whether it was having any effect.

There had been many times when, as a lass, she had dreamed of riding close to him like this, to be picked up and placed on his horse and told to hold on tightly. Now, it was too late, she told herself. Much too late.

In the strong light of day, the comparison with his younger brother was even more obvious. It was not only the four-year age difference, or Fergus's manly and graceful bearing that oozed sexuality, but his refusal to play by the accepted rules of courtly love, as his brother had tried so hard to do. It had, she recalled, been wearisome after several hours of flattery and adoration. Even so, the elder brother's methods were too much the opposite, and they would not do. No, they would certainly not do. 'Have you heard a word of what I said?' she muttered, studying the wide velvet-covered back and a straining seam.

'Your good name, my lady?' he said. 'Is that of such great importance to you, then? Is that why you spend so much time in the company of Jonathan Carey, Earl of Rufford? I'm surprised you think I'm more of a threat to you than a man like that.'

They turned on to the wide track that led down to the city walls, and Nicola was rocked as Fergus sought the higher grass verge instead of the dry deep cart-ruts. 'You speak in riddles, sir,' she said. 'A man like what?'

Fergus had never been one to let the grass grow under his feet. Over the past few frustrating days, he had made some investigations that George himself might have made if he'd taken his wife's concerns more seriously. Come to that, George should never have allowed his sister to live alone in the first place. That had been an indulgence of sheer folly quite untypical of George, and Fergus could only assume that he was humouring Nicola to make up for earlier deficiencies. 'Your aristocratic friend,' he said, stressing the high connections, 'has a loose tongue, I fear. That would not be so bad by itself if he didn't also lie and slander his friends. Sadly, he does.'

'If this is about discrediting my friends,' she said, 'I don't want to know.'

'We were talking about *your* good name, my lady. Weren't we?' he said over his shoulder. 'If you're really as concerned about that as you say, then you should know what your so-called friends are saying about it. Shall I tell you?'

Despite her resistance, she did want to know. 'If you must, though I don't know why I should take you seriously.'

'Well, then, I have a better idea.'

'What?'

'Don't take my word for it. Hear it for yourself. Come with me across the river to the Bear Gardens in Southwark where my man went last night, and there you can hear at first hand what your noble friend has to say about his chances with you. Oh, and by the way, he's married.'

The horse…the world…seemed to lurch beneath her as she stared hard at his back to keep her balance. She felt suddenly small and devalued as Lord John's teasing, his persistence, echoed through her mind, chilling her soul. 'Married?' she whispered. 'Are you…?'

He did not rely to that immediately, for he could feel her shock through his back. After a moment or two, he continued, talking low and evenly over his shoulder, trying to keep all signs of gloating from his voice. 'I thought you should know that. I'm acquainted with the Countess and her family. Needless to say, they live modestly well away from London, but she's in little doubt what he gets up to, mostly spending her dowry. She sees him rarely, and then only long enough to father another child. There were four when I last saw them and another on the way. I'm not sure how many bastards he has…well, I don't suppose he knows either…but by the sound of things he's relying on your co-operation to increase the number. You might ask him, one day.'

Nicola felt nauseous. Disbelieving. Confounded. 'Why has George never told me?' she said angrily to his back. *Why has no one ever told me?*

'I can't answer for George,' he said, stopping to let a loaded wagon pass by. 'Hold on. For one thing, he doesn't listen to gossip of that kind, nor does he keep that kind of company.'

'And you do, I suppose?'

'My man does when I tell him to, yes.'

She felt the thudding beat of anger in her wounded breast as the horse moved on again, and she longed to be home, alone and private. 'So what are you hoping to gain by telling me this, Sir Fergus? Revenge for my insults? An eye for an eye because I've refused you? You think that by saving me from scandal I shall be in your debt, and when you can't win me by your own methods you pull reputations apart instead? Do I have the general idea? Since when have you been mindful of me, sir? When have you *ever* bothered yourself about me or my good name? Have you forgotten how you recently wounded me and then shamed me so impudently as if I were a common serving-girl for your pleasure? Is all this meant to endear me to you in some way? Is your behaviour meant to be more gentlemanly than Lord John's?' Her voice echoed low through the Bishopsgate-house that was part of the city wall, and she saw how people looked at them, then at her angry flushed face, then at her own grey gelding being led behind. They would be putting their own constructions on the well-bred, well-dressed scene.

Fergus seemed unperturbed. 'It was certainly more private than his,' he replied. 'Otherwise no, I agree. We've not had a smooth start, have we?'

'And now you seem to believe that because we knew each other as silly children you can begin again as if nothing has changed. But it's not so, sir, and you must accept it. I know about winning too. I'm learning how to make my own decisions. I'm gaining experience, and I don't cry when I fall into the muck-heap any more.' She caught the smile he flashed over his shoulder at that and felt a mild surprise that he had remembered. 'You may smile at the memory if you like, but if my choice of friends is sometimes faulty, I think I can live with the mistake. My good name will probably stand it. Thank-you for your warnings, but I have other more loyal friends who'll be happy to protect me as you never thought to do.'

'And did they tell you about Lord John, these loyal friends?'

She paused. No, they had not. 'It doesn't matter. I was not intending to marry him. I'm not ready for marriage to anyone.'

'At twenty-four?'

Fortunately, she was not able to see his expression. 'Yes, Sir Fergus. And I shall never be ready to marry a Melrose at *any* age. Whatever your reasons for offering for me, which we are apparently not given to understand, you'll never convince me that either of us will be made happy by it, and I don't have a life to waste on more misery in your company.'

Nor could she see the lean tanned jaw that rippled with muscles, reacting to her scalding words and banishing any trace of mirth. His mouth was set in a grim line as they approached St Mary's Priory, his eyes narrowed to daggers. 'Is that so, my lady?' he said. 'Then we're going to have to settle for something more exhilarating than mere happiness, for I have a promise to keep to my father and, like it or not, Lady Coldheart, you're going to help me with it.'

She had expected more wrangling, more persuasive talk, but not an uncompromising statement of intent. But now they were turning into the stableyard at the side of her Bishops-gate home, and the stinging reply she had intended to deliver was lost in the business of homecoming.

Dismounted, he held her about the waist and, by the steely greyness of his challenging eyes, Nicola knew that the presence of the grooms would have not the slightest effect upon his intentions towards her. She had read those signs too many times before. She thought that, if she twisted on her way down, she might be able to escape him and then run. *In her own home? How undignified. Face him down, girl.* 'I am not,' she snarled, held in suspension between horse and ground. 'I am certainly not going to help you, sir. I don't even intend to try.'

'You'll like it,' he said, still holding her, making escape impossible.

'I shall *not* like it.'

'You haven't had a taste of it, yet. Not enough to change your mind.'

'Which I shall not be doing. Put me *down*.'

The stallion was being led away and they were alone

in the stableyard, and he was still close. Much too close. Suddenly her day was overflowing with a surfeit of emotion and the promise of more to come, and she was wading out of her depth with this great arrogant, over-bearing creature, as she had so many times before on a different level. Once, she had longed for his attention, his closeness. Now, she feared it. Now, he was a full-grown man and more of a threat that he'd ever been in his brief visits to her brothers, and she still did not know how to deal with him, or how to deal with herself. She wished with all her heart he had never returned to upset her so.

She breathed in his virile male odour of exertion and horses, and something else that lingered, enticing, ex-citing, increasing the conflict in her mind and slowing it over a recent memory, daring her to allow a repeat. Her defences weakened and faltered, and she failed to react quickly enough when he closed in. Then it was too late.

Never having felt the frightening restriction of a man's embrace until that night in Lotti's garden, she re-sisted him because she was too proud to be coerced in this shameful manner by one who had never accepted opposition in any form. Nor had she been swayed by his impertinent assumption that she would like it just because, for one weak moment, she had been stilled in his arms as he kissed her.

But her plan to fight him off was stillborn when he took her wrists in one hand and held them behind her back, and her cries of protest were stopped by his lips bearing down upon hers, warming and sensuous, softening her too soon, bending her into him. Then all the guilty dreams of the past few nights came roaring back to melt her thighs and to make of her a weak and impotent woman, weaponless against him. A distant voice called for her to come to her senses, telling her that this was all wrong, but then faded again as his mouth moved over hers, letting the first kiss run seamlessly into the next, and the next.

Unthinking, effortless, she responded. Holding herself in a kind of limbo, she followed his questing mouth to seek the next sensation as she had not done before, and it was the sound of a horse's neigh and the rattle of a bucket hitting the cobblestones that brought them back to earth. It took them both a moment to adjust.

Fergus watched her eyelids lift to reveal deep bottomless pools of uncertainty and some faraway pain, and he knew he still had much ground to make up before she would begin to warm to him. 'You thought to get rid of me, lady,' he whispered. 'Well, you will not. You should remember that much about me, if nothing else.'

The grip on her wrist relaxed, and she arched away from him like an uncoiled spring, bristling with indignation. 'I remember little about you, sir, except your rustic Scottish manners. Yet another demonstration of your lust, I see. Lord John manages to control his, so that keeps him in the lead still.' Words tumbled out madly in an effort to wound him.

'Not with bigamy or adultery as his intention,' Fergus said with obvious disdain. 'And wealth, of course. His gambling skills are very mediocre, so my man says. How much of your wealth has he helped you to spend?'

'Is there any other crime you can heap upon his head, while you're about it?' she snarled, trying to step out of his reach, but stopped by an open stable door.

'Plenty, but I'd rather talk of more interesting things like a date for our betrothal, for a start. You may as well accept it, my lady.'

She could have turned and walked away at that and he would either have had to follow, remonstrating or silent, or have held her back forcibly to develop the argument further. To go would have been the easiest and most sensible course for her to take, and yet she was to look back upon this episode in later years and wonder what it was that kept her there, bickering and upset, while the sounds of the stableyard floated around them as if life could not wait for them to make their minds up. It had to go on.

She had made it sound, or rather she *hoped* she'd made it sound, as if her mind was finally and irrevocably made up. And he was supposed to believe it. But the truth was that they had taken each other by surprise, and while Nicola's memories of him were fossilised in time, Fergus's memories of her had suffered on different grounds. It was understandable, but not to Nicola. For her, he should have remembered every single incident, every slight, and he should *not* have smiled when she mentioned the muck-heap, for it had been particularly distressing and she had stunk for days. More than that, he should have been contrite, apologetic and, if he really wanted her hand in marriage, the very reverse of how he used to be. Kind. Adoring. Eager to please. Like Lord John. *Was he really as bad as that?*

But Fergus had reappeared with all his old hauteur, plus an almost primitive sensuality that most men would give their eye teeth for. Not even Nicola could have missed that, having responded to his undeveloped magnetism at such an early age without being able to identify it except by the pain it caused her. Now, it had burst upon her with a terrifying speed when she had only resentments to protect her, except that they couldn't and didn't. And now, when he had kissed her so thoroughly and with such obvious spontaneity, it was as if everything she had ever wanted from him, ever, *ever*, had been granted in one huge portion. Too much, too soon. She was unready, and angry that he thought she might be, angry that he had made her respond. He would know now what she would rather have kept to herself, just to dent his pride. Now she was weak, and he knew that, too. Which was why, she supposed, he was keeping up the offensive as he had earlier with the rapiers.

Fergus was experienced enough to see that the opposition was almost at a standstill, though the battle was not yet won. 'Nicola,' he said, 'do you hear what I'm saying? I'm not giving up. We can fight in private as much as you wish, but in public you'll have to pretend.'

'Pretend what, exactly? I've no interest in fighting you in public or in private. In fact, I've no interest in you at all, and I'm certainly not going to—'

Her denials got no further before he pulled her back to him, angrily. 'Oh, yes, you have, my lass,' he whispered, harshly. 'You've done little else *but* fight me since I arrived and I only have to look at you to set your hackles up, don't I? You've tried every insult, deserved and undeserved, and maybe I should have put you across my knee there and then. Now all you can do is to fight like a wildcat because you fear what's happening to you.'

'That's rubbish!' she hissed, hearing the truth of it at last.

'Then what's this all about if not fear? Eh? You think I shall hurt you?'

'Let me go!'

'Tell me. Is it that you fear you're softening? Melting? Isn't that what I felt just now when you sought my kisses? You learn fast, my lady.'

Gathering together every past resentment into her last ounce of strength, she swung a hand at his head for what ought to have been enough to send it rolling on to the cobbles. But Sir Fergus had seen it coming, he was experienced, and the quick block of his arm caused her to yelp at the pain in her wrist. He caught her hand and held it behind her, and once again there was nothing she could do but wait, imprisoned, hurting and seething with yet another disability of her own making.

'That's how it will be,' he said. 'You'll hurt yourself, not me, and eventually you'll fight yourself to an impasse and I'll still be here when you've learned how to enjoy losing. You can, you know. Losing need not be painful any more. So until then you can *pretend* friendship, for your family's sake. Unless you want them to see you get hurt just as they used to. Is that what you want? To fight for the sake of it?'

With clenched teeth to prevent tears of pain, she forced out the first words that came. 'I hate you, Fergus Melrose. I *hate* you.'

'Yes,' he said. His grim expression softened as he thought on it a while. 'You wear your heart on your sleeve, lass, don't you? You always did.' Then, before she realised what he was doing, he lifted her aching arm to his mouth and kissed it, just as a mother kisses away her child's hurt. 'Come,' he said, holding on to her hand, 'we'll go inside where it's cooler, and you can practice your pretending where there's no one to see.'

Bitterly, she recalled a time when to hold her hand would have been the last thing on his mind. The warm strength of his fingers closed over hers. 'We are *not* friends, Sir Fergus.'

What a pity you could not have pretended all those years ago. And why did you call me Lady Coldheart when it was Muir who had used the name first? Is he also a part of your scheme, Fergus Melrose?

Chapter Four

They were met in the cool passageway by Lavender with a panting white rabbit in her arms, while from the garden beyond came the sound of the gardener's curses and Rosemary's attempts to soothe him. To add to the drama, a caged popinjay screeched a phrase so often quoted by Nicola herself, 'Tell-im-to-go-way!'

'Master Ramond is here, m'lady,' said Lavender, rather loudly, still holding the rabbit's ears. 'In the hall.'

'Tell-im-to-go-way!' came the indiscriminate squawk.

Nicola was not quite quick enough, however, to release herself from Fergus's possessive hand before her brother came to meet them and, with a cry of joy such as she would never have used on any of her other brothers, she almost bowled him over with her energetic hug.

Ramond Coldyngham, a sturdy man of twenty-six summers, didn't appear to be in the least put out. Nevertheless, his own warm greeting was tempered by amazement that these two should have been holding hands like lovers, and while he hugged his sister with genuine delight, his first question was to Fergus, delivered over the top of Nicola's head. 'What the hell are you doing here?'

'Thank you,' drawled Sir Fergus. 'How good to see you too.' He came forward, laughing at the reaction and waiting his turn for an embrace. It had been many years since their last meeting, and now soft punches to each chest were meant to span the missed seasons and to say what neither of them could put into words about their retrospective view of the gauche youths they had once been. Fergus had never understood weakness in any form, Ramond had never understood competition; whereas the former had had to learn of compassion, the latter had known of it since birth. Still, in the different lives they had chosen, there was room for acceptance and admiration.

Greetings over, Ramond placed an arm about Nicola's waist and pulled her to him teasingly. 'What's all this then?' he said, looking doubtfully at her. 'You two friends at last, are you?'

'No…yes!' The two replies fell into the same space, leaving Ramond wide-eyed and blinking.

'I see,' he said. 'So your holding hands is…?'

'Nothing,' said Nicola, quickly. 'Nothing at all. What are you doing here, love?' Gently, she disengaged herself and went to pour two glasses of wine, relieved that it was only Ramond who had seen and no one else.

His visits had not been too frequent in the last few months, though it was no great distance from Gray's Inn where he was a law student. Like all the Coldynghams, he had the height, graceful bearing and fine features that indicated noble stock, and already he had acquired a cultured and sober manner in the company of which both men and women felt safe. Not that he lacked sexual attraction, only that it was of a quieter sort than that of the Melrose brothers. Dark-haired, dark-clothed and neat in every detail, Ramond was rarely perturbed, though now his smile was strained, hinting at a problem.

'What am I doing here?' he said, peering through the panes of wobbly green glass into the sunny garden. 'I'm beginning to wonder. Perhaps…er…I think this may not be a good time.' With a slight sigh, he turned his attention to Sir Fergus. 'How are things with you, Ferg? Do you live in London now, or are you here on business?'

'Both,' said Sir Fergus, accepting the glass of wine from Nicola. 'I have a place near Holyrood Wharf so I never have to wait for the bridge to open to get my ships in and out.' He took a sip of the wine and placed the glass on the table. 'But if there's a problem, Ramond, surely you'll allow me to help? Don't let my being here change your plans. The Lady Nicola and I were only talking.'

They had not been talking when Ramond had first seen them, but his hopes of being a diplomat had taught him when to keep silent. He held his glass of wine up to the light before replying. 'It's Patrick. He's on the run. I can't keep him at my lodgings at Gray's Inn, so I thought he might…no…of course he can't. I don't know what I was thinking of.' He studied the wine, frowning at the reflection of diamond-shaped panes.

'Come,' said Nicola, taking him by the hand, 'sit down here at the table and tell me what's happened. What's Patrick been up to this time?' She made no sign that she minded when Sir Fergus placed himself next to her, nor could she explain the most unusual sense of support at his presence.

'He's at Oxford, you know,' Ramond said to Sir Fergus. 'In his last year. George is not going to like this one bit. Best if he doesn't know, I think.'

'Start at the beginning, Ramond,' said Sir Fergus.

Ramond took a sip of the wine at last, placing the glass down on the table with almost comical precision. He could ill afford to have any disruption to his studies, for he was ambitious and totally single-minded. 'It's a set-up,' he said. 'Anyone can see that. There are two brothers in Oxford who've accused him of raping their sister.'

'Oh, Ramond! That *can't* be true.' Nicola sat bolt upright in alarm. Patrick might be feckless, but he was not given to vices of that nature. 'There must be some mistake.'

'No, I don't believe it, either. As I said, I think it's a set-up to get him to pay for their silence. They want five hundred pounds from him or they'll tell the university authorities and get him imprisoned, sent down, the lot.

They say they have witnesses who'll swear that he was with her. That's the kind of scandal that won't please George one bit. He's hoping to be elected to office in the Mercers' Guild this year, you know.' What it would do for his own career he was too modest to say.

'How did you hear about this?' said Sir Fergus. 'Did Patrick send a message?'

'He's here in London,' said Ramond, 'with me. Those thugs gave him a good kicking, so his pals put him on a wagon going in this direction with enough money to pay for it. He's in a bit of a mess. Not our Patrick at all. But I can't keep him with me at my tutor's house, so I thought you might be able to find him a corner somewhere, just till he can decide what to do.'

'Here?'

'Yes, but on reflection I can see that it's not a very clever idea. They're bound to pursue him, and that puts you in danger.'

'You're right,' said Sir Fergus, 'it's not a good idea, Ramond. But has Patrick denied the charges?'

'Well, that's part of the problem. He doesn't know. He goes out to get drunk most nights because he can't face the studies, he can't debate or say what he means, and he can't remember who he's been with or where he's been. He talks about a dare made one night, but that's as far as he can go, so when these two brothers waylaid him and accused him, he had to admit he knew their sister but then he told them, foolishly, I thought, that it wouldn't have been necessary to rape her. Naturally they didn't appreciate that, so they beat him up.

They've given him till today to produce the money, but now I suppose they'll start to look for him. They'll know where to find all the other Coldynghams, too.'

'So he *certainly* can't stay here,' said Sir Fergus with unmistakable finality and ignoring Nicola's scowl. 'We have to find somewhere safer.'

'We?' said Nicola. 'Sir Fergus, this is between Ramond and me. I expect we'll be able to come up with some alternative. He can stay here a while until we can find somewhere else.' She owed it to Ramond to help him out, for once.

'*Sir* Fergus?' Ramond's glum face lit up at that. 'Well done, man. Do I have to bow and scrape now? Will it be my lordship next?'

Sir Fergus grinned. 'The bowing and scraping will do very well for the time being,' he said.

Nicola felt that her objections were being ignored, as usual. 'You can bring Patrick here, Ramond,' she said. 'And George *will* have to be told.'

'No,' said Ramond. 'George will hit the roof. Pat doesn't want him to know. He's sure it'll all blow over.'

Sir Fergus swung his long legs over the bench, signalling an end to the discussion, almost bumping Nicola with his back as he did so and having no idea how the warm scent of his body caught in her nostrils and sent a wave of excitement into her breast. 'He's not coming here,' he said, standing up. 'Come on, Master Ramond, sir. Take me to him. I know just the place.'

The deep crease in Nicola's brow did not escape the observant Ramond. He reached across the table to lay a hand on her arm. 'I know what you're saying, Nick. Thank you. I know you'd have him here, but it was wrong of me to suggest it. These two thugs mean business and they'll not let matters rest there. Fergus will help me.'

She could not explain; Ramond had already misread the situation. 'Yes,' she said. Changing to a whisper, 'It's not what you think, Ramond.'

He squeezed her arm. 'Tell me about it later.'

'You'll come back?'

'Course I will. Today. Later on. Promise.' His hand squeezed again as he took the glass of wine and downed the contents in one gulp. 'Too good to leave,' he said as he stood up. 'Oh, and it's time you either changed the locks on your doors or got a new steward. Anyone could walk in here.'

'Isn't that just like him?' Nicola stormed after the two men had ridden off. 'Absolutely typical. He walks in here and makes decisions and even now, after all these years, Ramond gives in to him as if he were a god. In spite of me saying I'd take Patrick,' she scolded her maids, 'I'm being told *in my own house* what I can and can't do. I *know* it would have been dangerous, Lavender,' she snapped as the maid tried to pacify her, 'but what are sisters for? How many chances have I ever had to pay Ramond back for caring for me? None. Until now.' She paced back along the passageway with the white rabbit bouncing in the wake of her long russet skirts. 'And then it's snatched away from me by that…that…upstart! Why does he always have to have the last word, I wonder?'

The creature stopped when she did and sat on her hem, waiting for a signal. Nicola turned and looked down at it. 'And what about you, Melrose?' she said. 'Are you going to follow me everywhere, too?' She bent to pick up the end of the blue leash. 'Tch! Come on, then, if you must.'

She discovered some of the answers to her questions about three hours later when Ramond returned as he had promised, bowing politely to two of his sister's friends who were taking their leave of her. 'Bit irregular, isn't it, Nick?' he said, throwing his felt cap down on to the window-seat and running his fingers through his thick hair. 'All those chaps coming and going? Who are they, exactly?'

'Just friends,' she said, kissing his smooth cheek.

'Don't you have any women friends?'

'Yes. Where's Patrick? Is he going to be all right?'

'Thanks to Fergus he'll be fine. Have you got any food? I'm starving.' Brushing himself down with sweeps of his hand, he turned to wash his fingers in the bowl held by the servant, wiping his hands on the towel over the man's arm. It was no imposition to Ramond to wear clothes of the correct length and colour prescribed for law students because, in his own way, he was content to be recognised as such. No jewellery, no ornament, no furs or feathers. Replacing his hat, he sat down to wait as food was brought from the kitchen: cold pies and roasts, herb-seasoned pasties, bread and salads and a dish of early wild strawberries. It was only when they were private again would he give her the news she waited for. 'He's at Fergus's house on the Holyrood Wharf,' he said. 'You should just see it, Nick. As fine a place as ever you saw. There's stabling for—'

'Are you going to tell me about Patrick?' said Nicola, watching her ravenous brother from across the table. 'I know diplomats never get to the point if they can avoid it, but I need to know about him. How badly injured is he?'

Unruffled, Ramond helped himself to a slice of lamb. 'A glass of that very good wine, if you please? He's pretty cut up, and sore, and I think he'll be glad to stay where he is for a while. But he's tough. He'll mend. Fergus's men are taking good care of him. Ferg says you can visit him tomorrow, if you wish.'

'Then why didn't he come and tell me himself?'

Briefly, Ramond looked up from his plate. 'Did you want him to?'

'No.'

'But you think he ought to have done.'

'Well, it wouldn't have killed him, would it?'

'So what's happening between you two, then? Is it to do with Father's promise?'

'Yes.' There was some relief in discussing the matter with Ramond, though even now she was not sure whether she had his full attention in view of the fast disappearing plateful of food.

'And you've agreed?' he said, still stuffing his mouth.

'No, Ramond. I haven't agreed. Nor shall I be doing.'

He turned a chicken leg over to see where next to bite. 'Right. So is that why you were holding hands?'

'That's his kind of persuasion. You know how he likes to get his own way.'

'Well, I can see why he'd want to get his own way if *you* were the one on offer. Fergus is not a stroppy young lad any more, you know, nor is he daft enough to try to persuade you, just to prove that he can. If he's offering for you, it's because he wants you.'

'That's exactly what George said. But you're wrong, Ramond. He's offering for me because he promised his father he would. He was killed last year, you know.'

'Yes, he told me.'

'He's not going about it the right way, either.'

'So how d'ye want him to go about it?' he said, quietly, laying down his knife and his food and wiping his fingers on the napkin. Giving her all his attention at last, he said, 'You want him to change. Is that it?'

Suddenly confronted by his intelligent brown eyes, she found the question remarkably apt. 'Well…yes. A little more gentlemanly humility. A little adoration… tenderness…an apology for…oh, you know.' Spoken out loud, the list began to sound like the weak men she had sent away quite quickly over the last few months. 'Is there so little softness in him?' she whispered, thinking of the white rabbit.

Ramond snorted, looking at her from beneath his brows and shaking his head. He leaned towards her, and she knew what to expect. 'Nick,' he said, 'he's Fergus. He's never had much softness.'

'Well, it's time he learnt, then.'

'No, it's not that he doesn't *know*, it's just not the way

he is. He's direct, not subtle. He goes in a straight line, not round the mulberry bush. That's how he wins. You can't change that, or pine because he's not like others. He's *not* like others, is he? And there was a time when you admired everything he did, but, unfortunately, you were a wee lass and you got run over from time to time. But you're not a wee lass now, love. You're a woman. You can deal with it.'

'I don't see why I should have to deal with it, Ramond. I don't want to.'

Ramond was sure that she could. In her own way she was every bit as determined as Fergus. There had been many times when, just to prove she could go it alone, she had refused help, her elbows and knees bleeding from falls, her lip cut from the mock jousting she had been determined to join in, just to be near him. She would never have allowed Fergus to hold her hand if she had not still harboured some feelings for him. 'I think you should,' he said, admiring the sweep of thick lashes upon her cheek. 'You're not safe here on your own, Nick, with all these people walking in and out. Fergus can protect you.'

'They're friends,' she insisted. 'Stop worrying about me, Ramond. I'm safe enough.'

'From those simpering swains?' he said, tipping his head towards the door. 'I should hope so. Who were they? Do they always dress like that?'

Nicola doubted that he needed to know. 'Ramond,' she said, 'would you do something for me? I need an escort. I want to go to Southwark.'

With a quick dab at his mouth, Ramond laid the napkin on the table before answering. 'Why on earth would you want to go there?' he said.

'Because there's a tavern where a friend of mine goes. I've heard he gambles and I want to see for myself. This evening would be best.'

Disapproval showed on every line of her half-brother's face, from creased brow to tightened lips, and she knew she should not have asked. 'Sorry, love,' he said, standing up. 'I have to be back at my lodging every night by nine. Rules, you know. And this evening I have to be present at a disputation. In fact, I'd better get a move on.' Brushing aside the request as if it had hardly existed, he kissed Nicola on each cheek and held her at arm's length. 'Now don't you worry about Patrick. He's as safe as houses with Ferg. You'll be able to see him tomorrow and I'll come as soon as I can get away. Lovely meal. Thank you.'

'You were right to come here, Ramond. God be with you.' She walked with him outside to his horse.

He smiled, detecting something in her demeanour. 'Why not ask Fergus to escort you to Southwark, if you must go?'

'Hmm,' she said, watching him take the reins from the groom. 'We'll see.'

His foot was already in the stirrup when he hesitated and took it out again, handing the reins back to the groom. 'Wait,' he said.

'What is it?' said Nicola. 'Forgotten something?'

'Yes,' he said, slipping a hand under her elbow. 'My

priorities. Come and sit over here a while and tell me the *real* purpose of this visit to Southwark. They can manage without me this evening, and I can pay the fine for being out all night. Family first, love.'

Resisting the impulse to throw her arms around his neck, Nicola perched on the mounting-block in the sunny courtyard while Ramond sat below her to listen to what Fergus had told her earlier that day about Jonathan Carey, Earl of Rufford. 'I don't know what to believe,' she told him, 'but it's clear I must try to find out for myself. It would be sheer madness to go there on my own, or even with one of the servants, but if you'd come with me, Ramond, I could put the matter to rest. I like Lord John, but perhaps I'm not such a good judge of character as I thought I was.'

'I agree that you must find out for yourself without Fergus being there. If you're going to hear slander in front of witnesses, they must be impartial. But the Bear Gardens are no place for ladies to go, no matter what Fergus says.' He swatted a buzzing wasp with his riding whip.

'Then I'll go as a lad,' said Nicola. 'I've had plenty of practice.'

'You can't do that,' said Ramond. 'What d'ye think George would say? Or Ferg, for that matter?'

'They'll not find out, will they? Look,' she said, smiling at Ramond's frown, 'all we have to do is wait till suppertime and then join the crowds. You know how they flock across the bridge then, and you'll be with your young brother Nick.' She dropped her voice a tone, accordingly. 'I'll wager I can throw a dice and use a dagger as well as you, Ramond.'

The frown vanished. 'You always could, pest.' He laughed. 'Oh, all right. But don't think I shall stay there a moment longer than need be. We find out all we need to know and no more. Understood? And I shall need to send a message to my tutor.'

'To tell him where you'll be, Ramond? Surely not!'

'No, silly. To tell him where I'm supposed to be.'

The village of Southwark lay on the opposite bank of the River Thames and could only be reached by crossing Tower Bridge or by taking a boat to one of the jetties. From the river, the impression was of fair orchards and gardens sloping down to the water, of thatched rooftops and a sprawl of timber-framed houses, the church tower of St Mary's Overy—over the river   and the road leading southwards. On closer inspection of the congested lanes one could find a proliferation of bathhouses known to Londoners as 'stews', gaming and bawdy houses, noisy taverns and cockpits, bullrings and bear-gardens where animals were baited for sport and bets were laid, dens where thieves, and worse, plotted how best to relieve unwary visitors of their money or their virtue, or both. Here, in the thriving thronging thoroughfares of Southwark, well-dressed men and women strolled to see the sights and to enjoy a kind of fun laced with danger, to recoup money they had lost the previous night, or to eye the Flemish madames brought over especially for the purpose of private entertainment.

Some of it, though, was far from private and very far from quiet. Women called to the two young men who sauntered along, the taller one of the two trying not to blush at the explicit suggestions thrown his way, or at the offers to show him what he might not find elsewhere. Failing that, there were signs painted on the walls facing the river, a boar, a swan, a bull and cardinal's hat: there would be no excuse for mistaking the address here, or the prices that were called out by cheeky young lasses and their brothers. Lamps had already been lit; business had already begun.

'This is weird.' Nicola giggled. 'I'd never have thought Lord John would come to such a place.' Well used to dressing and behaving as a male, Nicola had no need to practice the stride or the swagger, the hands-on-hips stance as they watched street-corner gambling, the quick glance at pretty women and at the weapons carried by their escorts.

As the laden wherries tied up at the jetties, apprentices swarmed in troubleseeking gangs, and Ramond nudged Nicola to one side as they passed. 'Watch out!' he warned. 'It's a may-ing time again. Better find what we're looking for and get away before the rioting starts. I suggest we go to the Tabard and make some enquiries.' It was, by coincidence, the shortest night of the year, when light lingered over the most distant reaches of the river, when it seemed as if all of London's revellers had congregated in Southwark to cause as much mischief as they could at the Midsummer Night bonfires in an orgy of merrymaking that for most of them would end in a stupor or in a new day, whichever came soonest.

By the time they had discovered where they might find Lord John and his drinking and gambling fraternity, Ramond was already doubting the wisdom of bringing his sister, for now her jaunty smile had begun to wear thin in the roguish masculine atmosphere around them. She was slight, her curves disguised by a thickly padded doublet that came well down over her hips, her hair enclosed inside a boyish plant-pot felt hat. And she was far too lovely to resemble anything except the most effeminate young man, which put Ramond in an unusually difficult position. He had seen people's envious grins and their unwanted interest.

They need not have been too concerned, however, about being recognised, for by the time they found the crowd they were looking for in a dimly lit and noisy tavern-cum-gambling-den, Lord John's eyes were focussed only on the wayward dice spilling across the table, and it was clear that he had been drinking heavily.

A shapely young woman tried to sit on his lap, but his bad-tempered push sent her hurtling into the arms of the spectators with an oath that took Nicola by surprise, coming from the suave companion she had been with only that morning. 'Interesting,' she murmured to her brother. 'Another side?'

'There's always another side,' he replied sagely, taking a sip of warm ale. 'If we wait, we shall see more of it.'

'How d'ye know?'

'He's losing.'

Ramond was right. Lord John's extravagant head-gear now lay in a pile in front of one of the three other players, his dyed kid gauntlets folded on top in resignation. With an angry growl, the loser stood up and stripped off the sleeveless jerkin of padded velvet and laid it on the table with a flourish. 'My best bloody pourpoint,' he yelled at his companions. 'Come on. You'll not win *that* off me.'

The three players leaned back, laughing. 'I'll wager you don't get the Lady Nicola's clothes off as fast as that, my lord. Do you? Eh? How long's it going to be before you see a bit more of her?'

Another one chipped in on the same theme. 'Ah, she's got him on a string, has the Coldyngham wench. He'll not get into *her* shift as fast as he gets into his lady wife's. Now there's a willing woman for you. A fifth bairn in the pot, is it?'

Nicola froze, feeling the hairs prickle over her scalp despite the stifling warmth of the stinking room. Was this what Fergus's man had heard? Her good name being bandied around a dice table by half-drunk lechers? Heaven forbid.

Ramond gripped her arm. 'Do you want to go, Nick?' he said, not bothering to lower his voice in the shrieking din of the room.

'No...stay. Surely he'll protest?'

But, far from protesting, Lord John saw the chance to elaborate, if only to delay the moment when he would lose his jacket, and he fell back on to the bench with a laugh that rose to a grating falsetto. 'Oh, no, my lord,' he mimicked, contorting his face to a mask of primness, 'the winner will be allowed to take me home, but no more than that. I'm a virgin, you see…' the accompanying bellows of laughter nearly drowned out the next bit '…and no one must remove *my* kirtle.' The voice changed, suddenly. 'Virgin my foot,' he roared. 'The chit is no more a virgin than I am, I'll bet my house on it.'

'Your house? You're serious, my lord?'

'No, you fool. But I'm serious about taking the Coldynghams for a ride, especially the wench. Silly whore! She's—'

Ramond's dagger was out of its scabbard before Lord John could tell them what else she was, pointing at the soft flesh of his throat in a very unaccomplished manner that betrayed his lack of practice. Even Nicola could see that this was a move motivated more by anger than ability. 'Which Coldyngham in particular, my lord Earl?' snapped Ramond. 'Will any of us do, or must he first be as drunk as you?'

'Ramond…Ramond…come away!' pleaded Nicola, tapping his back. 'Leave them to it, please. *Please!*'

The three friends were rising to their feet, feeling for their daggers, and, as Nicola drew hers in defence, Lord John sprang back out of danger, laughing at Ramond's threat. It happened very quickly, and Nicola wished with all her heart that she had accepted her brother's advice to go before things got out of hand. They were no match for four ruffians of Lord John's sort, used to tavern brawls.

Grabbing Ramond's arm, she swung him round to face the four of them with her beside him, praying that the wavering lantern flame would not illuminate her face. 'Back towards the door,' she whispered to him. 'Quickly, Ramond!'

'This dog has insulted my sister and my family,' Ramond yelled. 'He shall apologise to me, or pay the price.'

Carefully, and insultingly slow, Lord John withdrew his dagger and smiled, a canine grin that Nicola had never seen till now. 'Your sister, Coldyngham, is a teasing whore,' he said. 'Anybody can go in and out of her house at any time of day or night. It's time she was taken in hand, lad. Come on, then. What are you waiting for?' He held his arms out wide with hardly a glance at Nicola, though she knew that any move from her would be instantly countered.

The situation was critical. 'I'm waiting for an *apology*,' said Ramond, taking a step towards him. Then, seeing that no apology was forthcoming, he snatched at Lord John's abandoned heap of clothes and hurled them at his face, lunging forward as the Earl's attention was diverted. All at once, there was a wrangle of men throwing tankards, pulling and pushing, hauling on necks, throwing punches and slashing with daggers, howling like demons, tipping tables and benches, sending bodies crashing to the floor with ripped clothes and bloodied noses. Ripe for a fight, onlookers joined in, swinging fists at anyone. Nicola was knocked to the floor under a table, hitting one of its legs with her head and sending her hat rolling away.

She felt the collar of her doublet being pulled backwards and, despite her protests, she was hauled like a puppy into a space between several pairs of legs. 'This way, young sir,' said a familiar voice, implying a certain weariness with the process. 'How many times a day do you have to be rescued, for pity's sake? Come *on*. Stop struggling, lad. It's me.'

'*You!*' Torn between relief and humiliation, she struggled to her feet while making a dive for Ramond's arm just in time to prevent his dagger from sweeping across Lord John's shoulder and, at that moment, the eyes of her accuser opened wide as if his drunkenness had for that split second been suspended. He recognised her, tumbled dark hair, furious eyes and all. And in men's clothing.

'*Beware!*' he snarled.

'Ramond… come!' she called in her brother's ear. 'Come! Now!'

He would have ignored her, but he also was held back by the scruff of his neck and dragged to the door while the uproar continued unabated, and Lord John did nothing to stop them, for he also had recognised Sir Fergus Melrose, the large and intimidating Scot who had claimed that very day to be Lady Nicola Coldyngham's protector.

Nicola was bruised from glancing blows, her doublet slashed by someone's weapon, but Ramond had suffered a nasty cut on his head, and blood was streaming down his face. Just outside the door, he staggered and would have fallen but for Fergus, who supported him as far as the two waiting horses. Between them, he and his man took Ramond into a quiet back alley and there bound his head with strips torn from the sober gown of black, which was probably his best. And while Nicola held the horses and leaned against the wall, she watched how Fergus's fingers worked tenderly at their task, his concentration, his coolness. She recalled his solid and fearless presence when he was needed most, and could not help comparing him to that abominable man she had called her friend, whose tongue was vile with insults far more grave than any she had recently delivered with far less justification. His words still seethed inside her head, frightening her with their poison.

Moments later, dazed and shaken, Nicola was being held firmly in the crook of Fergus's arm upon the great bay stallion while Ramond, led by Fergus's man, swayed wearily behind them and tried not to fall off. It was very like old times, he was thinking, except for Nicola's elevated position.

'How did you know?' she whispered, looking down upon the crowds.

'Know where to find you? I didn't have to be a genius to work that out,' Fergus said, speaking into her dishevelled hair. 'You should have accepted my offer. I could have protected you better.'

'It's a family affair.'

'It is now. He'll not let it rest at that, you know.'

She recalled the look of astonishment that had quickly turned to anger, then to hate, the ugly twist of the mouth. *Beware*, he had warned her. 'Is Ramond's cut deep?' she said.

'Deep enough, but nothing you and your maids can't fix.'

She wished she had not asked, for now there was between them a vivid memory of another wound and its discovery, and the look in his eyes that he had not managed to conceal, any more than Lord John had. She knew she ought to thank him, but she felt nauseous and shivery and the words would not come, no matter how she tried to form them. In their place, Lord John's venomous insults cut a swathe through all else, hurting her again and again as the horse wove its way back across Tower Bridge. No longer could she maintain that her lifestyle was safe, for now it was glaringly obvious that her bid for independence had gone sadly wrong, that she was as vulnerable as George had warned, that she had indeed attracted the wrong kind of attention. After what had happened just now, and the gossip it would cause, how could she ever again expect anyone to separate the Coldyngham name from the taint of scandal? Especially in the light of Patrick's latest escapades.

Patrick! Was that what Fergus had come to tell me, expecting me to be at home? 'What of Patrick?' she said, brushing her cheek along his soft leather doublet. 'Where did you take him? Can I see him?'

The reply was enigmatic. 'Not for a while,' he said.

'Why? He's not…?' In a morbid lightning flash, the

worst possible fate rushed to mind, adding to her guilt about poor Ramond. Had he suffered a sudden weakness and died?

'Don't jump to conclusions, lass,' said Fergus. 'He's well. In fact, he should be well out into the North Sea by now, with a fair westerly.'

'What? The North Sea? What are you talking about?' She sat up straight, wrenching herself so quickly out of his grasp that she nearly overbalanced.

His arm tightened. 'Sit still. I've put him on one of my ships. It sailed out on the afternoon tide. Sit *still*! He was perfectly willing to go with my captain to Flanders instead of trying to hide with Ramond, and he'll be safer there than anywhere. He's certainly better off learning something useful than wasting time at Oxford.'

But this was too much for Nicola to bear. His timely but interfering appearances, his high-handed rescues that only a moment ago had been appreciated, as if they were all a bunch of children who needed parenting. It was *so* humiliating. 'You've *what*?' she screeched at him, turning heads. 'You've put him on a *ship*? Without letting me see him? How dared you do that? How *dared* you?'

'Hush,' said Fergus, gripping her. 'Save it till we get home.'

'No…get off…let me *down*! This is too…too…' Blinded by furious tears and a sudden topsy-turvy confusion of interests and emotions, she tried to beat at him, disregarding the curious stares and grins directed at the bold rider who appeared to be holding a struggling, scolding young man across his saddle.

Sobs shook her as she slackened in his vice-like grip, her screech of rage merging and muffling into a howl of helplessness smothered by his chest. The combined issues of her two injured brothers, her own animosities and wilfulness, Lord John's appalling treachery and the unwelcome rekindling of old feelings all welled up and overflowed on to the leather doublet to make dark spreading blotches as Fergus watched.

'What is it?' called Ramond, weakly.

'Nothing much,' called Fergus over his shoulder. 'Just tiredness.'

'We're very grateful to you, Ferg.'

'Think nothing of it, old friend.' Fergus smiled, caressing the shaking arm beneath his hand. 'It's a pleasure.'

'I think Nick should go and stay with George, Ferg. Don't you?'

'I certainly do, Ramond. I think we should see to it immediately.'

This exchange did nothing to stem Nicola's tears.

At the Bishops-gate house, there was hardly any need for Fergus to tell Lavender and Rosemary what the problem was as he handed the tear-stained and snuffling Nicola into their care. 'She needs some sleep,' he said. 'I'll be back tomorrow, but now I'm taking Master Ramond back to Gray's Inn, so keep all the doors locked and bolted, won't you?'

'Yes, sir,' they said, watching his feet as he turned. 'Don't step on Melrose.'

'Who?' He looked down at the white hopping bundle of fur.

'Melrose, sir. Until we can think of a better name for him.'

'Seems to be having the same identity problem as his mistress,' said Fergus. 'I assumed he was a she.'

Nicola's fatigue kept her asleep until almost noon. Having missed the day's main meal, she sat up in bed with a tray on her lap and the twitching nose of the white rabbit hovering possessively over a pile of pale green lettuce leaves. 'If Melrose deposits currants on my coverlet,' she told Rosemary, 'I shall blame you. Tell me again what Sir Fergus said, and get the kitchen lads to bring up the bathtub, will you?' Things, thought the maids, were returning to normal, though Nicola doubted that they would ever be the same.

It was while she was soaking in the half-barrel lined with a white linen sheet that someone at last responded to the steady knocking on the outer courtyard gate that they had been told to keep locked. Moments later, a piece of paper was delivered up to Nicola's solar, folded neatly and tied like a parcel with the kind of linen thread they used for mending.

Nicola examined it, then opened it. It was from the prioress of St Helen's Priory on Bishops-gate. 'It's from next door,' she told the curious maids, sitting up quickly and sloshing water over the side. 'She wants me to go and see her.'

'When?'

'Now,' said Nicola.

'Whatever for?'

'Tch! Just get me out of here and bring me some clothes. And if you two tidy up, you can come and find out for yourselves, can't you?' she said.

Nicola had not lived on Bishops-gate for long before she and the aged prioress had made contact. The church of St Helen's was open to the families of the girls who were educated there, and even Lord Coldyngham had attended whenever he was resident in London. According to the nuns, he had been a welcome visitor and a generous benefactor, and Nicola had assumed that the welcome the nuns extended to her was mostly for his sake.

Since their first meeting, Prioress Sophie and Nicola had formed an affectionate bond of the kind that Nicola had lacked in the days of her youth, a gentle hand to hold, words of wisdom, concern and a surprisingly worldly humour that had often sent Nicola away chuckling and thinking what a wonderful mother she would have made. Nicola always went round to the main entrance on the roadside, always well dressed, always taking a small gift, usually something sweet and soft to eat, for the old lady was frail. She had visited the prioress only three days ago.

The gate led directly into a cloister garden that adjoined her own, the roof of the walkway supported on wooden pillars entwined with roses in full bloom. The nun who escorted them beamed with pleasure. 'Sister Agnes has been tending them,' she told them.

'Are the young ladies allowed in here?' Nicola asked, looking for a sign of coloured fabric, of fur such as merchants' daughters wore. She was rewarded; a well-dressed girl of about fourteen stood in deep conversation with a dark-dressed young cleric and, from Nicola's glance through the rose-covered column, their talk was straying far from holy matters. The girl giggled, pushing at the cleric's chest with one hand then, seeing the visitors, she pulled him into the shadows.

The nun appeared not to notice. 'Only at certain times,' she said. 'They're embroidering this afternoon.'

'Have you any idea why the Lady Prioress has sent for me?' said Nicola.

'Not exactly, my lady.' The nun stopped and turned to her. 'But be prepared. Mother Sophie is not well. She took to her bed yesterday. I think she feels this may be her last summer, you see.'

The afternoon went suddenly cold. This was something that had not occurred to Nicola, nor could she make any connection between that poignant comment and the summons she had just received. She had dressed especially well as befitted a nobleman's daughter invited to meet a high-ranking lady, head of one of London's wealthiest priories. She would be expected to acknowledge the honour with a show of velvet and brocade, of silk and gold thread, fine veiling and jewels. The wide bands of violet satin across shoulder and breast, wrist and trailing hem was meant to complement the jewelled two-horned head-dress draped with floating gauze that left Nicola's dark hairline showing around its edges. Her tight sleeves reached as far as her knuckles like fingerless mittens, and the pale bloom of her lovely bosom showed through sheer silk edged with gold and pearls. She had intended to impress; now the prioress would have passed beyond that stage, for sure.

'I pray that the Lady Prioress may be mistaken,' said Nicola.

'So do we all, my lady,' the nun replied softly, searching the folds of her black habit for her chatelaine. 'So do we all.' The key was produced, a heavy door unlocked and re locked behind them, and then the world was very still and faintly perfumed with roses and cleanliness.

But it was not dark. Light bounced off a whitewashed wall on to a life-sized mural where figures strolled through a garden in costumes of the previous century. Ahead of them was a hunting tapestry side by side with painted statues of saints haloed in gold, and now there was no time to gaze, for the nun's head was inclined towards another door in anticipation of a signal. Apparently, she heard it.

Lit by the early afternoon sun from a row of narrow windows, the chamber was nothing like the stark cell Nicola and her maids had expected to see. Surrounded by long white curtains that moved in the breeze, the bed was high with feather mattresses, satin-bordered sheets and chequered white-and-grey furs. Huge pillows lined the soft nest where the white-gowned prioress lay and, if it had not been for the shell-pink face and hands, Nicola would have had to look hard to find her in the creaseless array. Swathed in a white wimple, the small head turned to look at the visitors with dark sunken eyes that seemed to fill her face, though the smile was the same as ever.

A white-robed novice stood up, curtsied, and silently withdrew. The nun had already disappeared. 'Come, my dear,' said the prioress. 'Take Sister Clare's seat, if you will.' The voice had once been powerful, though it wavered now at the end of the sentence as if the lungs were shallow.

'My Lady Prioress,' said Nicola, curtsying. 'You sent for me.'

A frail hand rose from the sheet and flopped again, and the eyes smiled at last, softening at some private jest. 'I've wrestled with my conscience like Jacob and the Angel,' said the prioress.

'And Jacob won?' said Nicola, sitting beside her.

They shared the smile. 'Well, somebody did,' said the prioress, 'and I'm not going to dig too deeply now you're here. You're so much your father's daughter. I'm sure you will understand.' Exactly what there was to understand was left unsaid until Nicola was seated.

Upon the smooth coverlet, Nicola laid a small linen parcel tied with ribbon that Lavender handed to her. 'Marchpane,' she said.

'His kindness, too. Thank you.'

'You knew my father well?' Nicola glanced at the window where the oak-shingled roof of her own house was just visible over the high cloister wall. Somewhere hidden in the roses was a door that linked their two gardens, overgrown and forgotten, and Nicola sensed that the time had come to talk of hidden things, of former friendships before it was too late.

The prioress's eyes followed hers. 'Yes, I knew him well. He came to worship at our beautiful church when he was in London. The public are not usually allowed access to convent churches, and for a man to enter the precincts of a nunnery is even more unusual, but we met while you were still a babe, and it seemed right for us to extend a welcome to our prestigious neighbour.'

Nicola thought it strange that her father, in all his widowed years, had never once mentioned attending the priory church.

The dark, deeply hollowed eyes slid beneath heavy lids that were slow to lift. 'He came regularly to church as other parents did whose daughters are sent here. There is a separate section for them, you see. We were always glad to see him, and he was extremely generous to us.'

'Yes, I see.' So this was to do with the hope of a legacy, perhaps. Had her father led the nuns to expect that he would leave them the house in which she now lived? If so, they would be disappointed.

'We were broken-hearted when he passed away last April. He was a good man, Lady Nicola. Was he also a good father?'

'I believe so. He cared for us well. The boys think highly of him. I saw him infrequently, but my memories are good ones and I doubt any father could have done more, except…'

'Except…to be there oftener?'

'Yes,' said Nicola, relieved not to have had to say it. 'He obviously found it too painful to stay for long at our Wiltshire home. My brother Daniel runs it for George as he did for my father.'

'And the two other sons?'

'Ramond and Patrick? Fine young men. We're a close family. Father left me the house next door, knowing that I like to be independent. It suits me well.'

There was a sigh from the frail immobile figure as if she needed to gather strength for what she was about to say. Then, when she spoke, it was as if she had read Nicola's thoughts some time ago. 'And I'm sure it will continue to suit you for as long as you wish. It's comforting to know that you and I have lived so close to each other, though I wish it could have been for longer. How shockable are you, my lady?'

'Oh, I know that we must all prepare to meet our Maker sooner or later, my Lady Prioress. My own mother went too soon for her to know me well or for me to know her. As for being shockable, well…my twenty-four years have not told me much about the world so far, I'm afraid, but I'm learning. Is your illness incurable? My father knew some good physicians—'

'That's not the shocking part, my dear,' said the prioress, gently interrupting. 'Death is not in the least shocking when you've been preparing for it most of your adult life. No, I asked you to visit me again today because I want you to do something for me before I go, and now I find I cannot do it without causing you some pain, which I deeply regret. Causing pain, I mean, not the pain itself. That was always mine, and deservedly so. I can feel it even now.' A delicate hand followed the other to lay upon her breast, pressing, quelling, silencing some terrible hurt that was quite obviously stronger than the thought of quitting life.

The prioress's eyes stayed wide open, holding some ghostly image along with the pain, and though Nicola was still young and innocent, the recognition of the other woman's harrowing emotion brought her instantly to her side to place a kiss upon the cool silk-skinned forehead. In that moment, they were as equals in the sorrows of womanhood, believing that no man could ever understand or share in them.

Nicola knelt on the wooden floor by the bedside and took one papery hand in her own. 'Tell me what you want me to know,' she whispered. 'A message, is it? Something of my father's? I'll do whatever I can to help.'

'You are free,' said the prioress, 'independent, and not without means. Yes, I believe you could do this. But where to start? Many a time I've considered where to start if ever I should tell it to one of his family. Shall I go to the beginning when you were still an infant and your father came to London, to Bishops-gate. You would hardly remember it.'

'I do remember. I had a nurse who bade me not to weep so.'

'He came here to ask about a place for you. He said

you would need female company, sisters as well as brothers.'

'And you were the prioress then, my lady?'

'No, not then. I was the sub-prioress and still only thirty. Can you imagine what happened, Lady Nicola? Have you experienced it yet, that terrible, instant, over-powering, uncontrollable love for a man? No, of course you haven't. You are still an innocent. I also was inno-cent then, and totally unprepared.'

'You began to love…my father? Did your faith not help you, my lady?'

'My dear,' the prioress said, gently removing her hand to touch Nicola's cheek, 'I didn't *want* it to help. Can you understand that? We were a liberal-minded community then. We socialised perhaps more than was good for us with the parents of our girls, we grew worldly and rather too fond of luxury. I'm afraid I've never quite accepted the frugality we were supposed to embrace as if it were a virtue. Our prioress was motherly and we looked up to her, and our lives were rich with every kind of love. Perhaps your father experienced that when he visited. He had already lost his first three wives by then and he was desperate for comfort, and I was willing to give it, and to accept whatever he chose to give. We complemented each other so well—' her voice broke as she whispered her longings '—and I adored him. It was wrong, I know, and I suffered penances for it, but now I believe I've paid the penalty in full. Now, I need to know where my child is before I leave this world.' Huge tears poured down her cheeks and she had no strength left to stop them.

Nicola dried them for her. 'You had a *child*, my lady? My father's? Did he know of it?'

Gasping soundless sobs, the fragile body shook the words out unevenly. 'Yes, a child…beautiful…little girl…we couldn't…keep her.'

A child? Her father's other daughter? The sister she would have so loved. His love-child, a secret for the rest of his life. How they both must have suffered.

Stunned by this news, Nicola mopped gently at the anguished face until it calmed, taking the glass of water that Rosemary handed to her and holding it to the sunken lips that had known an excess of loving. 'Don't weep, my lady. Please don't weep any more. I shall find her for you. Is that what you wish? She's my half-sister. I'll find her.' Without thinking, the assurances flowed even before the full import of them could be understood. The woman was dying and her tortured soul needed every help to find peace.

The haunted eyes, now red-rimmed, followed Nicola's movements, anxious to tell her the rest. 'I could not keep her here,' she said. 'That would have been unthinkable, for I would be elected prioress after Mother Sabina. Your father had no understanding relatives with whom he could share the child's existence.'

Nicola could believe it. Behind her father's kindly nature was a strong disciplinarian who would not have tolerated the idea of a mistress with bastards and the lies that would have to accompany it. He would never have revealed such a weakness in himself to his family, let alone take the child home to be reared. 'So where did the child go, my lady? Have you any names?' she said.

'Only one,' the prioress whispered, fast becoming exhausted. 'Lord Coldyngham had a good friend by the name of…Melrose.'

Melrose? Knots slowly began to unravel in Nicola's mind.

'Melrose in Scotland?' she said.

'Yes. A Scottish family dear to him. The lady had two sons, he told me, and desperately wanted a daughter, but could have no more children. She and her husband agreed to adopt our daughter as their own. She was taken from me…away up to Scotland…and I was not allowed…any contact.'

Nicola mopped the tears again, her heart wrung with pity. 'Hush, dear lady. Did my father give you no news of her?'

'No,' was the faint reply. 'It was agreed I should put her from my mind.'

Their eyes met in a long exchange of sorrow that Nicola realised was too much to expect a mother to bear alone. To put the child from her mind. That, she knew, was asking the impossible.

'And my father?' she said. 'You still saw him? Forgive me, my lady…' she touched the prioress's hand '…I have no right to ask you that.'

The hand held on to hers as a mother's would. 'Things could not continue,' she whispered. 'The prioress…the nuns…were merciful, but it couldn't go on. He came to the church when he was in London and as long as I knew he was there, he knew that I was too. We were next door for much of the year and I could see his rooftop. That had to be enough.'

Which, of course, was why he was hardly at home with his children. 'So you know nothing of this family…Melrose?'

'Nothing at all. I promised not to make enquiries, not to contact them, and I have kept my promise until now. And now I think the merciful Lord will understand, and pardon me.'

'I pray that He will, my lady. And I shall search for her and send you a message, I promise. She will be… what…thirteen summers?'

'She was born on the fourteenth day of February, St Valentine's Day, in the year 1460. Yes, she'll be thirteen summers, four months, one week and three days old.' The voice faded away at last and the deep sockets of the eyes slowly released their lids as sleep overtook her.

For some moments, Nicola stayed on her knees by the bed, watching the face and trying to accommodate the shattering news she had just heard. As usual, there was a keen sense of betrayal that this was also a part of her own life that had been withheld from her, albeit for the best of reasons. But the connection with the Melrose family was truly astonishing and must go a long way to explain the promise of marriage between the two friends. What else could it have been but to show gratitude to Sir Findlay and Lady Melrose for bringing up her father's illegitimate daughter as their own? That *must* have been the reason for it.

But how could she, Nicola, now refuse to carry out her father's wish to pay the Melroses back by sharing the Coldyngham family name? It was her half-sister's name, too, and, until she herself married a Melrose, that connection would never be made, her father's wish would not be honoured, and the Melroses would not be thanked as they deserved and hoped to be. But why had she never heard of a Melrose daughter? Thirteen, the child would be. How strange that they shared exactly the same St Valentine's Day to be born, eleven years apart.

There was a sound behind her as the door opened to admit the nun and the novice bearing a tray of medicines. Rosemary and Lavender drew forward to help Nicola to her feet, to dab at her face and to adjust her long sweeping skirts. She smiled at the two keepers and left the chamber with the linen packet still on the bed. How inappropriate, she thought. Marchpane. A bundle of sweetmeats. Of all the things she might have taken.

The sounds of laughter and distant singing, birdsong and the rush of the summer breeze were heightened, and the roses shone like pearls on a bed of emeralds as they passed through the gate on to the leafy stretch of track. In a sky of intense blue, seagulls wheeled and mocked with gaping beaks, and it seemed to Nicola that a new phase of her life was just about to begin as another's life was about to end.

Chapter Five

'No one must know,' Nicola told the two maids before they reached the courtyard gate. 'Promise me you'll not repeat a single word of what you heard just now. *Promise.*'

'We promise,' they said. 'May the Lord strike us dead if we break our word. And anyway,' Lavender added for good measure in case the Lord had not fully understood, 'we didn't hear very much, did we, Rose?'

'Very little. She spoke soft, poor lady.'

'Good,' said Nicola. 'Then it's to be our secret. Women's matters.'

Relieved to have some time to herself, to ponder over the prioress's tragic dilemma and her own part in it, Nicola divested herself of the two-horned structure, hoping that a head free of discomfort would help. 'Plait my hair,' she said.

'And your gown?' said Lavender. 'You wish to change it?'

Nicola was well into her pondering by then, so she stood like an effigy to be re-robed in a cool linen kirtle with a shorter houpplelande over it, its hem deeply scalloped and embroidered on a pale green ground. Absently, she picked up Melrose and a straw hat and went out into the sunny garden.

Partly covered by tall grasses, the door in the garden wall responded immediately to her hesitant lift of the latch and gentle pull. There through the gap was the cloister walk festooned with roses where she had walked, and there in one corner was the prioress's room. According to her there had been no contact for years with her lover, yet this easy access would suggest otherwise. Still dazed, Nicola closed the door and sought the turf bench where, shaded by rampant hops, she placed the rabbit upon her lap and leaned back with closed eyes to reconstruct the scene in detail, the tears, the guilt, the overwhelming misfortune of having to part with a child. The woman's pain was still acute, after thirteen years.

It would not be the first time such a thing had happened to a nun, nor would it be the last; that part had not shocked Nicola as much as the prioress possibly believed it might. What *had* shocked her, and what she had managed to conceal very well, was that the man involved was her father. The gap in her life created by his long absences had affected her deeply at the time, and now that she had learned the reason, she was unsure whether to blame him more or to excuse him. He had had another daughter. He had known of Nicola's need for a sister. Yet because of his wish to be seen as blameless in the eyes of his family, because of his pride, in short, the longed-for sister had been denied her. Surely he could have resolved the problem of guardianship? Surely he could have explained the child somehow?

I must find her, my half-sister. Her mother and I both need to know where she is. I shall have to make contact with the Melroses.

But wait, she told herself. Did they have a sister, those two? No mention had ever been made of one in her hearing and, as far as she was aware, no provision had been made for another daughter in Lord Coldyngham's will. Would he have ignored her existence, even at that late stage? Had he simply washed his hands of her by then? Wills were usually made when death was in sight, not before. Had he forgotten his love-child by then?

So what if the Melroses had decided, for some reason, not to keep her? What then? How could Nicola search for her without disclosing the reason? The prioress had waited until the very last moment and was relying on her discretion, unable to ask anyone else for help. Promises had been made that day which must be kept, even if it meant travelling to Scotland to keep them.

Then there was the other promise. Yes, it always came back to that, didn't it? Fergus was determined to honour his late father's wishes and now it looked as if she also would have to do the same for her late father and to please Lady Melrose, who was not likely to know

the mother's identity. There would, after all, be no reason for Lord Coldyngham to disclose it, in view of his
secrecy about the whole business. A mistress would
have been shameful enough, apparently, but a nun was
quite a different matter. No, he would not have told the
Melroses so much, Nicola was convinced of it.

It was not hard to visualise the infant in a nurse's
arms travelling over the bumpy miles to Scotland in the
spring of 1460, or the joy of Lady Melrose taking a
daughter into her arms at last, then the promise of a
daughter-in-law, the only Coldyngham daughter, no
less. Who was the most fortunate, Nicola wondered, her
father or the Melroses? Could she now continue to refuse them their due, knowing how important it was between men to pay back what one owed? If only her
father could have explained, and if only she had felt
content with what now seemed inevitable. But she was
far from content. Wanting him was one thing; marry-
ing him was quite another. Becoming his wife would
not change him in any of the ways she had mentioned
to Ramond. Even he agreed on that. It was the shortest
road to distress she could imagine, yet it was the one
that beckoned the strongest.

Wearing two tones of green, Nicola hoped to make
herself invisible long enough for Sir Fergus to make a
superficial search of the garden and then give up, as men
do. But Melrose had had enough of her lap, and her leap
on to the pathway towards the lettuces could hardly be
missed, even by a man.

A large pointed toe stepped upon the leash, thereby

preventing the threatened resignation of the gardener. ('Give it dandelions,' he had yelled at Lavender. 'There's plenty o' them!') Removing his extravagantly plumed hat, Sir Fergus picked the rabbit up and deposited her in it. 'Stay there,' he told it, adding a bunch of weeds. 'You're on probation.' His dark close-cropped hair shone with the bloom of chestnuts in the sun, and Nicola was spellbound by his masculine comeliness, his easy languid movements that belied the speed and power she had seen only recently.

He came to share the bench with her, placing the rabbit-filled hat on the ground between them, and she knew by the way he angled himself towards her that, though she had done nothing to win it, she was being made the object of his attention. She found it unnerving, and her unconscious response was to hold herself rigid and silent, unable to look directly at him. Would there be sarcasm, or politeness, or a reference to her earlier outburst?

'Better?' he said, softly.

She looked down at her hands, then across at his.

Deliberately, he opened one out to show her the injured knuckle, and she knew by the way he looked at her that he would have liked to review her wounds also. She had checked them only that morning, listing the cut and bruises with a mixture of wonder, anger and a sneaking glow of pride. She could find no answer to his question. He was the one on probation. Was that what he had meant?

'I had to get Patrick away,' he said. 'It was not how you think.'

'So you know how I think, do you?'

'Well, you've spared no effort to tell me, so far, but where Patrick is concerned you think I was overriding your wishes. George thinks it's the best thing ever, and so does Ramond.'

'You've been to see George?'

'Certainly I have, at his offices. I've told him about Ramond too.'

'And about last night?'

'Of course. I could hardly do otherwise.'

'So now my private affairs are common knowledge, and you both want to send me off to stay with big brother.' She leaned her head back against the massive hop-leaves, once more unwilling to meet his eyes, all her best efforts going sadly astray. She stared out across the raised beds of blowsy red poppies, the yellow St John's wort and the feathery fennel and thought that, had matters between the sexes been more equal, women's wrongs would be put right with more alacrity and severity than they were at present. Now George would be sure to renew his nagging about the safety of marriage.

Ignoring her pique, he stroked the rabbit's silky ears. 'George has left two men with Ramond,' he said. 'They have orders to guard him night and day.'

'Thank you,' Nicola said. 'Thank you for your help. You had no need to do so much.'

'Yes, I did. Unfortunately I'm about to make myself unpopular again almost immediately. I *am* taking you to stay with George and his lady for a while. He wants you to pack your belongings and close the house up.'

Regardless of her earlier thoughts along those very same lines, Nicola saw no reason to make things easy for him. 'Yes, I'm sure he does,' she said, 'but I intend to stay here.'

'That's what George thought you'd say. Well, listen to me,' he said. 'Apart from the fracas with Lord John, who will undoubtedly seek some kind of revenge, probably directed at you, there's also the threat from Oxford, directed at any Coldyngham, if they can't find Patrick. More than that, there are riots spreading all along Cheapside and Threadneedle Street and coming this way, midsummer foolery and apprentices all together, and already some houses on fire. You're in danger, Nicola, and, if I have to carry you there myself, you're going to George's. His orders. He's sending carts for your stuff and men to help. Or do you prefer to stay at my place on Holyrood Wharf?'

What if I agreed to that? Would you make love to me? 'No,' she said.

He smiled, a devastating smile that plundered her whole being and left her without a single coherent thought in her head, emptying her of every reason to fight with him. 'You care, then?' he said, still smiling.

I care. God only knows how I care. 'I'm pretending to. Remember?' She gave him no answering smile for, in spite of his efforts, it was too soon to deserve it, and the score must be evened at every opportunity. 'The riots are surely not going to spread as far as Bishopsgate, are they?'

'Quite probable. There's the Leathersellers' Hall and

the Parish Clerks' Hall nearby, and they've always been targets for rioting apprentices. Come on, my lady, we must be out of here before supper.' He got to his feet and held out a hand to her.

'But what about the priory next door? Are they in danger too?'

'Oh—' he glanced at the wall '—I shouldn't think so. High stone walls. They'll be safe enough.'

Ignoring his hand, she bent to pick up the hat with Melrose asleep in it, cradling it against her. Then she walked past him into the house, muttering, 'This is all highly inconvenient', but thinking that it was probably to be the first move down that dangerously beckoning road.

However much she disliked Fergus's authoritative and commanding manner when applied to herself, Nicola had to admit that there were times when it came in extremely useful. Take that afternoon, for instance, when they would certainly not have been out of the house on Bishops-gate by suppertime had it not been for his very unsubtle way with the men of her own household and George's men who did not agree on how things were to be done. A few crude and martial-sounding threats from Sir Fergus's deep bass, and the carts were soon stacked high, covered, and ready to go, and not another murmur was heard about who did what. It would not have been nearly so successful without him.

The carts were sent off down as far as Candlewick Street and thence along Trinity, Old Fish and

Knightrider up to the Fleet Bridge and along the Strand to avoid the worst of the revels. 'You'll ride pillion behind me,' said Sir Fergus to Nicola. 'Your maids will ride behind the men.'

'You *know* I can ride as well as any man,' Nicola protested. 'And we shall need our horses at George's.'

'We're taking all the horses with us,' he said, 'and it's your safety that concerns me, not your riding ability. Now, put that rabbit into its basket and fix the lid. She can go beside the bird.'

'Melrose will ride with me,' she said, defiantly. 'She'll be upset if she has to listen to that squawking popinjay the whole way.'

Sir Fergus eyed the bird with intent. 'I can soon put a stop to that,' he said. 'In fact…' Taking Nicola firmly by the arm, he walked her into the empty winter-parlour and closed the door behind them before she had an inkling of what he was about. Then she knew.

His kiss matched the mood of the last few hours, efficient, masterly and forbidding any more contrariness on her part, so thoroughly did he take possession of her mouth. It was not meant to gentle her, and she would have found it easy enough to match his urgency, kiss for kiss, except that it would have sent the wrong signals and he had already begun to anticipate her interest. She must not make matters worse.

'Fergus Melrose…no!' she gasped, her lips only a breath away from his. 'Stop, please stop! I don't know what you're thinking of, but whatever it is, forget it. This is all like a military operation to you, isn't it? But this is my house, sir, my home. Do you think I feel nothing at having to leave it?' She shook herself free but, with her back to the panelled wall, she was still captured. Her wound had begun to hurt her, and she put a hand up to comfort it, showing him by her frown that his strength was at fault. 'Leave me be,' she whispered. 'It's bleeding again. I need to attend to it.'

His voice was husky with tenderness as he replied. 'I can see to it. Come, I put it there, I can tend it too.' His hand took hers away as he spoke, forcibly overcoming her protests that were now on the brink of tears. 'It's all right…shh…come on, lass. We're going to be much more intimate than this before we've finished. Let me see… Look, I have a clean kerchief here in my pouch. If I place the pad just there, like that.' Once again, without her doing much to prevent him except by an ineffectual hold on his wrist, he drew the neck of her kirtle down to expose the full exquisite roundness of her breast and its wicked red line, placing the pad of silk against the skin, then drawing her clothes back over it while she stood there, trembling, watching his careful hands and not daring to think what he meant.

'All right?' he said, adjusting the shoulder of her houppelande. 'Will it stay there, d'ye think?'

She nodded. 'You should not have seen,' she said. 'Please don't speak of it.'

He placed a finger over her lips. 'Hush. Wild horses wouldn't drag it from me. Not even a hint, my beauty.' His hand slid gently down over her bare neck, lingering over the silken surface before daring to revisit the site where his kerchief lay hidden. As softly as a feather, his hand cupped the wounded breast as if in apology, and all that time she held his other wrist, watching, ready to stop him or to leap away like a deer. Neither of which she did.

Finally, she took his hand away and held it with the other upon his chest. 'This is not the Fergus Melrose I know,' she said. 'At least I shall be safe from you at George's house.'

'No, you won't, my lady. Come, it's time we were away.'

Although they chose not to acknowledge it openly, both Fergus and Nicola knew that their pretence at friendship had now moved beyond its first innocent phase into something more serious, for no woman would have permitted that degree of intimacy from a man, not even in an emergency, unless she meant to allow him more permanently into her life. For her to have stood still and done nothing much to stop him was a significant step forward that occupied Fergus's thoughts all the way to the River House and that, combined with the hand on his waist as she rode pillion behind him, was enough to put the glitter of triumph back into his eyes. At last now she had begun to talk to him without the continual tongue-lashing.

For Nicola, there was a mass of contradictions to straighten out, keeping her mind in turmoil all through London's rowdy streets, for she could find no good reason for her behaviour, nor any explanation why she should believe one thing and find herself doing entirely the opposite. Having gone so far, there would be no turning back. All she could do to slow things down would be to insist that her new civility was still pretence; but though that might deceive her brother and his wife, it would not fool Fergus.

Totally unfeigned, however, was the joy shown by George, Lord Coldyngham, and his wife, Charlotte, and such was the welcoming, the carrying of wicker baskets and bundles, the hugs, the questions and assumptions, that Nicola was convinced she had done the right thing even while she let them all believe it was their persuasion that had won. 'Only temporary, love,' she told her sister-in-law. 'Don't let George think I've come to stay. As soon as the troubles have died down, I'll return home.'

Lady Charlotte greeted Sir Fergus with a kiss to both cheeks. 'Did you see anything of the riots?' she said. 'George tells me they've started fires on the street where the Lombards live. You know how disliked the Italian merchants are.'

'We caught the smoke before we left,' said Sir Fergus. 'There's a strong south-westerly but still no sign of rain. Don't worry, it'll die down.'

Sailors' talk, the women's glances said. Lady Charlotte linked an arm tightly into Nicola's. 'You rode *pillion*?' she said.

'He wouldn't let me ride my mare. Bossy creature.'

'And you brought everything, did you?'

'Except for the heavier pieces. We left two men to guard it. No use leaving a house unattended.'

'Quite right, my dear. And who is this?' Lady Charlotte looked down at the white rabbit straining at the blue leash, obviously uneasy at the interest of two towering gazehounds.

Nicola picked her up. 'Melrose,' she said. 'Don't ask.'

'Well, well!' A white beringed hand stroked the silky ears. 'So it's gifts already, with jewels on the harness. Nick, have things…have you…?'

'No, nothing at all. And we haven't. This is to do with something that happened when I was a child and for some reason he seems to have remembered it, that's all.'

'Oh.' The disappointment in Lady Charlotte's voice would have been difficult to miss, but not the smile that followed. There was plenty of time and a few small indications. 'I've given your maids a room of their own,' she said, 'next door to yours. Come, I'll show you.'

But their hopes that the south-westerlies would bring rain did not materialise that night and, by next morning, the fires that had worked their way sporadically along the tinder-dry oak-shingled rooftops in the centre of London were now throwing sparks towards the lower end of Bishops-gate and, as fast as one fire was extinguished, another started.

The worse news came as Lord Coldyngham's riverside household stirred into life with the dawn when Nicola's two men arrived from Bishops-gate. Exhausted by their marathon, they came to tell her that her house was burning and that there was nothing they could do to stop it.

'Nothing?' said George, tucking his shirt into his braies. 'What d'ye mean, nothing? Where were the bloody fire-buckets, man? Did ye not stay to find out? What the hell d'ye think you were left there for, to watch it burn?'

It was rhetoric not meant to be answered but, in any case, there were no answers except the look of horror on Lady Nicola's face. She had lost her house and, with it, her hopes of independence. Shivering with shock in Lady Charlotte's arms, she heard how the men had been woken in the dark hours to find the place full of smoke and the roof well alight, the timbers already crashing into the stables and igniting the flammable straw. They dared hardly mention the illegal thatch on the service areas, for they were places the city aldermen had not checked too closely on their last visit. It had been a matter of expense, and Nicola's father had been complaisant.

'So the rest of the street's on fire too then, is it?' snapped George.

'Er…no, sir…your lordship.'

'Then where did the sparks come from? How did they reach Lady Nicola's house? Come on, man. *Speak!*'

'I don't…don't know, sir. Honest. We had to run for it.'

'Leave it, George, please,' said Nicola. 'The men are exhausted. Let them recover. It will have gone by now. Gone. I'll go and get dressed.' Her face was ashen. 'My lovely house,' she whispered.

'You might have been in it,' said George, tersely. 'I'll go there with you.'

Riding her own mare, Nicola set out with George and a party of armed men to reach Bishops-gate via a roundabout route intended to avoid the worst of the damage with the result that it took longer to get there, for all their speed. Many streets were blocked by debris and the evidence of uncontrolled hooliganism. Townspeople went about their business, silent and angry; they had seen it before. Men pulled at the rubble of houses, women scolded, children clung, dogs scrounged and yapped at homeless rats and, as every moment passed, Nicola thought of her comfortable house and those last few moments there with Fergus Melrose. It was as if fate was anxious to move things on quickly, before she could suffer a change of heart. Damned fate.

By the time they reached Bishops-gate, most of the signs of rioting had been left behind except for one heavy pall of smoke ahead of them, the smell of burning wood, and rivulets of water beneath their feet. Through the thick acrid haze, the eerie light of the sun struggled like a distant lamp and, more articulate than any call to prayers was the doleful priory bell, on and on. Coldness seized at Nicola's heart. It was the passing-bell.

All around them the trees and even the wild roses were singed, and where Nicola's timbered four-storey house had stood yesterday with bright herbs by the door, blackened posts pointed like fingers and sticks of smouldering incense. A massive heap of rubble lay beneath thick layers of hot white ash, rafters hung at strange angles and a doorway was still burning, the tongues of flame roaring and crackling in the breeze. Like a charred skeleton, the demolished wall spaces allowed a view through from front to back across the courtyard to the debris-covered garden, and from over the high wall came billows of smoke and greedily licking flames. The cloister next door was on fire, its thatched roof shrivelling in the heat. Sounds of crashing and showers of sparks were sent high into the air as the roof and pillars collapsed. Someone screamed.

The garden door, so long forgotten, burst open as George and Nicola drew to a standstill and a group of men and nuns headed straight for the fountain in Nicola's garden, making a chain of buckets and arms swinging in unison, as if to music.

'Quick, you lads!' George yelled to his men. 'Get in there and help.'

Moments later, two men on horses came galloping up the track behind them, throwing themselves out of the saddles to run through the hot embers towards the blazing cloisters. It was the two Melrose brothers.

'No…George…don't let them! Fergus…no!' Nicola yelled, then bit back her tongue. *Of course they must help. But please, God, don't let him be harmed.*

George looked at her and said nothing.

She had dismounted before he could help her, though he pulled at her arm to make her listen and wait. 'No…Nick, no! You cannot go in there.'

'Someone's been killed, George. There's a room at

the corner of the cloister. I must go and find out. Let me go, please.'

'No need. Look, there's someone coming out of the side door. Ask them.'

Two nuns emerged, followed by two more carrying bundles. They were crying and unable to recognise her with an old brown felt hat jammed down over her wimple, her plain homespun cote-hardie. 'Go back,' they croaked. Then, one of them stopped, blinking and frowning. 'Forgive me, lady…I didn't see…you were not in your home after all? Thank God.'

'No, I'm safe, as you see. But who's the bell for? Is it the prioress?'

The old nun's face crumpled and a hand trembled in front of her pale lips before it made the sign of the cross, telling Nicola what she needed to know.

'Not *burned*, sister?'

'No, thank heaven. Not burned, but overcome by smoke only a while ago, before we could carry her out. Her lungs, you know.' She patted her chest. 'She was so frail, but that was not the way for her to go. She deserved peace at the last, not that.' The nun had not intended it to sound like blame, but that was what Nicola heard, even so.

'Where is she, sister?'

'Over in the stone church on the other side. The fire won't reach us in there.'

Indeed, the fire would not reach them anywhere, for it had already begun to respond to the men's endeavours, sending clouds of steam to billow high above the wall and to enclose the human figures in shrouds of white.

But the appalling news of the prioress's hastened death, the damage to the priory, and the loss of her own home struck at Nicola's spirit with a pain so intense that, as the nuns continued on their way, she fell like a child into her brother's arms, shaking with distress and a numbing grief as if she had lost a kindred soul vital to her aim in life.

'Hush, love,' whispered George. 'These things happen. We'll rebuild it.' What occupied his thoughts at that particular moment, however, was to do with *why* it had happened when the riots had not spread this far, nor even as far as the Merchant Tailors' Hall, a favourite target of apprentices.

For two days Nicola kept to her room with neither energy nor inclination to share her convoluted thoughts with anyone. The certainty that Prioress Sophie had not been expected to live much longer was one thing, but it was an entirely different and horrifying matter to suspect that those few precious days had been stolen by an act of sheer depravity. Was it the apprentice riots, or was it, as George had said, altogether something more sinister? Nicola was sick at heart just to think of it.

Neither Fergus nor Muir had been hurt that day, but the memory of her fears and her spontaneous exposure of them to George stole into every small corner of her mind, giving her no peace during the day and no comfort at night. One dear friend had departed her life in a riot of violence and malice, while Fergus Melrose, whom she had never been able to call friend, had come to take her place with a velocity she was unable to stop. And now it looked as if she would have to swallow her hurt pride, after all her protests, and become his wife.

She was not ready. She would never be ready.

Casually, she had asked George if he knew of a Melrose sister, but he had disclaimed any knowledge of one. But then, Fergus's opinions about younger sisters were well documented. He had scarcely ever mentioned Muir, either.

Just as worrying was the way in which she would, before very long, be obliged to veer like a weathervane and startle them all, especially Fergus, by accepting the hand he was still offering her. It would seem, to put it mildly, like a typically female piece of whimsy without rhyme or reason when, in fact, it was anything but. Nor could she confide in Charlotte without expecting a strong bias in favour of Fergus. Would she ever be able to tell anyone the real reason for her apparent change of heart when the secret was not hers to reveal?

The real reason? Were there not two real reasons? Did those sneaking disturbing thoughts not also include memories of warm lips and a heady concentration of virile closeness, the touch of his hands upon her skin, tending her wound while making love to it, too? Was it not his strong arms and hard unyielding thighs she felt at night in the small dark hours when sleep would not come? And had any of those immature childhood longings been anything like the real thing? Physically, she was ready for him. Temperamentally, she was not. There was only one thing to do. Bargain with him. Reason with him. Put him off…stall him…try to make him understand…

Come on, lass. We're going to be much more intimate than this before we've finished. Was there ever a man so cocksure, so arrogant? Talking to him would be like talking to a whirlwind.

And so it proved to be.

Dressed casually in a blue linen bliaud and an old woollen sleeveless surcoat, she accepted the young groom's help to mount her grey mare, though she could have sprung into the saddle unaided had no one been around. A ride out through the fields in the sunshine would help to clear her head and blow away the nasty cobwebs of doubt, and she would escape before any of them could pester her about the wisdom of doing what she had always done at home in Wiltshire. Their protests whispered to her as she trotted out of the gates, as she broke into a canter upon the wide green verge that led towards Charing Cross and the open fields beyond. And though the canter could not last long because of the houses and people, it was enough to remind her of what she had missed for months, her own solitary company.

Her recent talk to Lotti about having her own circle of like-minded friends began to seem like wishful thinking after what had just happened, and the family she had been so eager to shake off since their father's death were the very ones who had her well being and safety closest to their hearts. With them, she could be more herself, as she was being at this moment.

Past the houses, she sped along the track towards a patch of dense woodland where a herd of black-and-copper-coloured pigs snuffled in the undergrowth, and noisy wood pigeons clattered upwards into the new foliage. The pigs ignored the pounding hooves, but the young swineherd called out a greeting as she passed, repeating it only a moment later, to Nicola's annoyed surprise.

She turned to look behind her and was both furious and excited to see the big bay stallion rounding a curve of trees, its rider sitting upright and holding the horse back, making no effort to catch her. 'Go away!' she called, hearing the emptiness of her command.

Digging her heels into the mare's flanks, she pushed on faster and faster, flying over the soft pine-needled forest floor, leaping fallen logs and ducking beneath the lowest branches, twisting and turning in the hope of out-manoeuvring the larger horse. It was a vain hope, for Fergus's horsemanship was legendary and Nicola knew she would be caught, if that was what he intended.

The mare turned sharply into deep shadow without realising how the ground raked steeply upwards into a tree-clad slope. She balked, pitching Nicola forwards over her neck, slowing and swerving, allowing Fergus enough time to come alongside and hold them at bay, purposely not allowing the horse enough space to turn round.

Nicola was breathless and not used to being brought

to a standstill while in full flight, especially not by Fergus Melrose, who had always been miles ahead and uncaring of her whereabouts. His attentions still alarmed her and, with hair beautifully awry in a dark tangle around her face, she scowled at him with unconcealed resentment. 'Leave me alone,' she panted. 'Just go away and leave me alone.'

It was the first time they had met since the disastrous fire, and his last sight of her had been as she rode away through the debris of her ruined house, white with shock. Now the wind had brought a flush to her cheeks and a new sparkle to her eyes, and Fergus would like to have pulled her into his arms and on to the thick carpet of wood anemones and bluebells. But he had learned some discipline during his years at sea, and so he dismounted and held the mare's bridle, mixing persuasion with compulsion. 'Come on,' he said. 'We have to talk some time and you've been avoiding me long enough now. Tell mè what the problem is and I'll listen.'

'Listen?' she snapped, pulling at the reins to free the mare. 'Listen? Men like you don't do that kind of thing, do they?'

'Yes, when it's necessary.'

'For what? Your comfort?'

'For my understanding.' Before she could pull away, he led the mare towards a patch of level ground where a tree trunk lay across the sunlit grass. Then, looping both reins over a dead branch, he came to her side with arms ready to receive her. 'We shall not better this for privacy, I think.' His hands waited, and he could feel the struggle within her as she deliberated. She could, he knew, just as easily have dismounted from the other side, alone.

At last she placed her hands on his shoulders, her body leaning down, and he felt the soft weight of her fall towards him as it had done so often in his dreams since that violent meeting in her hall. He felt her sweet breath across his face and then she was weightless between saddle and grass, and he could have kept her so, feeling that, for only an instant while her eyes rested in his, she might have allowed it.

Quickly, she moved away from him, breaking the contact that could so easily have become an embrace. Years vanished in seconds, and there again was that loaded complicated hostility that they had known as children, a confusion of needs that neither of them had been able to identify. Now, they both knew what to call it, and only Nicola remembered the pain. She took another step back, tripped on her long skirt and sat down with a bump on the log. She tried to untangle her heel and stand, but was held back by Fergus's arm as he sat astride, close to her.

'Hush,' he said, stopping her impending protest. 'Be still now. Things have moved on, my lady. We're not bairns any more. We can talk about it.'

Nicola was not so sure that she could. 'Everything has changed,' she argued. 'My needs have changed, too.'

He linked his arms about her tiny waist. 'Yes,' he said. 'Of course they have. It's a woman's privilege. And it's my privilege to change them back again.'

She turned to face him, a three-quarters view that almost stopped his heart. There were those same defiant eyes that had once galled him so, but now riveted him with their beauty, the wide soft mouth that had never smiled at him as the maids did, the hair that was never as tidy or as prim as his mother's. She was wild at heart, still struggling to conform, but wanting her freedom at the same time and angry that the two were not being allowed to work together as she had hoped. And now the foundations of that longed-for independence had begun to crumble. No wonder she wanted to escape them all.

'It's not like that. You can't just change them back as if they were the wrong buttons on a coat,' she said, crossly. 'You say we can talk about it, but you're already set on changing my mind even before you know what my mind is.' She looked away angrily, still smarting at the curtailment of her short freedom.

'Oh? I thought I did. I seem to recall you making it quite clear. Several times, as if I hadn't quite got the message.'

'I told you, my needs have changed.'

'Ah,' he said, softly. 'Your *needs* have changed. Not your mind, but your needs. Are you going to tell me of these… er…needs?'

'You ought to be able to guess.' Having nowhere else to go, her hands came to rest upon the arm that lay across her lap, her fingers idly pleating the folds of his grey embroidered sleeve.

Fergus was having some difficulty with his facial muscles. 'Yes,' he said. 'I'm sure I ought. I'm being particularly stupid. Do tell me.'

Hesitation turned into delay, delay into denial. Finally, Fergus helped her forward with a typical bluntness that shed some light on his understanding of the position, but did little for Nicola's dilemma. 'You've decided to accept me, is that it? And you're not sure how I'll take it. Am I right?'

'Fergus Melrose, I've lost both my house and my reputation, thanks to your interference, and since I have a promise to keep to my father, I must needs accept your proposal, in spite of all my objections. Better devil-you-know than devil-you-don't-know. I realise there must be a formal betrothal to make it all legal, but I told you before that there are…some things…to do with marriage that I'm…not…not ready for. If I had been, I'd no doubt have given myself to Lord John, but I didn't. Nor have I to anyone. I have not yet found a man to whom…' She looked sideways at him, and Fergus knew as well as she that she *had*, and that she could not bring herself to lie about it.

'That you want to go to bed with?' he whispered. When she did not reply, he went one step further towards the truth. 'Or perhaps that you *have* found one, but you feel he ought to wait. Is that what you mean? Because of what's happened in the past? You denied once before that you were afraid I might hurt you, but I think there's an element of that in it, too, isn't there. Eh? You think I should wait before I take you to bed, even though we're supposed to be betrothed?'

'Yes,' she said, blushing furiously. This was plain speaking indeed.

'But wouldn't that make a nonsense of the betrothal ceremony? Without the consummation, the vows are not valid. What then?'

'Then we have to trust one another. I'm not saying I won't marry you eventually. I'm simply suggesting… no, *asking* you to delay that part of it.'

'Until when?'

'Until I'm ready.'

He tightened his arms across her and pulled her to him with one hand beneath her armpit, wedging her head on to his shoulder, her hair tumbling like black-brown silk over his arm. Her mouth was soft, hesitant at first, then responding as he knew it would when she thought she had won. Moving his free hand up to her face, he held her pointed chin before sliding his fingers deep into her hair. 'Oh, no, my beauty,' he whispered. 'I think not.'

Her reaction was what he expected. Incredulity. Indignation. Then the struggle, which he held easily. 'What…why *not*?' Her hand pushed at his shoulder, but he took her wrist in his grasp.

'Why not? Because that's not the way it will be done. I'm a Scot, my lady. We don't leave things to chance, and, when we go through a ceremony as important as that, we like to finish it in the proper way. So if you've a mind to be a dutiful daughter and honour your father's promise, which is news to me since you've not so far shown any inclination to do so, then you'll have to accept all that goes with it. You can't pick and choose which bits to take and which to delay. Why, you could claim to be unready for years, my lady. I could reach my dotage.'

Her struggles became wilder as the teasing words matched her old image of him and, when he held her half-lying across his knee, the rage in her eyes signalled the kind of challenge he found hard to resist. 'That's it, my Lady Coldheart, fight me if you will, but hear this. You can choose whether or not to accept my offer, betrothal and all, but your answer must come before the sun goes down over yon horizon. Take all day, if you wish, but you miss that deadline and you can look elsewhere for a husband. Do you understand?' He knew she would not answer, but the scorching fire from her eyes told him that his message was clear. 'Good,' he said. 'Now we shall return to River House and you can give me your answer before your brother and myself, before Muir and Lady Charlotte and, whether you accept me or not, there'll be no going back on it. I shall do nothing more to persuade you. If you thought to run rings round me, my beauty, you don't stand a chance. That's not the way I do things.'

'Anything else?' she snarled.

'Yes, one thing.' His hand moved to her neck and was about to shift the linen down over one shoulder, but she caught at it.

'No…don't!'

'Let go of my wrist. I may not get to see it ever again, and I need to recall exactly where I put my mark on you. Let go.' He did not expect that she would obey without being forced to, but her grip on him slackened and, in truth, he did not know whether to take that as a good sign or the opposite. The fabric slid easily over her skin and this time he was less careful about not letting his hand touch her as he moved down to expose the voluptuous mound, with the slash now pink and healing.

He wanted to touch, to caress, to fondle, but this was not the time nor did he know for sure if there would ever be. So he gazed and watched the brown-ringed nipple harden with desire and then, because he felt it might be the only caress he would be allowed, he bent his head to touch the wound with his lips and to lick it with his tongue, tenderly. Her skin was like the softest silk, warm and moist, and she did nothing to stop him.

He watched her eyes as he covered her up, dark and heavy with yearning, and he wanted to insist, there and then, that she accept him once and for all, with no more delays, no more last chances. What if she refused, after all that?

Easing her upright, it seemed to Fergus that words had run out on them, that what might have been a long wrangling argument had come instead to an ultimatum of its own accord and a finale of the most paradoxical sort. Her rage might still be there, but Nicola wore her emotions close to the surface, and now he would have to put her to the test yet again and hope that the emotion she wore on the way home would stay with her a while longer, at least until sundown.

Chapter Six

Riding back to River House ahead of Sir Fergus along that wooded track, Nicola's thoughts centred around only two things: one was her body's craving to be near him, the other was her moral duty to keep the promises made to the prioress and to the Melrose family. The latter could not be avoided for any reason; it was now only a matter of hours before she would have to accept the inevitable, for Fergus himself was the key to discharging that duty.

The physical longing, though, had burgeoned forth like fields of flowers after rain, and the pain and bliss that followed in its wake were hard to tell apart. He had looked at her with unconcealed desire and her body had leapt at his lightest touch, but his kiss upon her breast would be his last unless she did something quickly to bind herself permanently to him. And therein lay the problem. He was skilled, experienced, and she would probably never know exactly what she meant to him personally after all the years of reticence. She could not act on desire alone, the dull ache of rejection being such a force to be reckoned with, and far from spent. She did not know how she would ever deal with that.

Nevertheless, the idea of having to make a formal declaration in front of her family at the appointed hour held no appeal for her; far better that she should tell him now and eat her words with an audience of one. To prolong the agony for the sake of it would give her little advantage.

With the words already forming—*Fergus, I need you, I've always...no... Sir Fergus, I have decided, after all...no... Sir, you give me no choice*—she slowed and pulled her horse round to wait for him to catch her up, staring in disbelief at the empty track. Fergus was nowhere to be seen.

There was the bend around which she had just raced, sure that he was only a few paces behind. Was he walking? Had the stallion cast a shoe?

'Fergus!' she yelled, putting her heels to the mare's side.

It was not Fergus who responded, but three riders who swept across the track from the dark woodland, circled her like devils, grabbing at the mare's reins and making her rear in alarm, and hauled her out of the saddle with exceeding roughness so that she fell some way on to the track under stamping hooves, dust and flying stones. 'Fergus!' she screamed. 'What have you done with— No!' Words were stifled by a black hood over her head, by hard uncouth hands that held her down into the grass, hurting her wrists and ankles with tight ropes that would have stopped a grown bull.

Shouting and fighting, she was nevertheless hoisted up into someone's arms, then came the claustrophobic experience of being dumped heavily into a creaking space with four confining walls that she knew to be a wicker basket like the one in which she had carried Melrose. The lid went down, pushing her head into a corner, and through the sides she heard muffled shouts, none of them decipherable.

A sudden lurch shook the basket like an earthquake, and she was thrown to one side into a dark, blind world where little existed but the fear and extreme discomfort of being helpless and of not having Fergus when she most needed him. The hardest thing of all to bear, though, was not knowing what fate he had suffered. Second to that came the guilty knowledge of how, but for her attempt to best him, this would never have happened. Even at this very moment they might be dragging him down, beating him, taking the ultimate revenge for his interference at Southwark. They would have no mercy. Perhaps, even as she was being carted away to heaven knew where, he lay at the side of the track breathing his last.

Over dry ruts that had hardened during weeks of drought, the waggon bounced her along, shaking her deeper into a nightmare of agony that Nicola truly believed was the nearest thing to purgatory she was likely to get. Hurt by the ropes, gasping for air, cramped and wedged with her back and neck aching unbearably, she prayed that whoever was treating her so badly had not treated Fergus worse, though there was little room for hope.

For mile after dreadful mile the torment continued

until the lurching slowed and the waggon rumbled to a stop. The sound of men's shouts, the yelp of seagulls and the general clamour of the river wharfs penetrated the dark hood, then the slap of water and the heavy patter of raindrops upon the lid of the basket. She felt the cold steady drip of rain on knees and shoulders and, now that the wheels were still, heavy rumbles of thunder replaced the jarring rattle beneath her ears. The basket swayed and tipped, creaking into a greying light with men's voices above it, then more bumping and shouting, the rocking of a boat, the squeak and rattle of oars and the rush of water. Where in God's name were they taking her? She began to shiver uncontrollably as a crack of lightning lit up the inside of the hood.

The first face Nicola saw did not surprise her for, in spite of the distracting pain of being tied up, there had been moments when she could short-list those who wished her ill. One was the Oxford brothers, who might be seeking revenge on the only female member of the Coldyngham family, the other was Lord John, Earl of Rufford, whose warning had not been an empty threat, after all.

'Ah my dear lady,' he said, bending down to brush the damp hair out of her eyes. 'What a sad state. I'm sorry these lads had to be so brutal, but it's a bad old world, isn't it?'

She had been tipped crazily at all angles to get her so far and now, at a nod from her erstwhile friend, the basket was kicked on to its side without warning, toppling Nicola out on to the floor like a bundle of laundry. Unable to right herself, she lay with her cheek on the dusty wooden planks only inches away from Lord John's pointed toes while her eyes tried to focus after hours of disorientation. She was in a small wooden room rather like a large crate, that much she could see through several pairs of legs.

'Out!' she heard Lord John say. Somebody began to argue about payment, but he was adamant. 'Later!' he barked. 'Get out!' There was more argument, then the feet and legs moved, a door opened and slammed and a pair of feet returned. 'Churls!' he said. 'Now, little lady, we're alone at last.' He cut through the ropes that bound her feet and wrists and hauled her upright with no trace of his accustomed charm. 'Get up!' he said. 'Stand.'

The effort was almost too much for her. On legs that had lost all feeling, she tried to stand and face him to find out why their friendship should have deteriorated this far. But before she could straighten, a blinding flash knocked her sideways, sending her crashing into the wooden wall, followed by a searing pain inside her head that she knew was nothing to do with the lightning outside. She lay there, stunned, shocked, hurt, uncomprehending and very angry while her ear buzzed and her cheek stung with pain. There was a taste of blood inside her mouth.

His face came down to her level and for the first time in all the months of their relationship, she saw the cruelty in the blue eyes fringed with fair lashes and a scattering of wrinkles. She had always believed these to be laughter lines. Now, she could see the other side to his complexion, the wolfish grin, the sharp canine teeth, one recently broken, the coarseness of his skin that he had told her was the result of a childhood illness, but which was more likely to be due to something more offensive than that. She had thought him good looking in an effeminate kind of way, tall and graceful, always impeccably dressed, his hair neatly bobbed, his skin fragrant, fingers tapering and attentive. Never had she thought them capable of delivering a blow like that to a woman. Never.

To guide her thoughts past the pain, she studied his clothes, rich crimson velvet, rain-soaked shoulders, pleats over a padded chest, false sleeves with silk linings and a hat with folds that helped to conceal some bruises to his face—the result, no doubt, of the fight.

'Get up!' he snapped.

Holding a hand to her face, she did as she was told, with difficulty. This was worse than the childhood muck-heap, she thought. This was deliberately aggressive, not accidental. 'If you're going to hit me again,' she mumbled, 'would you mind giving me some warning?'

'That was for your righteous brother,' he said. 'It was also for you, for playing the whore, my dear.'

'How *dare* you say that?' she said, furiously. 'You have slandered me in public, and now you dare to—'

His hand shot out only a split second after his eyes gave her the warning, this time to hold her chin in a cruel grip and push her back against the wall with a thud. Above their heads, the sound of running feet mingled with the crash of thunder, absorbing her cry of fear. His face became a mask of petulant animosity. 'Dare to what?' he snarled, pushing his nose so close to hers that she could smell the reek of stale wine on his breath. 'So, tell me exactly what you were up to in the woodland with that great lout only an hour or two ago? In his arms, weren't you, my dear? With your kirtle down over your pretty ivory shoulders. Eh?' Pinning her back to the wall by the throat, he placed his other hand in the neckline of her bliaud and, in one savage assault, ripped downwards, tearing the fabric like paper as far as her waist.

For all her pain and numbness, Nicola fought to keep herself together and his hands from doing more damage. But the harm was done, and the breast that had been the object of Fergus's attention was now exposed to Lord John's wrath. The wound had started to bleed again.

He stared. 'Little *whore*!' he whispered. 'Been playing games, have you, my dear? Is this how you like it, then? A bit of violence? And I've been tip-toeing around you all this time and getting nowhere. And no wonder. Why didn't you tell me? I could do the same...' He reached behind him for his dagger, but her hands grappled at his arm, fumbling, trying to out-reach the hand at her throat. Frantically, she clung to his arm, shaking with terror.

'No...no!' she cried, taking fistfuls of the soft velvet. 'He's my betrothed...we're to be married...I swear it. It was an accident, that's all.'

Relaxing his hold of her, he stood back, concerned

that she had pulled him out of shape, stroking the velvet into place. 'Oh, really,' he said, scathingly. 'So show me the ring.'

'There isn't one yet. I've only just accepted him. Where is he? Tell me where he is, Lord John.' The pain in her head made her see double and her eyelid was already swelling. 'Please,' she said, 'tell me what you've done with him.'

His face was twisted with hate as he watched her try to pull the edges of linen together over her nakedness. 'You would have me believe you were a virgin,' he said, angrily, 'and now I find that you're second-hand, and marked, too. What am I going to get for you now, I wonder?'

'Get for me? What do you mean? Where am I?'

With no man to oppose him, the Earl gave vent to his grievances, sparing her nothing of the malice he had kept carefully hidden until now. As she tried to cover herself, he pulled her hands away and ripped at the torn bliaud until she was again half-naked, shamed by his blatant examination. 'They were right,' he said. 'You *are* more difficult to get at than is good for you, *my lady virgin*. Maybe I should let them all have a turn on you, after all their efforts. Eh?'

'Please…Lord John…tell me what you've done with Sir Fergus. None of us have ever done you any harm. This is unworthy of you, my lord.'

His eyes never left her body. 'Oh, I don't know. I think it's very worthy of me. In fact, I think you'll be worth quite a packet. Enough to pay my debts.'

'What do you mean? What are you going to do? Where am I?' The words would hardly come out straight, so painful was her head and the scattering of stars that swam before her eyes. Never had she felt so ill.

'Where?' he said with a laugh. He released her hands, allowing her to hold her clothes together again. 'You're on a Venetian merchant galley, my dear lady. The captain is a friend of mine, a man who appreciates a good bargain when he sees one. He and my agent take good bodies like yours—*virgin* bodies, my dear...' he shoved his face nastily against hers '...fetch a good price on the slave markets of Turkey. Now don't tell me the idea doesn't thrill you a little, you with your open house and *vast* circle of friends. That'll be something for the grand Coldynghams to be proud of, won't it, my dear Nicola? Turn round!'

With unnecessary violence he pushed her round and held her wrists together behind her back, this time passing the rope round her elbows and pulling them inwards so that it bit painfully through the fine silken sleeves. When he threw her viciously to the floor, she saw the reason, for righting herself became almost impossible.

Without another word, he left her, shooting the bolts of the door and taking advantage of the poor visibility outside to make an exit that few would bother to witness. With clothes like his, Nicola thought, he would need all the diversions he could get.

It was to be her last thought for some time: the abuses

and injuries, fights and fears, the cold and wet, the terrible predicament of her surroundings now began crowding in upon her and with one fleeting vision of the man she wanted lying in a pool of blood on that desolate track, she succumbed to the icy sweat that crept along her limbs and into her head. Silently, she slipped into the inviting black oblivion.

'*Signora....signora!* Wake. Wake up, *per favore.*'

A man's deep voice pierced the haze in Nicola's mind, reducing the blackness to vaguely encouraging sounds, and hands lifted her, even though she could not understand her lethargy.

'Who are you?' the voice persisted. '*Santo cielo!* What's happened?' It was kindly, surprised and musically Italian. The face, when the swirling mists cleared, was bronzed, neatly bearded, and belonging to a man of mature years, judging by the lined skin and the wealth of experience in the sharp eyes.

She felt nauseous, but the man needed an answer. 'Lady Nicola Coldyngham,' she whispered. She glanced down at herself, flinching more at the pain in her head than at her semi-naked state, aware of each painful move as her bonds were cut. Her released arms returned as if on rusty hinges to cover herself, though she knew her rescuer must have seen. Was this the Venetian captain who traded in slaves? His manner suggested sympathy and concern rather than brutishness.

'*Vino!*' the man said to someone behind him. '*Pronto!*' He placed a pad of something behind her head and lifted her so that she could sip the wine, then he took off his own mantle of wet-smelling wool and covered her. 'Giovanni Foscari, captain of this ship,' he said. Then, picking her up easily as if she were a child, he carried her through the door and up the short flight of stairs to the upper deck.

Nicola blinked at the fading light and at the rain falling in sheets and bouncing off the boards but, up another short stairway, they were beneath a large canvas awning covering one end of the deck upon which the rain thundered unceasingly. Here, in this private tent, Signor Foscari placed her with hands the size of loaves and the gentleness of a woman on his own cushioned chair.

'Ees better,' he said. 'Piero!' he called sharply to the man who had brought the wine. 'What's been going on here while I've been ashore? Who brought the *signora* on board?'

'Your pardon, *capitano,* but I did not see her come aboard. All I saw was three men carrying a laundry basket and a nobleman following. They took it down there to the food locker. It had just started to rain, sir, and the oarsmen were dashing for cover. I didn't see them coming out or rowing away.'

Nicola saw the anger mounting in the captain's eyes and gestures, but the next part of the conversation was in Italian and she was little the wiser. She began to understand more when the captain released a volley of expletives as picturesque as Fergus's, and when she heard a mention of George's name, then Queen's Wharf, she realised that Master Piero had appreciated the urgency of his mission.

'I've sent him to find Lord Coldyngham,' the captain told her. 'Now, what can you tell me about how you came to be here on a Genoese galley, my lady?'

'*Genoese?*' Nicola whispered, accepting the glass of wine again. 'But…Lord John told me it was a Venetian merchant galley. Was he trying to fool me, or…?' She winced at the sting of wine inside her sore mouth, and her hand shook on the stem of the glass.

'Venetian?' The burly bald-headed captain turned aside to spit the word out, literally. 'Hah! Either your lord *was* trying to fool you, my lady, or he cannot tell one city's galley from another. He sounds like *un' idiota, si*? He did thees?' His fingers gently touched her cheek and swollen eye, though his own eyes strayed further afield.

She found it difficult and painful to speak, but this was important. 'Yes, he and some others ambushed me while I was out riding with Sir Fergus Melrose beyond Charing Cross. I have no idea what's happened to him. Please can you find him for me? They may have killed him.' Her eyes filled with tears.

The captain's face rekindled like a new fire. 'Sir Fergus was weeth you?'

'Yes. You know him, sir?'

'I should say I do, *signora*. Sir Fergus, 'e own half of this galley. I am his galley-master. I shall find him for you.' Nimbly, he disappeared through the canvas opening to lean over the rail above the deck, bellowing into cupped hands at the rowing boat pulling through the rain towards the wharf. 'Piero! Go to Holyrood Wharf first. Tell them to find Sir Fergus. *Pronto— pronto!* Beyond Charing Cross.'

There was an answering yell before Signor Foscari returned, wiping the streams of rain from his bald pate. He placed his hands like buttresses upon the carpeted table, leaning towards Nicola. 'He'll be back for you, thees Lord John, will he? Ees good,' he said, nodding. 'Then we shall be ready for heem, eh?' He smiled at her and then, as if he knew all about such things, he helped her discreetly to turn her bliaud round, back-to-front, so that her modesty was restored. Lifting her feet up on to a stool, he tucked his warm mantle and an extra blanket around her and begged her to excuse him. 'I am not about to leave you, *bella signora*,' he said. 'I shall be down below. Be patient. There is no danger.'

It was not the way Nicola preferred to do things, but she had to accept that a man's reaction would be to catch the man who had used his ship, mistakenly or otherwise, for his villainous schemes. If it had been left to her, Lord John could have rotted in hell for all she cared; her main concern was to find Fergus Melrose and to bring him back to her side. There were important things she had to say to him before the sun went down which, to all intents and purposes, it had already done.

She was to remember that dreadful time of waiting as one of the lowest periods of her life, for her battered body lacked the strength to rise above the deep despair in her mind that insisted Fergus was dead. After all the dangers he had experienced in his twenty-nine exciting years, this must surely be an attack he could not survive. The gang who had shown little mercy to her would show even less to him, and they would have been ordered not to leave him alive to tell what happened.

Drifting in and out of consciousness, the blackest and most terrible fears bore down upon her, obliterating her physical pains and the crushing shame of Lord John's scorn, the defamation of her character, his lewd and frightening threats, though these hung like ghouls ready to rend her delicate womanly essence. More, far more than those hurts was the terrible pain of knowing that, because of her waywardness, she had caused the death of the only man to claim her love. Yes, she loved him. There had never been a time when she had not, even through the fighting and slanging, the rejections and stalling, she had loved him. And now he would never know.

The pain was too great for tears. Once again, she passed out.

The torrential rain drummed upon the canvas awning, rattling it noisily and waking her with a start. She found that she was still shaking, as she had been through the black dreams, and her head was pounding to a sickly rhythm...or was that the drumming of feet she could hear?

Men's voices rose above the din, the clash of steel, bumps and yells, the hard slam of a door. Fergus? George? Had the Genoese captain caught Lord John, as he said he would? Would he come to tell her what was happening?

The thud of feet sounded upon the wooden stairway as Nicola heaved herself up in anticipation, then came the hat with many folds and, unbelievably, the surly wet face of Lord John, rising up to the deck like a dark menace from her worst fears.

She gasped, stumbling on shaking legs, clinging with tight fists upon the cloak and blanket, noting the greedy hard eyes of the four men who followed their leader. Sheathing their daggers and grinning at their most recent success below decks, they piled up behind him like so many soaked brigands drunk on killing, and Nicola's blood froze in her veins as she recalled Lord John's suggestion of their reward. Her mouth dried with a new fear.

'So,' he said, 'the good *capitano* brought you up here, did he, my dear? Well, it seems my boys had a problem telling a Venetian galley from a Genoese one, but no matter, we've sorted it out, and the *capitano* is not my friend after all, is he, lads?' He turned to them, laughing. 'I think he had something in mind for us other than the lovely Nicola. Pity. He didn't put up much of a fight.' He slapped the chest of a squat dark man who still breathed noisily from the exertion of boarding. 'This,' he said, 'is my Venetian agent Agostino who deals in flesh. Human flesh. Preferably healthy, reasonably comely and, above all, young and virginal. But that's something he'll have to find out for himself, since there seems to be some doubt about it. He has little English, but he's willing to take my word that you're unblemished. He'll take you.'

'What about us?' said one of the men, eyeing Nicola. 'You said—'

'Later, you fool,' Lord John snarled. 'I've told him she's a virgin, not a whore. I want his money for her first.'

Something in Nicola's mind snapped at that point, though she could not have said exactly what it was that triggered it—perhaps the men's barefaced leers, perhaps one insult too many, or the realisation that the expected help had failed. Without even thinking about the odds stacked against her, she freed one arm and, taking a bold stride forward towards her tormentor, swung a hand hard across his face, knocking his head sideways and sending his hat away across the deck. The incredulity in his eyes was worth, she thought, whatever punishment he had in mind for her, but she would make her point before it was too late.

'Swine!' she screeched. 'Low, filthy cur! You shame your own breed, whatever that is.' And before he could recover or refocus, she hit him again with a backhander that sent him staggering into the rail. It was the first time she had ever hit anyone in her life, but the rage that boiled inside her was also a first, as was every other emotion of the last few hours. 'That's for Sir Fergus Melrose,' she screamed at him. 'And the other is for me.'

She was in two minds, at that point, whether to challenge the whole pack of them or to keep the blanket tight in her fist and pray that they would keep their distance along with their amazed expressions and grins of admiration. Fortunately, she was prevented from choosing. Just when she had abandoned all hope of seeing her beloved Fergus and her family again, a slow movement along the bulwarks behind the crowd of men caught her eye, slow shining wet shapes, pouring silently, leg by leg, body by body, on to the slippery deck, daggers glinting in the fading light…faces grim…and there… yes, there was the unmistakable figure of…no…yes, it *was* him. It was Fergus!

She truly believed she was imagining things, her mind being so confused by loss, by pain, and now by the intoxicating gratification of physical revenge. She swayed on her feet, clutching at the captain's table, mesmerised by the slow advance of Lord John's ugly gang and of the silent crew who came up behind them, unseen and unheard. Lord John's face was contorted by fury. 'Take her, then!' he said. 'Do what you like with her!'

There was a concerted rush and a leap of figures, a struggle, some shouts of surprise and anger, and then it was all over for the surly and disappointed crowd of bound captives as Fergus and his men, far outnumbering Lord John's gang, took possession of their ship. The lovely, courageous and bruised woman with them said only three faint words before she was caught up by a pair of strong arms, scooped against a wet leathery chest to the sound of, 'Aye, lass. Well done, little tiger.'

'Fergus…oh, my love.'

But the noise was too great for Fergus to catch her

whisper and, even if he had heard, it is doubtful if he would have believed his ears. For Nicola, it was enough for her to be held safely by him during that hazy journey home.

From that glorious point onwards, things ought to have improved between the two of them, if only because they had found each other alive and relatively well. And indeed, after the first few moments of relief and euphoria, no one would have known any different, with so many male onlookers, that is.

It would have helped Fergus's cause, however, if he had been listening a little more intently to the advice given him by Nicola's brother on that critical day at Bishops-gate when they had breakfasted together.

'It doesn't mean she's tough or insensitive to pain,' George had told him. 'She's not. She's a woman now, with all a woman's needs, and she'll not easily be won over.'

Fergus *had* been listening, but he had not taken it in. Seeing her hit Lord John, moments before, had only reinforced what he remembered of her: tough, spirited, madly courageous and desperate not to show any sign of hurt. Many times he had seen her bruised and bleeding, stung and scratched, but never once had she whined like a girl or run crying to her nurse. She had changed physically, as one might expect, but that outburst and assault upon her male aggressors on the galley seemed to Fergus clear proof that she was tough, and she was able to handle pain as well as any man. She had raced against men only the other day, she had fought with them in Southwark, and now what more evidence did he need after her feisty performance today? She had a badly bruised face, but that was from the rough ride in the laundry basket, so she had said. Otherwise…? Well, she had been very quiet on the ride back to the River House, but that was not surprising after the ultimatum he had imposed earlier, now expired. No real harm done. Just another uncomfortable adventure, which would not have happened at all if she had not gone galloping off so far ahead.

Fergus himself had been dragged off his horse too, and had taken on three of them single-handed. It had been hard going, and by the time the three were laid out cold, the waggon had disappeared. Guesswork, intuition and luck brought Piero, Captain Foscari's lad, and Fergus together with the rest of the galley's crew, and not a moment too soon, for Lord John's men had been too many for Captain Foscari to tackle alone as he had expected to do. There would be no more trouble from Nicola's erstwhile friend, however. Fergus's Genoese galley could now boast the only real earl amongst its oarsmen.

It was Lady Charlotte Coldyngham, Nicola's elegant sister-in-law, who began to see, quite early on, that the adventure—as Fergus called it—had had a far more profound effect upon Nicola than on the brawny Scot, and that he was not taking her injuries with the required amount of gravity, however she had come by them. For her part, Lotti did not accept Nicola's explanation that the basket into which she had been bundled had grazed her face for, apart from broken skin, there were bruises, a cut lip and a swollen eye that was quickly turning purple. The tear down the back of her bliaud Nicola had tried to explain away as part of the struggle, but Lotti had known her for many years, and the dreadful melancholy that had descended upon her since the violent abduction was acutely disturbing and very untypical of Nicola's natural resilience. There was more to that torn bliaud, Lotti told herself, than a struggle.

Nicola's melancholy was no illusion, nor was it a pretence or a bid for attention, nor was she able to rouse more than a weak smile when Fergus went to speak to her the morning after. She had slept badly in spite of the sedative, tormented by nagging pains caused by the cruel ropes, cramps, the vicious blow to her head, and her reopened wound. Most disturbing of all was Fergus's failure to understand her fear that he might have been killed. Apparently no such fear had crossed his mind that something similar might also have happened to her, for he had related the details of the rescue to George with the same kind of understated directness he had used as a lad of sixteen when they had just beaten the neighbour's sons at jousting.

He found her out in the garden with her feet up on a stone bench, cushioned and swaddled like an infant in a blanket that Lotti had put round her. Her hair was in a simple plait, and the colourful bruising glistened with salve, her mouth was swollen and lop-sided, the bruises to her neck still showing. Quickly, she pushed the blanket up to hide them.

Fergus sat down next to her feet. 'Well, my lass,' he said. 'Feeling better now?' There were red weals on his cheekbones and the knuckles of both hands were raw, but he had not elaborated on his injuries and, apart from a certain wariness in his gait, he appeared not to be suffering.

'Yes, thank you,' she whispered.

He leaned forward, reaching out to touch her cheek, to caress it. But she shied away with a frown. 'It hurts?' he said.

'Yes.'

'Oh.' The hand dropped. 'I've told Muir about the Lord John thing. He sends his regards and farewell. He's gone up home today.'

'To Melrose?'

'Yes. His wife's expecting their firstborn in a few months.'

'His...his *wife*?' She looked at his hands, her mind temporarily blank. She looked up at his face, still heart-stoppingly handsome with the light scar that ran upwards from one eyebrow. His eyes were laughing. 'He has a *wife*? He told me he came down here to escape a love affair. He told me,' she said, indignantly, 'that he needed to stay. He flirted with me.'

'He told you it was an affair of the heart, lass. To bring the best physician from London for her. And that's what he's doing.'

'That's *disgraceful*! He deceived me. And he *did* flirt.'

'Not seriously. He had his orders.'

So, Muir had played her along and she had fallen for it. The two of them had schemed to get her into Fergus's arms that evening, making a fool of her, just like old times. ' I see,' she said, seething anew with hurt and resentment at this latest débâcle. 'Then you must both be feeling very pleased with yourselves. Have a good long laugh at your brief victory, Sir Fergus, but have the grace to wait till I'm out of earshot.' Humiliated, she turned her face away. 'I think you'd better leave me. Please go.'

'What about our deadline? We had an agreement, do you remember?'

'We both missed it.'

'It was you who missed it.'

'That was none of my doing.'

'Then I'm prepared to extend it.'

Nicola said nothing. She had been thinking that he might have changed, but quite clearly he had not. It was not going to work.

Fergus peered at her. 'Well? Are you interested?'

She shook her head. 'No,' she whispered, fighting back sudden tears.

Slowly, he straightened, rigid with affront. 'For pity's sake, Nicola,' he said, 'what's the matter with you? Is it about that silly prank with Muir? Forget it, it's nothing. Yesterday in the wood, you were—'

'I *know* what I did in the wood,' she snapped. 'That was then. This is now. Things have changed.'

'What…*again*? Hell, woman. Let me know when

you've stopped changing, will you, so that I can catch up? What is it *this* time?'

Too many to mention. She thought of Prioress Sophie, whose tragic story must be discovered, presumably from Fergus's mother. That now seemed like a distant promise with no immediate resolution. She thought of the thanks due to Lady Melrose from Lord Coldyngham, pledged in the form of her marriage to Fergus: that too would be withheld, and the connection would not be made, the house of Melrose to the noble house of Coldyngham. She thought of the much-needed protection so close to her grasp, protection necessary to a noblewoman of her age and wealth. Fergus could provide it, and had already done so, but something essential was missing. Had she any right to demand more? Was it a woman's right to yearn for husbandly devotion, for gentleness, for sensitivity and love? He had not breathed a word of that, only duty to his father, and deadlines. Only she had changed, not Fergus.

'Duty,' she whispered. 'Please go away, Fergus.'

He saw her trembling. He saw his chances slipping silently away with her refusal to communicate. He saw the woman across his lap in the woodland, her eyes full of desire, her willingness on the brink of surrender. He saw failure and, as ever, it was not something he was willing to accept.

He stood up and went directly to her side, squatting on his haunches so that his head was level with hers. Taking a hand to her chin, he tried to turn her face towards him and then, when her eyes would not follow, slid the hand down over the blanket to her wounded breast. 'Nicola,' he said. 'Look at me.'

Her recoil was instant, almost violent, her eyes wide, fearful, even horrified. Knocking his hand away with an arm beneath the blanket, she rolled off the opposite side of the bench, dragging the woollen wrap behind her like a train, stalking off on shaking legs along the gravel path where two screaming children hurtled towards her while trying to grab at the long blue lead of a white rabbit. Two nurses followed, white veils flying. Then came Lotti, Lady Coldyngham.

'Nicola, my dear. What is it?' She held out her arms.

But Nicola stumbled past, unable to answer.

Ahead, the large figure of Fergus Melrose slowly rose to his feet and waited for Lotti to join him, her concerned expression absorbing his look of blank astonishment. 'Something's wrong, my lady,' he said.

'Yes, Sir Fergus,' said Lotti. 'Something is very wrong. Shall we sit?'

As a result of their long talk, Fergus sent for the captain of his galley, Signor Foscari, for a full explanation of exactly what had happened to Nicola below decks during that torrential thunderstorm. He hoped the good captain had fully recovered from his unconsciousness. When Signor Foscari had answered every question regarding his gentlemanly care of Nicola, with whom he had fallen more than a little in love, he noticed that the Scot's face was not only pensive but as white as a sheet,

his mouth set in a dangerous line that all his employ-
ees knew to beware of.

'You did well, *signor*,' said Fergus, with a grim se-
riousness. 'I am most grateful to you. I wish I could say
the same for myself.'

Chapter Seven

Following her two boisterous children up the great carved staircase at a more sedate pace, Lady Charlotte Coldyngham espied the faded blue and violet surcoat and kirtle and thought at first that her sister-in-law appeared to be weeping. She then saw to her relief that she was mistaken when Nicola's hands left her face to pick up her skirts ready to walk away. 'Nicola, don't go!' she called from halfway up the stairs.

'The children went that way,' said Nicola, tonelessly.

'Yes, my dear, I know. Wait.' Why was it, Lotti wondered, that Nicola had chosen to wear her oldest and most-mended clothes these last few days? Surcoats had gone out of fashion years ago, and so had the bliaud that she'd worn yesterday, and Nicola had always been ahead of such things. Was this some form of protest at the way her life was moving, or a reflection of her state of mind?

She lifted her own sunny skirts into the crook of one

arm and took the last few steps, sensing the reluctance in Nicola's waiting stance and being aware yet again of her own self-reproach that her two guests had come to such harm while sharing her hospitality. George had said it was hardly her fault if they chose to go off unescorted after all that had happened, but still Lotti's days had been darkened by guilt, and she had tried to compensate by sparing no effort to relieve the effect of their separate ordeals.

Signalling to the children's nurses to go on ahead, she stopped by Nicola's side, saddened to see the lovely and usually lively face mottled by an angry flush, the skin so marked, the perfect mouth still swollen. The lustrous brown eyes were guarded, holding no smile before they looked away, and Lotti sensed that a private talk was something Nicola would refuse, if she had been asked, for there was something raging angrily inside, toiling alone, and bitterly. She took one of Nicola's limp hands between her own. 'Will you come with me to the still-room? I've made something new for you. I think it may help.' She felt the hand between hers respond with a gentle squeeze and took this for an answer, leading Nicola along the passage to a small room overlooking the kitchen gardens where an outer door led to a flight of stone steps.

Nicola looked down from the high vantage point into the sparkling greenery where, at the far end, a gardener pulled up radishes to pile into his wheelbarrow, unaware of how his lettuces had been discovered by a white rabbit.

Lotti's mixture of treacle, rosewater and wine was offered in silence and, just as silently, Nicola accepted it and stirred some more, staring into the swirls. 'Thank you, but I didn't want this to happen, Lotti. It's not what I had in mind for my twenty-fourth year. If he'd stayed at sea in one of his ships, all this wouldn't have happened, would it?' She knew that Lotti and Fergus had been talking about the situation and that she had been caught for a similar talking-to.

Moving slowly so as not to disturb the unexpectedly private comments, Lotti came to sit on a stool next to the basket of lavender and began to gather a handful of stalks ready for tying. Like her husband, Charlotte knew how to wait, though on this occasion she could not have predicted its length and the sigh that was to mark its end.

'I can't talk about it, Lotti,' Nicola said at last.

'I understand. A little sip?'

Obediently, and out of politeness, Nicola sipped, took a closer look at the concoction and sipped again. 'Nice,' she said. 'Mmm.'

'Nicola, my dear, if you're concerned that what you say to me will be passed on to George and then from him to Sir Fergus, don't be. There's no question of me breaking a confidence, even to your brother. I know you're taking the blame for some of the happenings, but I think you're being too hard on yourself. And I know how you must be feeling about Sir Fergus when you were so...'

'You *don't* know how I feel, Lotti! *Nobody* can know how I feel.' The words were cried straight from the heart, fiercely grating and passionate, cutting through the peaceful room and shaking the potion in her hands so that the spoon rattled.

Lotti leaned forward to remove the drink and place it on the table, taking Nicola's hands once more into her own to feel their icy chill, despite the warmth of the sun. 'No, my dear. You're quite right, I don't know. If you could tell me, talk to me about it? It often helps if you can let it out. Did Sir Fergus ask what had happened to you? Was he concerned?'

'He asked,' she said.

'And you told him?'

'Only some of it.'

Charlotte released her hands. 'Only some of it. Was that because you thought it not important enough or because you'd rather he didn't know?'

'Neither. It was because he didn't pursue the matter. Perhaps he thought he could guess, or perhaps he felt it was too unimportant to bother about. I'm not surprised. He was never one to dwell on injuries, especially mine.' There had been recent exceptions to that accusation, but those were entirely out of character and certainly not to be shared with anyone. 'Anyway, I couldn't begin to tell him how I feel about what happened. I don't know him well enough to confide in him to that extent. He cannot *possibly* understand how a woman feels to be so treated...' Her voice shook and faded away as the air in her throat became tangled in memories and emotions.

Lotti handed her the treacle mixture and watched as

she took a sip, then another, admiring the way she collected herself so bravely. She removed the drink again. 'No, probably not,' she said, 'but I can. I can understand it. Can you share it with me, dear one? I can help, if you'll allow it.'

Looking down at her lap, she saw it all happening again in every terrifying detail. 'A man would think nothing of it,' she whispered, shaking, 'but I've never been struck before. Never in my life. I've had more than my fair share of injuries with the boys, but never like that, Lotti. There were several men. Ruffians. They pulled me off the mare and trussed me, blindfolded me and threw me into a basket. It hurt, Lotti. I was terrified by what they might do to me. But worse than that was him, that dreadful man. I felt disgraced, bullied, threatened, insulted. He called me a *whore*, Lotti,' she whispered the word, 'because they'd seen us in the woodland when I believed it was so private…and special. He tore my bodice and threatened me with his dagger, and I felt dirty…so dirty when he looked at me.' Covering her face with her hands, she shook like an aspen leaf, and Charlotte ached with sorrow for the suffering and for the spoilation of a moment that, left alone, would have remained private and special for ever. This pain was far worse than bruises and would take longer to mend.

She took the shaking Nicola into her arms and held the dark head upon her shoulder, smoothing her back with motherly hands, appalled by this news.

'He knocked me to the floor, Lotti.'

'Oh…Nick! You told us it was the basket that—'

'I didn't want to speak of it. It was so…' At this point, the control she had tried so hard to maintain was torn from her in the too-recent and vivid memories that haunted every waking moment, and her softly muffled howl became a roar like that of a trapped animal, pitching her into a crashing wave of grief and pain. Rocking in Lotti's arms, the rasping sobs broke upon the softly comforting shoulder until at last they subsided into half-words that sounded to Lotti like apologies.

'Hush, sweet,' she whispered. 'Let it go now. Let it go. If only we'd known. Hush now. I didn't know the tear was done deliberately. It was down the back of your bliaud.'

Hiding her swollen face in Lotti's shoulder, Nicola explained, punctuated by convulsive sobs that fractured her words. 'The captain helped me to reverse it, to cover me. He saw me too, but he was kind. But I'm so shamed, Lotti. I'd begun to enjoy being admired and respected, and then to find that the man I called my friend could hardly wait to slander and betray me, to sell me, even. That's…that's disgraceful. He could have asked me for money if that's all he needed, and I'd have given it him. He had no need to do what he did. And now, the one man who seems not to care how sullied I am is the only man I've ever tried to impress by my superiority. I've never said half the things to anyone that I said to Fergus when he first offered for me, Lotti. I never had any desire to convince anyone of my worth. I said things to wound him, and he knows that, but after what's happened I don't think I can ever give myself to him without remembering that man's insults and his vileness, his hands on me, his coarse talk of my virginity. Fergus is not going to want me for a wife once he knows how I feel. It's too soon…too soon. It's spoiled, Lotti. Spoiled.'

Charlotte took her by the shoulders, holding her away to look at her, but knowing that her own eyes were reflecting pity instead of the strength that she intended. 'When it comes to giving yourself,' she said, 'I think you'll find that Sir Fergus will understand your fears once he knows what you've been through. I believe he's quite an extraordinary man, you know.'

'Yes, I do know. He was quite an extraordinary youth, too, but I never thought that sensitivity was one of his more outstanding qualities. And if he could understand any of my fears, Lotti, he'd not have told me just now how he and Muir lured me into his arms that evening in the garden, would he? He would have saved it until a more appropriate time.'

It took Charlotte only a moment to recall Nicola's angry demeanour and their palpable hostility. 'Bragging,' she whispered, consolingly. 'How men like to brag about how they got a woman into their arms, but it's the timing, isn't it? Of all the things that men are not so good at, and there are quite a few, their timing is the worst, I've found. But forgive him. There'll be compensations.' She took Nicola's weeping face between her hands as if she'd been made of eggshell. 'Such a very special, courageous woman,' she whispered, 'and so very much loved by us all. Bruised, and hurt, and confused too. But the hurts will fade, dear one, like the problems, if you give them time and stop berating yourself. Give your love time to grow too. Men in pain don't always say the right things, you know.'

'Give my love time, Lotti? What love are you talking of?'

Charlotte could not hold back a mischievous smile. 'Oh, you cannot conceal it for ever, you know, though you may try. You may want to believe Sir Fergus is thinking only of his father's wishes in this affair, but, believe me, it's Fergus Melrose's wishes he's thinking of far more. He's about as transparent as you are, my love.'

'You see too much, Lotti,' Nicola said, wiping her face with a knuckle. 'And what did you mean about men in pain? Were you speaking of Fergus?'

'It's time you two had a long talk about things,' Lotti said, prosaically. 'You both have a lot of ground to make up. Yes, Fergus was injured too. A broken rib, for one thing. He wouldn't tell you that, of course.'

'No, he still thinks of me as an eleven-year-old child at heart.'

'Well, you'll hear no more from Lord John, my dear. Sir Fergus certainly knows how to deal with people who step over the line, doesn't he?'

Nicola shivered as the hairs on her arm stood on end. Yes, I shall find little softness in him, it seems. To insist that I ask him to agree to a betrothal was a heartless move to boost his own score, not the act of a lover. She took a last sip of the treacly drink to avoid answering.

Lotti dusted down her gown with well-manicured hands. 'Now let me put a dab of this new salve on your poor lip, then we'll go along to the solar. I'm going to send for a bath, so we'll take all the fragrant essences with us, and the body lotions, and then we'll find something pretty and comfortable for you to wear. Who does your hair best, Lavender or Rosemary?'

But Nicola was not listening. A white rabbit had found its way up to the top of the steps and was being stopped from entering by its blue leash caught on the ledge. 'Melrose,' she whispered, picking her up and savouring the warm softness against her skin. 'What am I going to do with you?'

The lovely face was still blotchy with the ravages of weeping, and there was nothing that Lotti could devise that would quite conceal the swellings and bruises, but the transformation was nevertheless truly remarkable, in spite of Nicola's protests that this was all rather a waste of time. Lotti knew what she was doing, and insisted on choosing Nicola's most becoming apricot silk with a twining pale aqua motif woven in. The deeply scalloped sleeves reached the ground, and the high-sashed waist hinted at the full curves that she swathed in layers of gossamer around the shoulders and neck like a tantalising mist. They had bound up the glossy dark tresses with gold braids and ropes of pearl, listening to no protests. They had salved, creamed and perfumed her and, hanging pearl pendants from her ears, had unanimously declared the effect simply irresistible.

'Irresistible to whom?' Nicola said, looking with suspicion into the mirror. 'It's a bit late, isn't it? Sir Fergus will have gone home, surely?'

'I think you'll find,' said Lady Charlotte, 'that he's been waiting to speak to you this last hour.'

Nicola stared at her sister-in-law's reflection and saw that she was serious. 'Lotti…no! I don't want to talk to him. I don't want him to start probing about…oh, you know…I can't…Lotti. Please tell him to go away. It's not going to work. I thought it might, but I was wrong.'

Lotti caught her as she flounced away, knowing that it would not, *could* not be as Nicola feared. 'Give him another chance, my dear,' she whispered. 'It's worth another try, isn't it?'

For many reasons it *was* worth another try, if not for Nicola's own happiness then for Lady Melrose's and for the memory of Prioress Sophie.

Still confused, angry and defiant, and still trying to quench the love she had only just begun to acknowledge, she passed through the door that Lavender held open, expecting to have some time to think, alone. But it was not to be, for there by the upper passageway, leaning against the wooden panelling, was Fergus, and she was unable to escape as she had hoped. Nor did he intend her to.

Even on the shadowy landing it was plain to see that something about him had changed, something less easy to define than Nicola's outward appearance, something in the eyes that showed a softness, less challenging than their usual sweeping assuredness. The hauteur was now replaced by a tender appreciative smile that promised more than arguments and unnecessary deadlines, and it was this disarming expression that made Nicola check the refusal she'd been intent on delivering. She knew then that she would *have* to give him the chance to speak.

Even now, his look made her blush and stammer like a girl. Any look at all from Fergus Melrose was unfamiliar, but this one roamed from the dark pile of hair to the hem of her gown and back to her face, lingering sadly upon the tell-tale marks of her suffering in Lotti's arms. 'My lady?' he said. 'Nicola?' There was a pleading in his tone she had never heard before. The door to her room closed quietly behind her, and they were alone. 'Can we begin again?' he said. 'Please? I cannot lose you.'

Her breath welled up into a hard mass, refusing to help. She shook her head.

'I've been with Signor Foscari, Nicola. He's told me—'

'*No!*' The word exploded angrily, squeakily, and she tried to turn away, anticipating the probing questions that would be sure to follow. But Fergus reached out to catch at her hand, and the gentle restriction became a tug-of-arms, then a beating at his breast that flared like tinder into a fight, blind and instinctive on her part, purposeful and restraining on his, a brief skirmish she had no hope of winning, even on a good day. Then she was in his arms, hitting at his charcoal-grey doublet in helpless rage, her voice entangled in a mesh of scalding rebukes that came out sideways and backwards and every way but straight as if they'd been under compression since her childhood.

Raging and pounding at him still, she was held securely against his chest until, panting for breath, she wound down like clockwork with one last feeble shove and the typically female conclusion that made him smile, unseen. 'I have *nothing* to say to you, Fergus Melrose.'

The smile widened before he could pull it back. 'No, sweetheart. But will you hear what I have to say?'

'I've *heard* what you have to say. I'm *tired* of hearing what you have to say. If you did less talking and more…'

He waited. 'More what?'

'Nothing. And I'm not your sweetheart. You can take your damned deadlines…and conditions…and…'

'Shh…hush, lass. I have no deadlines or conditions.'

'What?' Lifting her flushed face, she wiped a knuckle across her damp nose in a child-like gesture that tugged at his heartstrings. Worn down by the earlier storm, her voice now grated sexily, making her rebukes sound more like caresses.

'No deadlines, no conditions,' he repeated. 'There are some things that we both need to know, sweetheart. Things we should have known before. As I said, I've been listening to Signor Foscari. He's a wise man, is my captain. He agrees with me on this matter.'

'On what matter?'

'That I would be a fool to lose you, having got so far. He's right; I *cannot* lose you. Can we talk now? Which is your room?'

'That would be unseemly,' she sniffed, intent on being contrary.

'Not for a betrothed couple, or even a couple about to be. Which one? This?' Keeping hold of her waist, he opened the door through which she had just passed and steered her inside, holding it open as Lavender and Rosemary departed with lowered eyes and tripping curtsies.

The room had been tidied, and the sounds of happy children and deep laughter floated through the open window, reminding them both of how time had suddenly crept up on them before they were ready for it.

They listened, then Fergus drew her towards the window-seat and sat her opposite him, each to their corners. 'Does the light hurt you?' he asked, letting go of her elbows. 'Here, let me put this cushion behind you.'

The wariness must have showed in her eyes as she followed these small attentions that, apart from the tending of her wound, hardly typified his earlier manner towards her. 'What is all this about?' she said, with more than a hint of mistrust. 'You think to change my mind again, don't you? Well, I think I should warn you that—'

'No, don't warn me. It's much too late for warnings, sweetheart. I want you to tell me, not warn me. You've suffered, I know.'

Instantly, she was back on the defensive. 'You do *not*

know, Fergus Melrose. Why does everyone think they know how I feel? How could you possibly know? You're a man. It couldn't happen to you.' She had begun to tremble again, aware that her outburst could sound pettish, like the silly ramblings of a girl with her first lover. 'That kind of thing doesn't happen to men,' she said, lamely.

'No, it doesn't. And I blame myself entirely for getting you into such danger and then for assuming that nothing much had happened, since you still had the energy to thrash your attacker. I had no right to assume anything of the sort. Nor had I the right to assume that you are as tough a nut as you used to be as a child. I can see that you're not. How could you be?'

'I never was, Fergus. You assumed then that I was impervious to hurt because it suited you to. But I never was then, any more than I am now. You've always assumed too much. Even after the brawl at Southwark you never once asked if I'd been hurt, though you must have seen what happened.'

'I thought—'

'That because I didn't list my bruises, there were none? Well, I got hurt in places where ladies are not supposed to get hurt, and although you could say it serves me right for dressing as a man, it would have been nice to receive *some* sympathy. And I don't want to tie myself for life to someone who thinks I'm just an inferior breed of man, like the lad I used to be when we were young. I've told you, things have changed. I knew what *you* were like, Fergus. I have only myself to blame for letting things get this far.'

'Is it really too late, Nicola? Is it too late for me to make it up to you? I heard what the captain had to say. He told me…oh, God…sweetheart, show me your poor wrists… come, show me.' Taking her fingers, he gently eased back the silk sleeve to expose the red and purple pattern of the twisted rope on her skin. Bending his great handsome head, he put his warm lips to it, kissing every part of her wrists while she watched and felt each healing caress steal down to the soles of her feet. And when he had done that to his satisfaction, he pulled the sleeves back into place and drew her into his arms with none of the resistance her words had led him to expect. 'Your beautiful eye, your lip, too,' he said, studying them so closely that she could see herself reflected in his eyes.

'Did the captain tell you everything?' she whispered.

'Yes, he told me what he saw. Now, you can tell me the rest.'

'No, I can't do that. I won't repeat it. It's far worse than Southwark.'

Fergus's eyes hardened with rage. 'I need to know, Nicola.'

Her voice shook. 'They told him what we were doing in the woodland, and he was angry because it was you and not him. He was crude and disgusting, Fergus. He's spoilt it. I was going to stop on the track…to tell you…that I wouldn't wait till sundown…to tell you…you know. But now it's spoilt. I can't tell you what I was going to say. I feel cheapened. Defiled.'

'Did he touch you?'

'Except for hitting me and holding me by the throat, no.'

'Show me.'

Without shame, she let him move the gauze aside to study the blue fingerprints, watching again as his lips approached to lap tenderly at them. 'I shall keep the dog at those oars till he drops,' he said. 'I swear it. Is there anything else I need to know? Nay, lass. Do not look at me like that. This is not going to change anything between us. Did you believe it would? You belong to me, Nicola Coldyngham. You were mine before this happened, and you still are. You were on the verge of accepting me, and it was insensitive of me to impose a time limit. I can see it now. That's not the way to win a woman.'

'You're sure you still want me?'

'Am I sure? Good grief, woman, I'm more sure of that than I am of my own name. You'll never know what torments I suffered when I almost lost you. Did you know that I broke three heads that day, and nearly tore London apart?'

'No. No, I didn't know. You didn't tell me what had happened to you. Lotti told me about the rib. I'm sorry. Does it pain you much?'

'Several ribs. It's nothing. Were you concerned for me?'

I died a thousand deaths for you, that day. 'Yes,' she said. 'I was.'

'So do you think it's time we started to confide in

each other a little more? We *shall* be betrothed, my lady. You may as well accept it.'

'All this in the name of duty to your father, Fergus?'

His reply to that was not quite what she had expected. With no thought of his broken ribs and the pain any movement caused him, he slid a hand beneath her knees and lifted her into his arms, carrying her the three strides to her canopied bed as if she could not have walked. As softly as thistledown he laid her there and stood over her as he had done once before, with his arms like a cage on each side of her. 'Let's just leave the duty out of it, shall we, sweetheart? Just tell me what you were going to say on the woodland path before you were prevented. Come on, I need to hear it.'

The time for prevarication was past. 'I was going to say…' she looked away, but he moved her chin back into place with tender fingers '…that I will marry you, but you don't deserve my co-operation.' The hard words were softened by a smile that reached her eyes as well as her swollen mouth; for all Fergus cared, the reprimand might just as well have been a declaration of love.

'No.' He grinned. 'But you've said you'll have me.'

'Yes.'

'Then I shall work harder to deserve you, Lady Coldheart.'

'My heart is not cold, Fergus.'

'I'm relieved to hear it, sweetheart. So, as soon as the ceremony is over and you feel well enough, we'll go up to Melrose to see my mother. Come, lass,' he said, sitting beside her and enclosing her with his arms, 'tell me that we're friends now. I've seen you smile for the first time in days. Is that a sign of your recovery?'

He was close again, close enough for her to feel his warm breath upon her face, and all she had to do was to lift her arms and cradle his head, and feel the shivers of desire start under her fingers, flooding her body. She had accepted him. There would be no going back.

Fergus's intention to work harder to deserve that lady's thawing heart was taken rather more literally than he expected and, in view of his broken ribs, too soon. Nevertheless, no one made any objection to the events that Nicola had planned, for while some doubts still lingered in her mind, she would need to put Fergus to the test, one way or another.

The arrival of Ramond at River House was just the opportunity she needed, for with two brothers to bolster the competition, she believed that Fergus would surely revert to his former ways and forget to include her in any of the sport. Though it was good to see them together once more, swapping news and teasing, in spite of Fergus's plea not to make him laugh, Nicola could scarcely hold back the strange feeling of déjà vu and the anticipation of dread.

Less surprised at the impending betrothal than George expected him to be, Ramond was predictably diplomatic, entering into the spirit of Nicola's suggestions as if she had always been team leader instead of Fergus. A boating party found favour with them all.

But the brothers would not allow Fergus to row, relegating him to sit in the stern of the narrow launch with both arms around Nicola, his hands over hers, beneath her breasts and only a move away from a public caress. Fortunately, Lotti and the men were far too occupied with keeping Roberta and Louis still to notice where Fergus's hands were straying, or how tenderly she was being held against his warm body.

She felt his whisper on the patch of skin behind her ear. 'Got you, my beauty,' and until then she had not known of the link from there to her woman's parts. The rush of excitement was like a vibrating bowstring, keeping her breath deep inside her lungs.

'What do you do for a ship now it's on its way to Flanders?' George called, heaving at one pair of oars. 'Wait for it to return?'

'No,' Fergus said. 'I have my Genoese carrack filling up at Holyrood Wharf. Have you not seen her? Smaller sails and fewer men, but she carries a massive cargo. I'll show you round if you have time. You may want to send some of your wool in her.'

'Where will she be bound?'

'Scotland. I have Queen Margaret's shipment from Genoa.'

Testing him, Nicola said, 'Perhaps we could row up there to see the ship?'

'Ooh…yes!' the children shrieked. 'Can we, Papa? *Can* we?'

Fergus's arms tightened, his laugh sending shivers into Nicola's seat. 'We're rowing the wrong way,' he said. 'We'll go tomorrow.' Typically, he had taken charge, but the old brutal coldness was now replaced by a gentleness as his hands fondled her arm underneath the woollen wrap, and she would not for the world have argued with him.

'It's the prioress's funeral rites in a day or two,' she whispered over her shoulder.

'That's all right, sweetheart. Time enough.'

'Are you going to take a turn at the oars, Fergus?'

'D'ye want me to?'

'No.'

'Then I won't. Besides, you want me here, don't you?'

'Yes.'

'That's what I thought.'

The next trial, sure to demand more from Fergus than a ride on the river, was a game of cricket on the lawn of River House. He had always been extremely competitive in this, and Nicola's memories of him angrily yelling at her eleven-year-old incompetence was hard to forget. But once again, her brothers were protective of Fergus's broken ribs, refusing to allow him either to bowl or to bat, sitting him on a stool from which to umpire and to flout every rule. It turned out to be the most hilarious game of cricket any of them had ever played, with Nicola, Lotti, the children and the white rabbit all taking part on both sides and Fergus notching up an outrageous score in their favour. It ended when the ball flew far out into the river with a splash and Nicola collapsed at Fergus's feet, speechless with laughter. Again, her plan had been happily turned on its head.

Noticing the change in his sister since their last meeting, Ramond could not help but question it. 'What's happened, Nick?' he said. 'Why have you accepted him after all that protesting?'

'I can't tell you,' she said. 'It's to do with Father. Don't ask me.'

'How did you find out?'

'Recently.'

'So all this affection Ferg is showing you, you think it's a sham?'

'No, not a sham. But it's a result of what happened. The assault.'

'You were in his arms before that, Nick.' Ramond had his own thoughts about what was happening, but he saw that there was only so much one could say. So he took her hand in a brotherly clasp and held it upon his lap for a few moments of silence. 'My tutor wants me to take some time off,' he said eventually, leaning his sculpted head against the roses. 'I think the threat of those Oxford brothers is worrying him and his wife. They have a daughter, you remember, and I've had Ferg's two men with me constantly since it happened. It's all a bit too much for the family, so he's suggested I take some leave until it settles down. Perhaps a month or so.'

'Oh, Ramond, I'm so sorry.' Nicola leaned over to place a kiss upon his cheek. 'But you've not had a break for over a year, have you? What are you going to do, keep on studying, or find a job? Are you very disappointed?'

'Not as disappointed as I thought I'd be. To be honest, I don't fancy my chances at the royal court just now with things being as they are. It's more dangerous to be in Edward the Fifth's service now than it's ever been, with all those Yorkist and Lancastrian family quarrels going on and members changing sides every few weeks. Clarence and Gloucester will never see eye to eye, and I don't think I'd sleep safe at nights, so I can appreciate how my tutor and his wife feel. I don't know what I'm going to do, or even whether I shall go back to law. That's why I came to talk to George about it.'

'And what do you want George to do, offer you a position?'

'It had occurred to me. Perhaps Fergus might need somebody. Does he have a secretary?'

'I have no idea. I know little about him or what he does except to own some ships that ply between here and Genoa.'

Ramond stared at her in astonishment. 'You're going to be his wife, for pity's sake,' he said. 'Hadn't you better show more interest than that?'

'Yes, I suppose I had,' she said, smiling at his scolding.

Taking advantage of the lapse in conversation, the men in the group joined in, bringing Rosemary and Lavender with them. Soon, there was laughter and admiration, witty conversation and rapport on a level that Nicola had not enjoyed for quite some time without the overtones of rivalry or serious flirting, of carefully defensive replies to veiled proposals, or wondering how to get rid of so-called friends and hangers-on.

Still expecting to find a way of verifying Fergus's new loyalty to her, she suggested a game of cards after supper. The meal had been unlike any of those at which Fergus had been present as a young lad when, seated by her side at the Coldyngham table, he had pretended she was invisible. This time, he held her hand under the cloth, fed her with the choicest pieces, and let his gaze wander over her face and bosom as he did so, unable to keep the smiling approval from his eyes. But the card game was as much an indication of the new Fergus as were the previous activities for, with Nicola as a less-than-useful partner, they managed between them to lose most of Fergus's clothing and then to start on Nicola's, until Fergus put a stop to it. There would have been a time, she recalled, when he would have delighted in embarrassing her, but not now. However much she had tried, she could not fault his care of her.

'An evening ride into the town?' she suggested, quite late.

Ramond glanced at her from beneath his dark brows, but it was Fergus who replied, 'No. The apprentices are still rioting at night. I heard they attacked one of the Lombard's houses. It's best to keep out of the way.'

'A visit to Southwark, then. It's on the opposite side.'

Straight-faced, Fergus stood and, taking Nicola's hands, pulled her to her feet, escorting her from the chamber and into the dim hallway that glowed pink with the last reflected rays of the sun. 'Now,' he said, leaning a hand against the wall above her head, 'what's all this about?'

'What?' she said, resisting the temptation to finger the cleft in his chin and to feel the soft dark hair around his ears. 'All what?'

'You know what I'm talking about. You're avoiding being alone with me, is that it? You fear it's all going too fast for you?'

'I have accepted you. Isn't that enough?' She was glad he had got it wrong, for once. It would not do to have her strategies exposed every time.

'No, my beauty. You know it isn't. I want to get close to you. I know that recent events are still on your mind, but we'll go at your pace, I promise. Don't run away from me now, Nicola. I'm trying so hard to show you my other sides. Have you not noticed?'

At last she smiled, letting her breath out with a gush. 'Yes, I noticed. I think everyone else noticed, too.'

'Good. I found it came easily to me. I can't think why I've not tried it before. You see what your good influence has done. What did brother Ramond have to say?'

'He wants to know if you need a secretary. He needs some temporary employment. That's why he's come to see George, but I wondered if you…well…if…'

'If I could give him a position in my household so that you can have him near you. Have I read you correctly, my lady?' There was laughter in his deep voice, and the tightening clasp of his hands made her blush to be found out so easily. 'I'll speak to him. I'll see what I can do.'

'Oh, you mean it? Really? Thank you. So he can be with us, can he?'

'Is it worth a kiss?'

She leaned forward and tilted her head to one side, allowing him to take as large a payment as he could get before she drew back, holding her sore mouth.

'It's been a long day, sweetheart, and an emotional one too. You're a remarkable woman. I should have got to know you sooner.'

She knew what he meant to say. He had had the chance, but something had stood in the way and now there were obstacles to be removed before they could read each other's minds. 'Give me time, Fergus. You always *did* go too fast for me.'

'That was before,' he said. 'This is now.' Slowly, he gathered her into his arms as if at any moment she might break away, and his last kiss of the day seemed to reinforce all the trials they had been through together, all the discoveries, and the beginning of a new understanding.

Chapter Eight

If anyone had told Nicola, as a young child, that Fergus Melrose would one day say to her, 'I want to get close to you', she would have either laughed or cried. Even now, the nagging shades of cynicism passed over her like a beloved enemy and then disappeared, waiting to return. At the time she was sure he had meant it, but only time would tell. She would have to accept whatever was in store and pray that the new tenderness of the last twenty-four hours would not fade too soon, breaking her heart in two.

It was an augmented family party that rode down to Holyrood Wharf the next morning to inspect Sir Fergus's impressively large Genoese carrack; though Nicola and Charlotte could tell that he was in some discomfort, his wish to please them was even more obvious. Through the early morning streets, along Thames Street that ran parallel to the river, past glimpses between houses of steps and sails and bobbing boats, dodging overhanging house signs and men with loaded backs, carts, packhorses and stacks of barrels, Sir Fergus kept a leading rein on Nicola's bridle as if she were a novice, regardless of her exasperation and her brothers' undisguised amusement.

But the streets became more and more difficult to negotiate with the paraphernalia of shipping, and Nicola began to see the wisdom of it when George did the same for Lotti. Crossing the road that led to the bridge was a nightmare; Holyrood Wharf was several stops up from there, part of the great Billingsgate complex where the grain and salt markets were held twice weekly. What Nicola had not known was that from Thames Street down to the river, Sir Fergus owned six shops where he sold his imports to merchants in East Anglia and Hampshire, to dyers in Suffolk and Wiltshire, and directly to customers in London.

'What d'ye sell to Londoners?' said Ramond, pulling his horse round a pile of manure.

'Wine,' said Sir Fergus, 'and beaver pelts, saffron, licorice, alum and woad to dyers, wax and linen to drapers, green ginger to the sheriff of Middlesex, silk to silkworkers and oil to cooks, wainscot boards to carpenters, copper, lead, millstones, precious spices and silks from Genoa and Venice. Whatever folks want, I can get it.'

'I'm going to enjoy this,' said Ramond. 'When do I start?'

'Just observe for a while first,' said Sir Fergus, winking at Nicola. 'You can start after dinner. Have you brought your tool kit along with you?'

Ramond did not go far without his quills and knife, papers, parchment, inks and sealing wax. 'Yes,' he said, glancing at George who was keeping a circumspect silence about his ignorance of Fergus's trading activities. He had known of the shops, but had no idea that they belonged to his friend, and that did not go down too well with one who believed he knew as much as anybody about how merchants distributed their wares from the port of London.

He caught Ramond's beaming face and knew him to be well pleased by Fergus's offer of a position. It could not have come at a better time. 'What are we to call you now?' he said. 'Master Secretary Coldyngham, is it?'

'If you please,' Ramond replied. His answer would have been longer, but for the spectacle of his new employer helping Nicola from the saddle and across the muddy wharf to the waiting boat that would ferry them to the carrack. He suspected that, but for the painful ribs, Fergus would have carried her.

To Nicola herself it seemed that she was learning, moment by moment, what those other sides were that Fergus had kept hidden from her for so long, for this was a far cry from the arrogant and intimidating man who had taken up a rapier against her almost two weeks ago. In the rowing boat, he held her close as if he knew how she had suffered during her last boarding experience and, when it came to walking up the ridged gangplank to reach the high deck of the ship, he went before her to help her over the side, his hands never very far away from her.

There was no danger here: Signor Foscari and his cargo had weighed anchor from the Galley Wharf on the early high tide, and the layout of this large ship was altogether different, relying for manoeuvrability on many sails rather than many oars. Instead of the canvas awning over the balconied stern there was a double tier of cabins for the captain and passengers and, over the painted bows, yet more platforms for guns as well as people. Deep in the belly of the ship, bales, boxes and chests held merchandise for Scotland's young Queen. The cabins were lined with shelves, cupboards and tables of polished oak, curtained and hung with fair tapestries, windowed with thick glass and lit with gleaming lanterns. The beds appeared to be inside cupboards, an idea that particularly intrigued the women.

'I could lock him in,' said Lotti, naughtily.

'Or out,' said Nicola, opening the cupboard doors and testing the feather-filled mattress. 'I think I could sail in a ship like this, Lotti. What an adventure. Just think of it—the wind, the sea, and freedom.'

'Quicker than horseback, too. And probably more comfortable.'

Nicola ran her palm over the shining oak panelling. 'Then why could we not go up to Melrose by sea instead of by road? Do you know?'

'No, not exactly, except that Melrose is not on the coast, is it?'

'No idea,' said Nicola. 'I'll ask Fergus.'

George ducked his head as he entered the cosy cabin.

'Ask Fergus what?' he said, readjusting his padded and draped hat.

'Why would we travel up to Scotland by road when we could go with the cargo? Could we not reach Lady Melrose from the coast?'

'Lady Melrose will *be* on the coast at Whithorn, with the Queen. I believe it was Fergus's intention to—'

'Intention to what?' said Fergus from the doorway. 'Is there room for me in here?' Like George, he had to stoop and step over the high ledge, his head almost reaching the beams of the roof. 'Now, what's the problem?'

'No problem, Ferg,' said George. 'The ladies think it would be better to go by sea to Scotland than on horseback, that's all. I thought you had some cargo you particularly wanted to take by road.'

'Hmm,' said Fergus, looking at Nicola. 'I do. I had not thought that my lady would relish the idea of a sea voyage at this time. Am I mistaken?'

As always, when he looked at her like that, her knees turned to water. 'I *would* relish a sea voyage in a ship like this one,' she said, quietly. 'And if it would mean we reach Lady Melrose sooner, then it makes some sense to go this way.'

'The only problem is,' said Fergus, leaning against the door, 'that the captain will be sailing in three days from now.' He began to fold his arms across his chest, then decided otherwise and placed his hands over his hips instead. Because there was a strained silence loaded with unspoken queries, Lady Charlotte took hold of her husband's arm and steered him out of the cabin and out of earshot.

Fergus closed the door. 'Well, my lady?'

'Three days, you say? That's not long, is it?' Nicola said, feeling suddenly vulnerable in the confines of the panelled cabin. 'But you must agree it would be kinder to your ribs than having to ride a horse all that way. Wouldn't it? Are there enough cabins for us, for you and the captain, for me and the maids, and Ramond?'

'More to the point, Lady Coldheart, is whether there's enough time for our betrothal,' he replied, softly. 'Isn't it?'

'I wish you would not call me that,' she said, turning her back on him as he took a stride to reach her. 'I've told you, my heart is not cold.' The many-paned window leaned forward at an angle to give views of the brown swirling river below, making her clutch at the edge of the table for support.

His arms caught her, enclosing her in a protective embrace while with one hand he searched gently for her heartbeat. 'No, I believe you're right. It's getting quite warm, isn't it?' he said into her braided hair. 'So what about this betrothal, then?'

'It could be brought forward.' She placed her hands over his, idly fingering the dusting of hair on their backs. *Would his chest be the same? Would he be this colour all over?*

'It could. Tomorrow? Or the day after?' he said.

'The day after is the prioress's funeral.'

'Oh. I cannot see the two ceremonies mixing well, can you?'

'No, it will have to be tomorrow, then. Of course, if it doesn't suit George and Charlotte, it could be a small informal affair with just a couple of witnesses. It's just as valid. You've already talked about money, I suppose?'

'You were expensive.'

'Blame George. He's the merchant.'

'Is that what you'd prefer, an informal ceremony?'

When she did not answer immediately, he turned her round in his arms and held her close so that he could find it in her expression. 'Are you ready?' he whispered. 'I'm not going to rush you into this, but if you really want to go up with the cargo, we shall have to do it soon. But you need not fear that I shall insist on the consummation, not with broken ribs.' He smiled.

'If it suits you to wait, then I don't—'

'It doesn't suit me to wait, I can assure you. Am I to take it that your mind has changed about that?'

My mind is changing every moment I'm in your arms. Don't ask me about my mind. I know little of it. 'No,' she said, 'my preferences are the same on that score. I'm glad to hear you have your own reasons for accepting them.' Almost out of habit, her words were uncompromising, but underlying them was a strange sense of disappointment at the inevitable delay. After this recent and conspicuous display of concern for her welfare, she was gradually accepting the notion that there might be less to fear than she had thought. But was this too soon for her to relent, to show him that he had warmed the heart kept on ice for so long?

Placing his knuckles beneath her chin, he lifted her face to his, obliging her to read from his smiling eyes how far they had come from the bristling antagonism of that first meeting, but finding no answering smile in her eyes. 'We shall see,' he said. 'It will be a shorter journey, but still time enough to make some progress in other directions too. I have no objections to a small betrothal ceremony. Shall I put the idea to your brother?'

'Yes,' she said, having less interest in what he was saying than in the nearness of his firm mouth and in the long lean pressure of his body against hers. *How will it feel? Will it be fierce, as it is in my dreams?*

Softly, as his lips touched hers in the lightest caress, a flame leapt out of control deep within her body, its heat igniting her, tightening her fingers involuntarily upon his back, pressing them through the fabric into hard muscle while her mouth waited upon his, suddenly reckless and contradicting all her cool intentions. *Fool. Foolish woman. This is no way to punish him. Turn back, before it's too late.*

But he knew how to read even the smallest sign, and the quick pressure of her fingertips told him all he needed to know about the conflict raging inside her, the passion she had always struggled against, and the reawakened adoration she had once held for him. The teasing of his lips sensed her tingling anticipation and the verge of her surrender, and he closed his mouth over hers with a kiss that had begun as a token but now roared into flame like a heath fire in a drought.

Unthinking, she cried out into his lips a soft mew of submission and then, swept up into the blaze, felt the soaring heat of his desire fuse with her own years of yearning. Distantly, the urgency grew within her womb with the need to know him intimately, and the ache between her legs was stirred by the hard strength of his arms and hands that bent her to his will. She had been convinced that she would care about the hurts sustained in being his; now it mattered least compared to the overwhelming need to be taken, possessed, and sweetly conquered. While his lips kept her mind in turmoil, his hands urged her further into abandonment, searching over breasts and skilfully questing beneath her skirts, setting alive her sensitive skin.

As if they had both been waiting for some signal, even though it was before time, their needs swept them past any reservations that would otherwise have made them more cautious. Neither of them paid any heed to the poor timing, or to the mental barrier that Nicola had erected, or to the physical problems, or even to her total lack of experience. When Fergus shed his doublet with some difficulty, she helped him, and when she showed no qualms at the sheer pace of his ardour, it was he who reminded her that she was yet a virgin, giving her the choice to wait for a more appropriate time.

Then, it was if she was fencing with him again but wanting to be both winner and vanquished, held, and taken forcibly, and made his for ever. She took his head between her hands in a sudden frenzy of irresponsibility, releasing everything she had held dear and close, ready for the right moment. Whispering against his lips, she told him her secret desire. 'It's yours, Fergus Melrose. Take my virginity now, here, while it's still mine to give, freely. I give it to you if you can take it here, before they come looking for us. Can you do it? Broken ribs and all? Can you take what I offer you and still accept me tomorrow in seeming innocence? Quickly, Fergus Melrose… can you do it?'

'Is that what you want, truly?' he said, scarcely believing her.

'Yes, it's what I want. Now. Here. Or are you in too much pain?'

He spoke between hungry kisses. 'Never mind the pain. But I wanted to take you through it slowly, Nicola. Infinitely slow. To seduce you and make you want more, and more. This is going to be—'

'I know, I know. I will want more. Take it.'

He did not wait to argue, but bent his head to kiss her again with a new ferocity she recognised as the acceptance of her challenge, for that was what it was. A challenge he could not have refused, coming from her.

She could not have known, at that stage in their storm-driven relationship, that for Fergus there was more to it than that. As they kissed, he sensed in her the duel of excitement and curiosity, of fear and driving force, of the need to fight him and to be conquered on her own terms, not on his as it would be from tomorrow. Everything that had happened between them so far had been the result of his intervention and insistence, her independence having been rudely snatched from her. He knew that this was the reason why, earlier, she had balked at the idea of consummation, as a desire to keep some control of the one precious thing she owned. Or so she thought. This was a challenge in the guise of a gift, and vice versa, one she would not want him to refuse because the timing was not perfect. Nor did she want to win it. It was his task to make it memorable for her in the most difficult of circumstances with a crowd of her relatives waiting outside the door, and now was not the time to remind her that this was not the only precious thing she had to give. Nor did he think that her expectations were even remotely realistic.

Despite the soreness of broken ribs, he placed his hands under her thighs and lifted her, swinging her round to the open bunk bed padded with furs, parting her legs with his own as he sat her on the edge. Huskily, he whispered. 'Hold on, beautiful woman. I'll try to be careful. Pull your skirts up out of the way, sweetheart.... Oh, Nicola...I cannot wait for ye...I shall be useless...forgive me if I hurt you. Hold fast, sweet thing, and don't cry out. This is your gift to me; mine to you will take longer than this, I promise.' His fingers wrestled impatiently with the points that tied his hose to his shirt, finally releasing his throbbing hardness.

He sought her mouth, gentling her with his lips, feeling her eagerness unabated, her co-operation ungrudging, her hands clinging and caressing, urging him on. All the nights of wanting and the days of imagining poured into his being at the moment of entry, lending him the power he needed to pass the first tender barrier. He pushed, withdrew, and pushed again more slowly but with force, and her lips parted with the pain of it. He heard her stifled yelp, the gasping cries and felt the sudden struggle against him, just as quickly checked. 'Go on,' she whispered, shakily. 'Go on…it's all right. Do what you have to do, Fergus. Don't hold back.'

In his fantasies, he had talked to her and made long slow love to every inch of her body, drawing her together along every delicate strand. Never had he thought it would be this way, in the dark undercurrent of his dreams where he became silent and grim in the grip of the primitive urge to possess. But that was what she wanted from him, something she knew he was well able to perform, for to conquer came naturally to him.

Half-blinded by his unleashed passion and on the very edge of control, he braced himself against the panelled bed and moved rhythmically into her, seeing the woman with the lad's trews clinging to her legs and her hair falling down, a rapier poised in her hand, then the haughty viper-tongued noblewoman who lashed him with insults, and last the chastened and bruised woman from whom he had demanded a proposal of marriage. Recalling all this in the space of one moment, he was caught in the surge of power far too soon, as he had known he would be and, unable to delay it for even a second, he was thrown into the maelstrom while his body, ignoring the pain, delivered the vigorous thrusts that rocked Nicola without mercy. From deep within his chest came a muffled roar that he stifled in the rich mass of her silken hair while she clung to his neck and shoulders as if to a bolting horse.

Cradling her like a child in his arms, his hands smoothed her over the rich stuff of her gown, his eyes searching her lovely flushed face for a sign of tears and distress. The one tear hanging upon the thick lashes he removed with lips and tongue, opening her eyes to him. 'Nicola,' he whispered. 'My beautiful and courageous woman. I took your gift. I could not refuse it. Can you forgive me?'

Breathless, as she had been after their fencing, she let her gaze feed on him as if he had answered some mysterious question she had long asked herself, searching his contours and using her fingertips to confirm his expression of contrition, tenderness, longing and… yes…some triumph, too. 'There's nothing to forgive,' she whispered, taking a nip at his chin with her teeth. 'It was a wound I sought from you, this time, but on my terms. Do you still want me for a wife, Fergus Melrose, or am I free of you now?'

His kiss was hard upon her mouth, drinking in her sweetness as if his thirst had only just begun. 'How can you ask it, woman?' he growled. 'You will never be free of me. I have marked you and possessed you. You are mine and mine alone, and you will make your vows tomorrow. What's just happened between us was not meant to free you of your obligations, but to bind you. Do you understand me?'

'Yes, my lord,' she said, hiding her smile in his shirt-front.

He lifted her chin. 'Now we have to emerge from here and put on a front of extreme boredom. That will be our test. Can you stand?'

The next few moments were indeed as much of a test for them as anything they could have devised, and though Nicola was practised in the art of recovery after a mishap, this experience was unique in many ways, and she needed the support of Fergus's hand as they stepped nonchalantly through the cabin doorway. Helping each other without the aid of a mirror, they had repaired damage to clothes and hair as best they could, though it remained to be seen whether their seemingly casual chatter would convince the waiting companions.

'My apologies,' called Fergus cheerfully to the group. 'We've finally come to an agreement of sorts. We shall go by sea after all. It's sure to be easier, and quicker too, unless we run into a storm.'

'Glad you've decided,' said George, missing nothing, as usual. 'We've been taken round by Captain Munro. It's a fine ship, Fergus.'

Ramond was mounting the steps up to the forecastle, but Lotti took Nicola's arm to turn her round the way she had come. 'And you look as if you've already run into a storm, sister dear,' she whispered. 'Don't tell me it's taken you all this time to decide that.' Not expecting an answer, she busily tucked a lock of dark hair back into the gold caul behind Nicola's neck and replaced a hairpin that had come adrift, noting the flush that had not had time to fade. 'You are all right?' she breathed. 'God in heaven, lass, but he's a powerful creature, is he not?'

Nicola's secretive half-smile was more convincing than words that she was indeed all right, her brief nod of agreement as close as she could get to explaining the euphoria of being desired by Fergus Melrose, no matter how hurried or unglamorous the act of love itself. He had accepted her gift with all the care he could afford and with far more than she had expected, and she herself had led the way, and he had followed. *Just this once, she had led and he had followed, and she had allowed herself to be conquered only because it suited her to do so.* Fortunately, there was no one who would ask her to explain herself, for she would not have known where to start.

In one sense, Sir Fergus's doubts concerning her expectations were justified: she had not been satisfied in the same sense that he had been, as men usually were in these matters, however scanty the preparation. Having no experience of what that satisfaction might entail, she knew only that she had given away what was still hers to give to the man she wanted to receive it and, whether on the spur of the moment or not, hurriedly, poorly timed or ill advised, she had no regrets. His promises to make it last longer in the future sounded good, but had little meaning for her except in terms of time and, if she still wondered whether the combined presence of her brothers would make a difference to his attitude, she was relieved and happy to discover that this newest intimacy meant as much to Fergus as it did to her. She was kept close to his side all the way to his grand house on Holyrood Wharf and all through the mid-day dinner that followed.

Physically, there was a problem she was obliged to share with her two maids, who found a way of tearing Rosemary's chemise to clean up the inevitable signs of a first loving, after which she was more comfortable. If they were surprised by anything, it was Sir Fergus's house that impressed them rather than what they saw as Nicola's sudden capitulation. Who would not capitulate, they wondered, given the chance?

The meal, beautifully prepared and served on the finest silver plate by liveried servants in a large oak-lined chamber, impressed the Coldynghams to a man, keeping the conversation flowing throughout the meal. But the one whose mind could not be engaged fully was Nicola herself; she could not summon, like Sir Fergus, that extra reserve of equanimity needed to sail through the event without looking as if something monumental had just happened to her. For one thing, the memory of his ardour had taken her aback for, though she understood the basic mechanics of coupling, her education had been deficient in the details. She had not been aware, for instance, of how much physical effort was involved, not only by him but by her, too. The fierceness of her dreams had fallen some way short of the realistic; the actuality was both exciting and frightening, for there had been moments during the heat of the action when he had seemed like a stranger to her once again, a man in the throes of some unstoppable force that had little to do with her as a person.

Afterwards, in the short time allowed to them, he had tried to explain that that was not how it should have been, leaving her wondering how it should have been, if not like that. In her giving had also been her receiving, though he had not appeared to think so. Was it possible, then, that he had more than that to give? Would there be a time to find out soon, while her curiosity was at its peak?

Concerning her apparent inconsistency, the niggling question remained. It had been less than a fortnight since her first scathing attack upon Sir Fergus's pedigree, character and status, and now here she was, on the eve of a betrothal, giving him a part of herself that, if she'd kept to her original intentions, she could have withheld for some considerable time. Was there, after all, an element in her that refused to conform to her new independent image, the one she was so sure everyone had recognised and understood?

'Inconsistent?' said Lady Charlotte, examining Sir Fergus's grapevine along one sunny wall. 'Well, of course you are, love. So are we all, to some extent. Very few people are consistent all the way through. People do the strangest and most unpredictable things, quite out of character. That's what makes them human. Take Ramond, for instance.'

Nicola squeezed a grape but found it still hard. 'Ramond?' she said. 'You mean suddenly changing tack? But that was circumstances, Lotti.'

'Maybe, but I'll wager that this experience as Sir Fergus's secretary will take him in a completely different direction. He's not too concerned about giving up his studies, is he, after all he's said for years about wanting to be a diplomat? Of all the Coldynghams, I think that Patrick is probably the most predictable, and even he may surprise us.'

'So what about George? And you?'

'In our own ways we're not nearly as typical as we appear, love. We give the impression of being sober and civilised and very proper, but, believe me, that's not how we behave in private. Love's like that, dearest. It allows you to do anything with your loved one that makes you both feel good. Did you think it was a well-mannered and gentle business?'

There was a silence between them, of recognition and accord, and Nicola realised that those had been her thoughts, even the more ferocious ones. 'You knew, then?' she whispered.

'Yes, love. Women usually know. There's a difference, somehow. I could tell. Did he persuade you? Is that what happened?'

'No, it isn't. He didn't. It was me. I wanted him to take me, there and then. Can you believe it?'

Lotti smiled and placed a soft hand fleetingly over Nicola's. 'I certainly can believe it,' she said. 'So you think that's your inconsistent side, do you? Well, if it's any comfort, love, I wouldn't even try to find an explanation for it. The only one who needs to know what you're about is Sir Fergus, and it looks to me as if he has a fair idea, in spite of those worries we talked about the other day. You'll be hand-fasted tomorrow. Leave it at that. You've done all the right things for all the right reasons.'

If only you knew the whole story. 'Thank you,' said Nicola, placing a kiss upon her sister-in-law's cheek. 'I'm glad I have you.'

But when it drew near to departure time, Sir Fergus took Nicola away from the good-natured brotherly bickering. 'Are you all right?' he said, taking her carefully by the shoulders. 'Would you prefer to stay here overnight and return to River House in the morning with me? I have a room for your maids too. We can spend a quiet evening here.'

'Just you?'

'Just me. I shall make sure you have everything you need.'

Cocking her head to one side, she could not resist a touch of mischief. 'Everything?' she whispered.

His grin was only just short of a laugh. 'Everything,' he said, softly. 'I even have a pair of rapiers, should you get a sudden urge.'

'But what's George going to say? What will your chaplain say?'

'I never pay a great deal of attention to what my chaplain says. He's mostly for show. As for George, he'll understand.'

George did, though he took care not to betray any sign of approval. 'Hmm,' he said to his lovely wife. 'A bit unorthodox, isn't it? It was only a day or two ago she was balking at everything to do with him. What's changed her?'

Lotti passed him his convoluted head-gear, smiling

as he searched for the part to put his head in. 'They're an unorthodox pair, George dearest,' she said. 'Nicola will be quite safe. Ramond will stay with us tonight.'

George handed the hat back, defeated. 'Here, you put it on me, love. I shan't be ordering another one of these things. I'll have one like Ferg's with an ostrich feather to show me where the back is.'

'Yes, dear. You might consider having your hair cut like his, too.'

'Mmm. Fancy him, do you?'

'Well, I fancy the ships and shops and sealing-wax…' her white teeth and pink tongue tripped over the esses with a smile '…but I'm stuck with a lord, so I'd better be satisfied.' She sighed, dropping her tone to a minor key.

'I think it's time I got you home,' said George.

'Yes, dear. Keep your head still, will you?'

While Lotti's words of wisdom afforded her some comfort, Nicola realised that it was not only her own inconsistency that was so remarkable, but Fergus's too. She could not have dwelt upon this to her sister-in-law, however, when only days before she had grumbled to her about his singular inability to change. Now he had changed and she could hardly bring herself to believe that it was either genuine or permanent, in spite of her recent experiences of men's unreliability. Putting it to the test was one option, but with a betrothal looming so soon the result would be more academic than useful. Nevertheless, put it to the test she would, while the chance to assert herself still existed.

Fergus's beautiful house on Holyrood Wharf was strangely silent after the departure of Nicola's family, though not the same kind of silence she had encountered as a child when, almost invariably, she had known the deep despair of being left alone and nettled by their too-rough horseplay. On this occasion, the one most responsible for those particular childhood grievances was by her side, holding her hand in an unmistakably possessive grasp even after the boat carrying her family had dwindled into a speck on the gold-washed stretch of river.

'Better if they return by barge,' said Fergus. 'It'll be safer at this time of day, and more comfortable. And the tide's just on the turn, so they'll make good time on the current.'

'What about the horses?' said Nicola.

'They can stay here overnight. The men will take them back in the morning.'

'Fergus,' she said, hesitating, 'there's something on my mind.'

'About tonight, you mean?' He smiled, swinging her arm gently.

'No, not exactly. About us. You in particular.'

He saw the slight frown as she watched the craft on the river scudding through the sunset. 'What is it about me you want to know, sweetheart? Relationships?'

'Not past ones, no. That's your affair. What I want to know, I suppose, is whether you'll want to stay with me after we're married. I don't particularly like the idea of being left on my own while you go off round the world as soon as I'm…we're…you know what I mean. I saw so little of my father, Fergus. I expect he came down to London for…well…for some relief, once there was a child on the way.'

Fergus put an arm around her, smiling at her concerns and wondering who had put such notions into her head.

'Well,' she said, sensing the impending laughter, 'I think it's sad if a man can't contain himself for nine months while his wife is bearing his child. I suppose there was some excuse once my father was widowed, but…well…I just wondered.'

Fergus's arm tightened around her waist, pulling her off-balance so that she had to walk with him towards the house and away from the shouts of sailors and dockhands, ferrymen and messengers, away from the rocking masts of ships being loaded. He was laughing. 'You are a delightful innocent,' he said. 'Do you think that, once a woman finds herself with child, she ceases to go to bed with her husband? Eh? Do you?'

Nicola blushed, suspecting that he was about to tell her what her mother should have told her years ago, if only she had been there. This was the kind of detail that not even her Yorkist guardians had explained. 'I don't know what I think,' she whispered, 'but from what I've heard so far, that's how it looks.'

He stopped as they reached the wooden porch that led into the shady house, a place where lavender and marigolds crowded around the pillars. Holding her against one of the carved wooden posts, he made her escape impossible, lowering his head to whisper against her brow. 'It may be so with those who have no desire for each other,' he said. 'Then their duty is done until the next time. But for couples like us, sweetheart, love-making can continue as long as the pregnancy lasts. Not fiercely; more like the way I shall show you tonight… and tomorrow…in bed. Carefully. Slowly.'

Her face burned. 'You talk of dutiful couples, but is that not what we are?'

'Not exactly, no. We are fortunate. We can oblige our late fathers at the same time as pleasing ourselves. Were you pleased, Nicola? Just a little? Was it wrong of me to have taken you there, like that?'

'No, it was not wrong. You did what I asked of you. I had my reasons. You must have realised by now that there has been nothing ordinary about this agreement of ours, neither in the wooing nor in the resolution. I am not in an ordinary frame of mind, Fergus Melrose. I never have been when you were around, and I still don't know whether I'm doing this for all the best reasons or for reasons that are simply the strongest ones at the moment. I can only pray that I don't regret it too soon.'

'Love, you mean? Is it love you're talking about?'

The shake of her head was the merest movement that caught the low sunlight in her dark lustrous eyes. 'No, that's not what I'm talking about. There is duty involved, despite what you say. Obligations to others. It's no use pretending otherwise. But there's something else, too.'

'What? What else is there?'

'It's too difficult to explain properly. Something to do with…you know…the way things used to be. I know I should have put it behind me by now, and I thought I had, there in my little house on Bishops-gate. But you've brought it all back, and I find that I cannot go meekly in a straight unwavering line to the altar, as you expect me to do. I cannot!'

'You need say no more, sweet lass. I know what you mean. And you have every right. I hurt you, I treated you shamefully, and now you need to be sure of me by getting some of your own back. It's natural. That's partly what that was all about, isn't it?' His dark close-cropped head tipped towards the three dark masts of his carrack out there on the shining river.

'You knew?'

'Not at the time. But now I know. I'd expected to take you in my own way and in my own time, and you decided to stop me, even at the risk of being hurt, or disgusted, or both. You tried to take the lead in our games more than once, didn't you, rather than be left behind? And I wouldn't let you beat me in the fencing either. Tch! That was churlish of me. Shall we try it again, then? Tonight? Winner takes all, and no recriminations?'

'I don't want you to let me win out of pity,' she retorted, hotly.

'I won't. I'm not so stupid. I intend to win as much as you do.'

'All right. Winner takes all. After supper?'

'I shall keep you plied with wine.' He smiled, standing upright and taking her hand. 'If I have to fence with sore ribs, it's only fair that you should have a woozy head.'

Having been warned about the wine, Nicola was careful to drink only spring water that Fergus obtained from Malvern, after which she was reasonably confident that his sore ribs would be such a handicap to him that she stood a good chance of winning the contest this time. And when she won, she intended to deny him her bed, not because she did not want him there, but because it was time the score was evened in her favour. That was the theory.

The reality was rather different, for he staged the event to look so like the first that she was set back in time, seeing him as she had then with her heart thudding to the same uncertain rhythm. He lent her some lad's breeches and a shirt to wear, and she had told Rosemary and Lavender to stay out of the way until she should send for them and, instead of the morning sun to light their way, they had tones of apricot across the bare floor, long shadows, and an atmosphere of drama. The hall was larger than hers, and the long table had been moved to one side, the silence of his entry alerting her to his mood of quiet determination.

As before, he advanced with the tip of his rapier describing irritable figures of eight just ahead of his toes and, for a disquieting moment she was assailed by doubts that she could, after all, best him in this when not even her brothers had managed it. He was stripped to his long-hose, soft boots and shirt, exuding fitness and strength in spite of his injuries, his eyes darkly unreadable, his wide straight mouth unsmiling. 'On guard,' he whispered, extending his rapier towards her. There would be no facetious chit-chat.

This time, Nicola was cool and more in control of herself than on that earlier occasion. This time, she knew what to expect from him, more prepared for the clever subtleties of his attack and defence, for the way he would lure her forward and drive her back. But this time was different too, when every so often he took on the role of fencing-master, correcting her, advising, showing her how best to breach his guard, how to defend herself better, how to deceive him. Once or twice he actually lowered his weapon to explain to her what she could do and then, when she learned faster than he expected, settled grimly into the contest with no more tutoring, no more concessions, and she would never have guessed by the skill of his sword-play that he was in pain.

In the end, it was as it had been before when his stamina exceeded hers, when her legs ached unbearably from the strain and her arm failed to respond with anything like the speed she required of it. A moment of extreme weariness together with a lapse of concentration, and the point of his rapier spiralled round hers, lifting it out of her hand just as she had done to the surprised young swain at Bishops-gate. With a noisy clatter, her rapier flew across the floor, leaving her at his mercy and no sign of humour to soften the humiliation.

Panting, she knew the kind of panic that a rabbit feels when it can flee the stoat no longer. Nor did he lighten the defeat with condolences, but held her at bay with the point of his rapier just touching her breast, backing her slowly against the wall and closing in on her before she could summon the strength to fight him off. This time, she was too weak to lift an arm.

He did then what he had wanted to do after their first contest and with no more gentleness than he would have done then, had she not been wounded. Taking her loosened plait in his grasp, he steered her face to meet his, holding her still while his kiss slanted across her mouth, disregarding her exhaustion and taking his fill from her lips as if this, and only this, had been on his mind since the beginning.

Without a word being spoken, her hand was being clasped in his and she was taken, almost at a trot, first to collect her rapier and then out of the hall and up the staircase, past the maids' small closet to the chamber she had been allotted.

Fergus's manservant had been instructed to furnish the lady's chamber with quantities of hot water and, as they entered, the steam rising from two deep brass-bound buckets swerved away from the draught like a swirling mist. Whatever Nicola had expected, it had not been that.

In her large tile-floored room, one wall of which was almost entirely taken up by a stone fireplace, was a wooden chair, several chests and a large green silk-covered bed, the canopy of which was suspended by ropes from the rafters. Diamond-shaped glass panes reflected the soft glow of two lanterns while the sky on the other side had turned to deep purple. They must, Nicola realised, have been fighting in near-darkness.

Fergus drew her further into the room. She was still breathless and damp from her exertions, her legs quaking with fatigue, and she was sure he could have brought the contest to an end much sooner if he had wanted to, for he was sweating but certainly not exhausted. Removing the rapier from her hand at last, he placed them together on the chest then, taking a folded sheet that was lying there, he shook it out with a crack and laid it on the floor, lifting the steaming buckets into the middle.

'What are you going to do?' she asked.

He held his hand out, pulling her forward. 'Take off your slippers. There, now come over here. It's bath time.'

She was in no position to argue. He had always done things his own way and surely he was enough of a gentleman to leave her to bathe alone. His eyes roamed over her, noting the damp patches that clung to her body. 'Undo the breeches,' he commanded.

'Er…' she stammered, 'I can manage to bathe on my own.'

'This time we shall do it my way. Undo them. Slip them off.'

She watched his hands, willing them to stay away. 'Yes, but I can send for Lavender and Rose…please…' she whispered, catching at his hand.

He caught hers instead and held them away. 'Nicola,'

he said, 'we agreed that the winner takes all, did we not?'

'Yes.'

'And I won.'

'Yes, damn you.'

He smiled as she swayed wearily towards him, catching her soft body as her hair fell in a thick veil around her bowed shoulders. 'Shh, honey. I used to walk away laughing, remember? Not any more. Now I stay with you and reward you. I wash you down after a contest. If I can do as much for my horses, why would I not do the same for a future wife? The main difference is that I don't make love to them afterwards. Come now, sweetheart, if the winner takes all, he needs to take a look at his prize. And I've waited long enough. Stand still…let me help.'

Too spent to protest any more for the sake of modesty, and now trembling at the touch of his fingers, she stood with her head bowed as he peeled the breeches away, leaving her with only the linen shirt to cover her nakedness. 'Arms up,' he said.

'No…I…no, Fergus…please!'

Taking her wrists from across her body, he held them up in the air and plainly expected them to stay there. Instead, they dropped to his shoulders while he lifted the shirt up over her head, turning her to face the buckets so that she could not tell where he was looking. And though it passed through her mind that this could have happened sooner, if he'd had a mind to it, she knew that she would have fought him tooth and nail if he'd laid a finger on her then.

'Step into the bucket. Go on, into the water. It's not too hot.'

Her elbows were supported by his hands as, reluctantly, she stepped into one of the broad-based buckets and felt the soothing water steal up her shins, and she wondered how many times he had done this for a woman before taking her to bed. But she was not allowed to dwell overlong on aspects of his past, or her modesty, for already his hands were twisting her hair into a rope that he held on top of her head. 'Hold it up there,' he said, expecting no resistance.

Closing her eyes, she did as she was told, feeling the gentle touch of his wet fingers upon her neck and throat, the trickle of water being sluiced over her, the sweep of his hands over her skin. And there was no chatter to interrupt his concentration. Although not as vigorous as those used on his favourite stallion, the ablutions were not lacking in direction along every surface of her back and beautifully rounded hips. Sloshing the water in cupped hands, he reached her buttocks and thighs at which moment the hair was suddenly dropped and one of his hands caught.

'Fergus!' she gasped, ready to step out of the bucket.

'Yes, I know. Stand still.' He held her with one brawny arm round the waist and continued, his feet wide apart as he bent to wash her lower reaches, and she was obliged to remain there with her feet trapped, shaking at this unprecedented familiarity until he had finished and gone round to the front of her so that she had no need to turn.

He started again with her face, carefully wiping along her brow and cheeks, kissing her closed eyelids to open them and to show her the desire and hunger in the now charcoal-grey eyes. Resting one hand on his shoulder, she watched as his head ducked to reach the other bucket and swing back up to her level while his hand poured water over her throat, following it down to her breasts, grooming and smoothing so slowly, erotically, that caresses now took the place of cleansing. 'Fergus…no more!' she whispered, trembling.

'I haven't finished,' he said, kissing the long pink pencil-line scar that ran down one curve. He lapped water from the tip of one nipple, arousing it.

'Please stop.'

'Take one foot out.'

She had been prepared to step out with the other one also until she discovered that there were some places he had not yet attended to, and now her eyes closed in ecstasy as he sluiced the water over those parts that, earlier that day, had received his most vigorous attentions, parts that now felt used and experienced. Gasping at this intimacy, she caught his wrist yet again, holding it as it continued the foray into her softest folds, washing and salving while water trickled down her legs on to the soaking sheet. Purposefully, his hand lingered, drawing forth a moan from her throat, and she closed her eyes as his lips found hers, almost swooning with the ache that consumed her. 'Not yet,' she murmured against his mouth. 'It's my turn, Fergus. Let me…please?'

It took all her efforts to remember what she had to

do. Holding on to him, she stepped out of the water and tugged at his points to unlace his hose, then, dragging his shirt off over his head, she threw it aside. 'Off,' she said. 'Take off your boots, man.'

Laughing at her commands, he shed his clothes in two quick moves while Nicola saw, for the first time, the full extent of the injuries he had received upon his beautiful hard-muscled body, the awful blue-black, red-green weals and cuts where boots had kicked and fists had punched, the long cut where a dagger had caught his shoulder blade, still beaded with dried blood. And for the first time also, she began to understand the full cost he had paid on that day and the pain he'd had to suffer since then, far worse than hers. But for her, he would still be recuperating slowly. But for her, he would have been spared the difficult ride through crowds this morning, the fierce coupling on the ship, and the duel this evening that had lasted far longer than it need have done, for the sake of her pride. And after all that, he had tended her as if she had been the one who needed it most.

'Oh…oh, my God…Fergus! What in heaven's name…? Why did you not tell me?' she whispered, appalled. 'I should have known about this.'

For once, he had no ready answer. It would have taken too long.

Shaking her head, she brushed her hand lightly like thistledown across his ribcage and felt the flinch inside him, saw the sharp parting of his lips. Here was the shapely and superbly fit Fergus Melrose, now outwardly marred by injuries that would take weeks to mend and, internally, some that would take longer. How could she not have realised?

Overcome by guilt, contrition and pity, she drew him towards the two buckets, poured the contents of one into the other, and then began to do for him what he had just done for her, well aware that she was affording him a view of herself in action that she had been reluctant to reveal until now. Punctuating the process with kisses to his wounds, she washed every part of him with extreme tenderness, drying him with her mass of hair and pouring water over the soft bristles of his head that had darkened with new growth since their first meeting It was the most sensuous lesson she had learned in her life, for until now she had not known which bits of a man's body were hard and which were soft, or whether the dark mat of hair on his chest and down his stomach would be rough or silky. She found that his navel was not quite like hers, nor were his buttocks, though his sensitivity was indeed very similar. There was yet another marvel to be witnessed lower down which, in her innocence, she did not know how to address, whether to ignore it, or to appeal to its owner to exercise some control over it while she dried him.

'Sweet lass…' he laughed, cupping her chin in one hand '…I cannot. He has no manners, I fear. None at all. When he sees something he wants, he refuses to lie quiet. Can we not appease him now?' His hands slipped down to her breasts, setting her alight once more.

'I want you desperately, Fergus, even more than I did

this morning. We both want it, the way you've been waiting to show me. But come,' she said, drawing him towards the bed, turning down the covers and easing him backwards on to it. 'I am willing to wait longer, for I am not going to allow you to exert yourself again today. If I'd known, we would have stayed at my brother's house, though I'm glad we didn't. But enough is enough, Fergus.' She laid a finger upon his lips as he began a protest. 'No, I'm not going to leave you alone in my bed. Not after all that.' Pulling the covers over him, she went to the lanterns to put out the flames before climbing in beside him, half-laying her long smooth body over his, her arm resting gently across his bruised chest.

'Now I'm just Nicola Coldyngham lying naked in bed with Fergus Melrose,' she teased him, 'and he's not going to make a move because he's never taken the slightest interest. In fact, he's already half-asleep with boredom without knowing how she let him win, just this once.'

'Wicked, wicked woman,' he whispered, grinning. He turned himself to her, trapping her under him. 'I can take you any time I like. D'ye think a few bruises can stop me?' His hand started to wander before she caught it.

'Not bruises, perhaps, but my common sense can. Let's keep the best till the morrow, Fergus. Or perhaps the next day? Sleep in my arms now, while I examine your bruises more carefully. I might have missed one.'

'Nicola, I want you.'

'No, you don't. And I don't want you, either. Not really. Never have done. Go to sleep.' Snuggling closer, she pushed him back and hooked one leg over his, letting her hand begin its journey while her heart melted in the unaccustomed security of his embrace.

As for Fergus, it was some time before his aching body would allow him to sleep, for the part that ached most would not settle under Nicola's lightly questing hand. Moreover, he knew that, had he taken her without the preamble, she would not have had the opportunity to see the injuries that had racked her with pity and concern. The interruption, however, had not been altogether wasted, having given her another chance to control a situation that had initially been quite out of her hands. And if anything could be guaranteed to salve her wounds, that could.

Chapter Nine

The wavering glow of a candle broke into her sleep, making her wonder drowsily what it was that her maids needed to see. She turned her head away to avoid the light, putting out a hand to pull the sheet over her shoulders, but touching instead the forearm of the one who had occupied her thoughts before she slept. 'Fergus?' she said, blinking up into his eyes.

He was leaning on one elbow, gazing at her as if sleep had evaded him altogether, his knuckles hovering over the point of her shoulder, hesitating. She could not fathom his mood, though the eyes gave something away.

'You lit the candle?' She yawned.

'Yes.'

'Why?'

'To see you.' His face was close, his hand even closer, close enough to take the sheet from her fingers and draw it downwards, slowly, as far as her waist, resting his hand lightly upon her warm skin.

No, it was not a dream. She had never dreamt this part.

'Is that all?' she said, finding herself suddenly short of breath.

It was some moments before he brought his gaze back to hers. 'No, woman, it's not all. You said wait till the morrow, so I've waited, and now it is the morrow, and I want you, Nicola.' His hand moved down to rest on her hip with the pad of his thumb settling neatly into the hollow of her groin, and the temptation to protest, argue, delay, was snuffed out like a flame.

She lifted a hand to caress his strong face, knowing every line of it, sliding her palms over his close-cropped head, touching the fine white scar on his forehead and teasing his firm lips with her fingertips. 'Then show me,' she whispered. 'Show me how it should be, Fergus. Your way.'

What Nicola had learnt by her previous experience on the ship was hardly relevant this time under Fergus's tuition, for there had been no real lovemaking, only the powerful urge to be taken, then and there, in the manner of her choosing. Now, in direct opposition to that hurried event, he took her carefully and tenderly through every sweet phase of loving, stoking the fires that lay perilously close to the surface and skilfully holding her at the point where her cries became pleas for him to take her without more delay. But delay was what he intended.

Blissfully, she gave herself yet again to the mastery of his mouth, to its journey over throat and breast, to the exquisite fondling that sent waves pulsing into her womb as never before, quivering the chords like harp strings in her thighs. She moaned when his hand sought out her most sensitive parts, gasping at the flood of excitement, though his lips were close enough to drink her cries into his mouth. The sensations were almost too much for her to bear.

Quite unprepared for these new and overwhelming needs of her body that exceeded by far the excitable longings of the previous day, she prised his head away to free her mouth. 'Fergus…I want you…now, now. I can wait no longer.'

She thought he was about to oblige her when he nudged her legs further apart and covered her, letting her feel the bliss of a man's weight upon her, briefly. Then he crouched, raining kisses upon her flat stomach, her hips, her groin and down the inside of her thighs, reminding her once more of how little she knew about the art of making love, how poorly the first time compared to this, how she should follow his lead and learn to trust him.

His shoulders moved upwards like smooth boulders beneath her hands, hard and wide. 'Fergus,' she whispered, opening herself wider to him, 'will it pain you too much?' She saw his face in the candlelight before it came too close, craggy and deep-shadowed with a flash of white teeth and a spark of laughter in his eyes.

'Not as much as it would to stop, sweet lass,' he said, guiding himself into her. 'But we'll take our time, shall we? I want this to be for you too, not just for me. Let's make it last.' Following his words, his entry was leisurely and tender while he watched her eyes widen and blink in astonishment at the incredible rippling, dilating invasion and the stealthy advance at each move of his body.

Her eyes flickered and closed, then opened again, bleary with desire. 'I didn't know.' She sighed raggedly. 'I didn't… know…it would be like this.'

'Shall you let me teach you now? Have you begun to trust me a little? Eh? Is that good, Nicola?'

'I scorned you. I wanted to hurt you.'

'Aye, lass. I know that. It made me want you more. You were magnificent, spitting fire. I wanted to take you right there, to subdue you, make you rue your words, proud woman. Like this…and this…to quieten you.' His loins beat gently against her as he spoke, scattering her thoughts into fragments, then melding them into sensations of pristine newness.

Quiet she was, except for the mewing of pleasure, the sighs that seemed to spread into her limbs to hold him close, binding him to her. Like her sighs, her hands swept over him, softly exploring. 'Make this last, Fergus,' was all she said, not realising how her head tossed from side to side on the pillow of dark silky hair, forecasting that it would not, could not, last.

A new and unexpected wave of excitement began to grow from some deep place within, making her cry out and curl her fingers into the hardness of his arms, gripping her in its power as she gripped him. Fergus responded, quickening his plunging strokes, deeper and deeper as the fire in her rose to the surface and exploded, consuming her with a force all its own, and Fergus went on, fiercely pulling her back as she arched away as if to escape him. 'Mine,' he growled. 'Mine. At last I have you.' His groan was soft against her neck, and Nicola could not be sure whether it was for relief, or pain.

Shattered by the experience, she rose slowly to the surface of reality, dazed and breathless, smoothing her hand over the velvety cap of his hair and finding an ear to fondle, then his muscled neck damp with sweat. She had never thought to find such pleasure in the aroma of a man's heat, but nor had she known anything of real men till now, only of duplicity and shallowness.

Was now the time to tell him of her feelings, her love? Was it safe to trust him with her heart so soon after trusting him with her body?

Caution, memories, and a remnant of fear held her back, still too aware of lingering doubts to lay herself open completely. 'Fergus?' she whispered. 'Are you all right? Did it pain you badly?'

Lifting himself from her, he tenderly brushed the dark veil of hair from her face. 'Woman of my dreams,' he said, 'I am more than all right. But 'tis I who should be asking you. I used you roughly at the end, but you ride like the wind. Did you know that?'

His teasing words made her blush. 'I am a novice. I need more lessons,' she said, touching the dimpled corner of his laughing mouth.

'You learn fast, too. But last time I told you that, you

tried to box my ears. Shall I teach you more, lass? Shall we fight and make love all our lives together? Shall you obey me in all things?'

'Highly unlikely, sir, unless it pleases me.'

'I can find ways of pleasing you,' he whispered, looking deep into her eyes with a sudden change of mood. 'I think I've already found at least one, have I not, my lady?'

It was true, though it was not only the lovemaking that pleased her, but the whole experience of being the centre of his attention after so many years of neglect. Something warned her that it could not last or be true, and something also reminded her that, for both of them, there was a strong element of duty tied up in this affair, and to put all this down to coincidence was stretching credulity to its limits, for duty to one's parents was hardly ever of this order. In her own experience, never. Now, however, she must go through with it and hope that her discoveries in Scotland would lay her concerns to rest once and for always.

Meanwhile, she could do no other than agree with Fergus that she had indeed found as much pleasure in his expert tuition as he had in her innocent eagerness to learn. Allowing her to boss him gently and to try out some skittishness only made him laugh with delight, both of them knowing where it would all end. The dawn came well before they were ready for it.

Master Secretary Coldyngham, as his brother George had called him yesterday, had certain business to attend to before the unexpected voyage to Scotland with Fergus and Nicola. Some of it was his own, and much of it was his new employer's, for being secretary to a prosperous merchant shipowner was going to take all Ramond's organising skills. Having taken his personal belongings on board ship and arranged them in the small cabin he'd been given, he went to Fergus's larger cabin to attend to the boxes of paperwork sent over from the Holyrood warehouse, bills of sale, receipts, lists and orders, IOUs and bags of coins, books of accounts and letters. He had been instructed to sort them out.

In the arms of a helpful young seaman, the bundles of papers and log-books teetered precariously as the lad stepped over the ledge, but he was caught by the swinging door and knocked sideways. 'Whoops!' he yelped, grinning. Half of the pile slithered out of his arms, the rest followed soon afterwards. 'Sorry, sir. Shall I pick 'em up?'

'No…no, thank you,' said Ramond. 'Leave them. I'll manage.' He sighed, casting an eye over the sad beginning to his organising attempts. The task was almost complete when his eye was caught by a certain piece of folded paper upon which the handwriting was uncannily familiar. 'Father?' he whispered. 'What are you doing here?' There was no envelope, but the paper was folded diagonally to look like one, and sealed with a blob of dark red wax, his father's arms impressed upon it. The seal was broken; there was the address of Sir Findlay Melrose, Bart., Fergus's late father, at the

Sign of the Thistle, Holyrood Wharf, London, and the letter invited him to read what he knew to be none of his business.

No one was there to see him read it twice, then stare at it for quite some time before making a copy of it on his own paper. He then restored the original to the pile of letters and carried on with his task, forcing himself to keep his mind on the job. And having done that to his satisfaction, he hired a wherry to row him to the River House where his sister and his employer were about to celebrate their betrothal. He had the entire journey in which to wonder how much of the matter Nicola knew, whether this was the business to which she had mysteriously referred and, if not, whether he should discuss it with her. And why was his father expressing gratitude to Sir Findlay Melrose? He realised that he would not know the answer to any of these questions unless he revealed to her the contents of the letter, and that if Fergus were to discover that he had already taken advantage of his privileged position, he would lose it. The quandary occupied him for the whole watery journey while the copy almost burned a hole in his leather pouch, though he did not believe that Fergus had been aware of the letter amongst his late father's effects, otherwise he would surely have put it in a safer place.

In view of the limited time before their marriage, the informal ceremony that Nicola and Fergus requested took place in the garden at River House quite near to where they had first kissed, though no one else knew of it. It caused some teasing whispers in the lady's ear.

Nicola had dressed for the occasion in pale rose silk and silver tissue with a brocaded pattern in a deeper rose, cream silk sleeve-linings and underskirts, and borders of silver-fox fur, not only around the wide neckline but trailing behind her, too. Over her swept-back and braided hair she wore a huge Flemish-type butterfly of floating white veils anchored with pins to a wire frame that needed several pairs of hands to construct it, causing the men to comment outrageously on alternative uses for it. Fergus's reaction was to duck as if a seagull was about to attack him, but was forgiven when he told her how beautiful she was and how determined he had been to win her, after the fierce opposition.

On purpose, Nicola had not sent invitations to any of her London friends, for not one of them had bothered to offer condolences or help after the disastrous fire or tried to contact her, not even the few women she knew. It had become clear to her that they were fair-weather friends she could well do without. The main guests were her close family, with Fergus's chaplain, his sea captain and senior members of his household, but the scene was almost stolen by the arrival of two enchanting children and one indulged white rabbit wearing aquamarines.

The ceremony was brief and simple: an exchange of vows to marry in the future at some time convenient to them both, an exchange of rings and kisses, and some tomfoolery which was quite the norm when brothers were present. Then the signing of agreements stating Nicola's dowry and jointures that would come to them

both from their relatives, but, since they were both independently wealthy, this was relatively simple and
Fergus's comment that she had been expensive was
more to do with effort than money. Not unnaturally,
there was some loud banter about the lady's change of
heart after her emphatic denials that she would ever
marry Fergus Melrose. What had he done to her? they
wanted to know.

They were not the only ones who wanted to know.
'Something's happened to her,' said George, only stating what the rest of them knew. 'I think she's in love
with him all over again.'

'Yes, dear,' said Charlotte.

'I shall go and have a quiet word with her before they
leave.'

Charlotte held his arm. 'I think, dearest, that it may
be best to say nothing at this stage. You've done all that
an eldest brother is required to do, and now they need
to be left alone to sort themselves out. Ramond will be
with them, remember. He'll tell you if there's anything
you need to know. Don't look like that, love: it's far too
soon for Nicola to be able to tell you how she feels.'

'What should I do, then?'

'Just remind her of our support and protection,
that's all.'

'In case it all turns sour, you mean?'

'Of course it's not going to turn sour, dear. Why
should it?'

George swiped a hand across his mouth, remembering Nicola's invective on that day of their first meeting

as adults. 'Yes…well, he said he'd not be put off, and you have to give him full marks for determination. Now, it's that funeral tomorrow. Perhaps next week we can settle down to some real work.'

After the congratulations, the cosy feast, the giving of gifts and the inevitable laughter, Fergus took his newly betrothed in his beautiful canopied barge on the last tide to Holyrood Wharf. Rather than risk shooting the dangerous current as it passed under London Bridge, they walked the short distance while the empty boat was taken through, for Fergus would not jeopardise his passengers' safety. Once again, Nicola could not resist the comparison between this new Fergus and the one she had known as a child who would have risked everything and everyone to prove how skilled his boatmen were and how little he cared for safety.

She twisted the new gold ring on her finger, stealing a glance at its beautiful workmanship, two linked hands with diamonds at their wrists, a businesslike symbol that carefully omitted any suggestion of love and lovers. Sure that he must by now have guessed something of her feelings for him, she had carefully avoided any mention of love, even though he had given her plenty of chances, for there was one more barrier to cross before she would give him her heart as well as her body.

One rather interesting development to make Nicola smile more than ever that day concerned the attachments made by Ramond and Fergus's sea captain to her maids, Lavender and Rosemary. She had seen them pair off and stand in deep conversation or wander off, ostensibly to admire the gardens and orchard, and she was pleased, for Rosemary's hazel eyes had widened at the powerful physique of Master Ben Munro who, although not a young man, had all the vitality and quick wit of one who had lived and loved and seen the world. Their attraction for each other had been evident from the start.

The bond being strengthened between the gentle Ramond and Lavender, both the same age, was equally discernible, as it had been to Nicola even at Bishops-gate, for the maid's blue-eyed fragility was much to Ramond's taste, as was her trim figure and neat attire, and though she was not of noble birth, the Coldynghams could afford to overlook that. Her dearest wish being to please people, she was exactly what he needed, and she glowed whenever he spoke to her.

The evening at Holyrood Wharf was unforgettable in many ways, not only for the genial company that eased their hearts past the previous turbulent days, but also for a new and kinder relationship that gave Nicola hope that Fergus's desire for her would last. He had been so attentive, dispelling her fears of a return to the former aloofness, keeping hold of her hand, protecting her from her brother Daniel's tendency to coarseness after a little too much of George's best Rhenish.

'I'm getting to like your other sides,' she whispered to him as they took the staircase to the upper floor. 'Are there any more that I haven't seen?'

'Plenty, my lady,' he said. 'Turn left and I'll show you some.'

He did, and they spent another night of bliss, wrapped in each other's arms.

They had been relieved to know that, because of the number of guests expected at the funeral of the prioress, it was to be held at mid-day instead of the more usual eventide. Their re-visit to the site of Nicola's Bishops-gate house was, however, an extra reason for deep sadness, for now the blackened frame had been felled and laid to one side ready for removal, and the whole of the ground cleared to give an uninterrupted view of the garden beyond, now laid waste and trampled by many feet. Roses still festooned the high wall, but the door that once had been concealed was now open, half-hanging off its hinges, showing all the world of the connection. Not for anything would Nicola have broadcast that private relationship to those who stared on their way to the convent next door.

As they expected, the service and mass was attended by everyone who had known Prioress Sophie, and the church of St Helen's Priory was packed to capacity, with many more hearing the mass from outside the west doors. The Coldyngham family were led to a place at the front where the plain coffin rested on a white-draped bier, and from there Nicola could easily visualise the petite figure who had wanted her to know the secret she had held in her heart for thirteen years, far too soon for the pain to have abated.

If that part of Nicola's affairs had tended to lose impetus in the last week or two, it now rushed to the fore again as her resolve to keep her promise strengthened. The prioress had known her life was drawing to its close, but not even she could have known how fine she had cut her meeting with her next-door neighbour, or how unexpected the manner of her demise. It was all heart-breakingly sad.

At the end of the mass, Sister Agnes, the one who tended the roses, whispered a message to Nicola as the company of nuns and priests gathered into the nave for the private burial in the crypt. 'Sister Clare requests,' she said, keeping her head low, 'that you meet her after the interment.'

'Yes…where?' said Nicola.

The nun's eyes shifted under the frown of a passing priest. 'In Mother Sophie's room, if you please, my lady.'

'Alone?'

'Oh, yes, alone.' The nun bobbed a curtsy and glided away into the black-and-white robed procession.

Accordingly, having asked Fergus to excuse her for a few moments of privacy, she made her way along the denuded and charred cloister, past the broken garden door and the sad glimpse of her own garden, through the smoke-blackened portals of the annexe that had been the prioress's last abode, and into the deserted room where the bed was as white and flat as a marble slab.

Sister Clare was waiting for her, her eyes red with weeping, her hands clasping a leather-bound book of psalms. 'This was hers,' she said, softly patting the book. 'I had to go through her belongings, but, since we're not supposed to have any, it didn't take long. Thank you for coming, my lady. I don't want to detain you.'

Her demeanour was so forlorn, her voice so pleading for comfort, that when Nicola opened her arms to her, she came into them like a child, clinging and trembling, seeking warmth. 'The smoke came in,' she whispered, her eyes filling again. 'When I returned that night, the young novice was overcome with coughing and Mother Sophie was gasping. I had gone to sleep, you see, and the fire was blowing this way. And I could not carry her alone. I had to go for help…but…'

'Yes, it was too late. There was nothing you could have done, Sister.'

'There was not even time to shrive her, m'lady.'

'But she would have received absolution long before that, surely. She knew her end was near.'

The nun drew away, fumbling at the book and opening it to reveal a small flat package from between two pages. 'I found this. It has your name on it. See…Coldyngham, it says. She must have wanted you to have it, eventually. Shall you take it?'

The package was only half the size of a page, made from folded parchment and very fragile after many openings and closings. Nicola took it and sat down on a stool, opening it on her knee, taking advantage of this moment of isolation to find out what it could be that had her name on it. Momentarily, the meaning of the contents took her breath away: a shining curl of hair, just enough to wrap around Nicola's forefinger like a ring, the colour of new copper and finer than anything she had ever seen, like strands of finest silk. Baby hair. On the inside of the package were scrawled the words in faded pencil, *February 14th 1460.*

Nicola's breathing returned slowly as if she'd been wakened from a dream. *Her half-sister. The same birthday as her own. Her father's love child, conceived in a nunnery. She would have to show it to Fergus's mother and ask her where she was. Demand to know, if necessary. She had promised to find her.*

She folded the precious keepsake back into its packet and placed it in the embroidered pouch that hung from her girdle. 'Did you know of this?' she asked.

Sister Clare nodded. 'Only myself and two of the older nuns,' she said. 'No one else. The priest who knew is gone from us now. She was an exceptionally good prioress,' she added, tearfully. 'She understood all our weaknesses.'

It was those kindly words that Nicola took back with her to the group who stood talking together with some of the parents whose daughters were pupils here. George knew many of the merchants, and so did Fergus. 'Come, my lady,' he said, going to meet her. 'Why, what is it? You look pale, sweetheart.'

'No, I'm all right,' she said. 'I've just been to the prioress's room. Just think, my father might have sent me here for my learning.'

'And then we would never have met as children, would we?'

* * *

Later on, Nicola and George had the chance to tell the acting prioress of their decision to rebuild the house as part of the priory at Nicola's expense as a kind of memorial to their late father, though Nicola knew as well as George that it was more as an atonement for the distress at the hands of the fire she had unwittingly caused them. Overjoyed, almost overcome by gratitude, the nuns and priests were led around the shell of the house, the men discussing technical problems, the women putting their needs first and foremost, while Nicola found it almost impossible to dismiss the recurring thoughts of her father stealing out through the garden door in search of the love he had discovered. Having discovered it herself, she could understand how such a thing could have happened.

'Be sure to keep this door in the plans,' she said to George as they passed from the cloister into her mangled garden where Melrose had stolen lettuces. 'The wall is still good, isn't it?'

'Oh, yes,' he said, 'we'll build it in. It's a perfectly good doorway. Besides, I wouldn't be surprised if Father used it more than once, you know.'

The hair prickled at the back of Nicola's neck, and she looked at her brother carefully to see if he was being uncharacteristically frivolous. But he was not. 'Used it?' she said, stopping by the well. 'What for?'

'Visiting,' said George. 'Something I heard when I was a lad with ears that flapped whenever there was talk of women and such. You know,' he smiled, sheepishly.

'What did you hear? Who from?'

'Oh, the cousins, who'd heard it from Father's sister, who'd heard it from others. You know how it goes. There was talk of Father having set his eyes on a cousin of his who was sent into a nunnery to stop the relationship developing, and they seemed to think it was St Helen's Priory. If it was, and I have no proof of it, then he'd be in a convenient place to make contact with her again, wouldn't he? Strictly against the rules, of course, but these things do happen, sadly. And Father did spend a lot of time here, didn't he? You remember?'

'I remember only too well,' said Nicola, remembering also the prioress's account of how they first met. Love at first sight, she had implied. Or had it been love at second sight, as it had with herself and Fergus?

'Were they young when they fell in love?' she said. 'Or was it after my mother died?'

'Oh, this was well before he was first married. But you know how it can be when you carry a flame for someone. It can keep alight for quite some time, can't it? And this cousin, if there was one, must only have been in her early years when she became a novice. Parents were so terribly strict in those days, Nick. Thank heaven ours were not like that.'

'We saw very little of them, didn't we? So this early love of Father's was a cousin, was she? They couldn't have married, then, because of the close relationship. Is that why she was sent here?'

'Well, I can only suppose so, unless she preferred the cloistered life to one without the man she loved. Anyway, it's only hearsay. It's just that the presence of the door in the wall always makes me think it could have a grain of truth in it. Of course, we'll never know now. Come on, love. We must make ready to go.'

A cousin he could never have married. Yet they had had a child, in the face of every opposition. Was that courageous, or foolhardy?

But by the time they had reached Fergus's grand house, the question was still unresolved, for she knew in her heart that the answer lay elsewhere.

It crossed her mind more than once that any sensible person would have asked Fergus himself what he knew about his parents' adoption of an illegitimate daughter, and indeed she came close to it in the time allowed to them between their betrothal and their departure. But she was reluctant to disturb their new relationship and there was so much else to keep them occupied, luggage to prepare, last-minute purchases to be made from Cheapside and essential ingredients to gather for her simples-chest. Time for talk of that nature would have to be held over for the days of their voyage.

Fergus's injuries were responding well to her intimate treatments, though any physician would have scolded, telling them that the exercise they were getting was hardly the best way to a speedy recovery. She did try, that night, to get him to rest more, even threatening to make him sleep alone, but Fergus had his own ideas about what constituted rest. 'Are you tiring of me, sweet maid?' he said, holding her in his arms. 'Is that what you're trying to tell me?'

'I'm very tempted to say so, just to make you rest more.'

'So it would be untrue, would it?'

'Very. I have always wanted you. You know that I have.'

He leaned over her so that she felt the warmth of him upon her cool breasts. 'Is that true, lass? Is it true that you've always wanted me? Even when…?'

'Yes, even then. Always. But you've changed, Fergus. You're much kinder.'

'Yes, forgive me. There was a reason for it, I think, but perhaps now is not the time to go into all that.'

'I know. There'll be time to talk about the whys and wherefores in the days ahead. Sleep now. We have to be up at dawn to catch the tide.'

'To please you, then.' He lay back, wrapping his arms around her and letting a hand wander along her silky thigh. 'I've won you, Nicola Coldyngham,' he whispered, yawning. 'I've won you. I am ten feet tall.'

She smiled and kissed his jaw, thinking of the day just past and of the days ahead.

The Coldyngham family were there again early next morning to see them set sail out of the port of London, to watch them head eastwards to the estuary; from there they would sail southwards to the Channel, westwards across the south coast and from there northbound through the Irish Sea. With some good south-westerlies, Captain Munro predicted a voyage of about four or five days.

To Charlotte's fears that Nicola might be seasick, there was only laughter. But there had been tears at the thought of losing Melrose the white rabbit until Fergus suggested that Philippa and Louis should be her keepers only until Nicola's return, when they would have to give her back. It was agreed.

Out into the choppy waves of the wide estuary, Lavender and Rosemary went hurriedly to lie down on their bunk-beds, leaving their mistress to stand with Fergus and Ramond on the forecastle with the wind whipping her face and the sound of the waves against the bows, pluming along each side, white and sparkling in the sun. Fascinated by the diminishing landmarks along the Essex and Kent coastline, her admiration of Fergus's knowledge grew with each hour, and it began to seem that there was little at which he did not excel.

The crew cast sideways glances at their employer's woman, approving his choice and vying with each other for one of her shy smiles. The cabin-boy, a mere fifteen years old, fell in love at first sight, to Fergus's amusement, as did the cook. Ramond decided he had work to do, but Nicola stayed on deck for most of the day, marvelling at the distant coast, the sheer expanse of sky and water, the swooping of seabirds and the nimbleness of the crew. And Fergus was never far away from her side. At dusk, they weighed anchor at a small fishing village on the Isle of Wight, where the ship rocked gently on the swell to the sound of slapping water and creaking boards, and Nicola knew the stealthy anticipation that soon her mission would be complete, after which she would be able to attend to the all-important business of her future with this enigmatic creature called Fergus Melrose.

Recalling their first hurried, even frantic, experience of Fergus's loving in that cabin, Nicola now had to admit that her determination to make decisions affecting her life, although rational, had not always led to perfection. The so-called seduction was a prime example, the attempt to live alone and unchaperoned was another. It was, she decided, an overreaction to events in her life that had led to a lack of faith in men. No one man in particular, just men, and a belief that she could do better. And for once in her life she was coming round to the idea—only coming round to it, mind you—that she had discovered the one man whose way of doing things was good enough for her to follow, after all.

Turning herself to him in the narrow bunk, she felt for his face and velvety head, still awed that he now welcomed such intimacies. More than welcoming, his embrace pulled her under him once more. 'Nicola,' he murmured, kissing her. Not once had he used the childhood Nick by which her brothers knew her.

'Fergus?' she whispered.

'I want you.'

'Again?'

'Again, and again, and again…'

So far, the few times of their loving had been different, for now he was teaching her how to make it last through phases that ebbed and flowed like the tide, leaving room for laughter, teasing, words of admiration and gentleness between more urgent spells. Sometimes, like this one, they were silent and submerged in the intensity of their passion, using only body signs to express their needs and intentions. Finely tuned to his commands as she had always been, Nicola followed his lead, finding no reason to do otherwise when all he did seemed to be for her pleasure as well as his. And now, instead of being puzzled by his lack of words, she found it exciting to be swept along in the flood of his desire, and she began to improvise, silently fighting him, nipping at his upper arm and warding him off with hers, and refusing to co-operate with her legs.

She felt his silent laughter upon her face and knew that he had correctly interpreted her mood of contrariness and, for a while, as he toyed with her struggles, they were well matched and attuned, making a game of something they would both win, eventually.

But Fergus's main advantage was in his injuries and in her care of them, and she would not beat at him as she might otherwise have done. 'You will not always win, Fergus Melrose,' she panted, writhing in the grasp of his hands over her wrists. 'I shall not take pity on you for much longer, so be warned.'

'That's my beauty.' He laughed. 'You can fight me now as much as you wish and I shall only win when it pleases you. Is that it, Nicola Coldyngham, termagant that you are? I can tame you, lass.'

'So is this the best you can do, then?'

'It'll do for now. We've plenty of time, and I know a good way to quieten you down. Be still now.'

'I shall not be still and I shall not be quiet.'

'I think you will,' he whispered. His mouth silenced her, his hands skilfully lured sighs of delight, melting her legs and opening them softly to his signal, receiving him like a victor, her arms wreathing his head.

* * *

In his new position as Sir Fergus Melrose's secretary, Ramond made a point of being seen to be working, not taking advantage of his relationship with his employer. There was plenty for him to do, and his basic training in law was already a good foundation for many of the things he was expected, and not expected, to do, which would save Fergus the expense of a qualified lawyer. They spent some time together going over problems that had accrued during Fergus's absence, and Ramond dealt with them all with impressive efficiency. Nicola went to his cabin expressly to tell him of the appreciative remarks Fergus had let fall.

With papers stacked on almost every surface, the cabin did not at once reveal where his bed was. 'Under those ledgers somewhere,' said Ramond, waving an arm. His dark head was still bent over a sheaf of papers, though there was no disorder; with a last scribble of his quill on a list, he lay it down and swivelled round on his stool. 'Well, Almost Lady Melrose?' he grinned. 'You're looking happier by the day. I take it things are going according to plan?'

'There was no plan, Ramond. You know that.'

'Not on your part, no. But you were convinced Fergus was only performing a duty. Now it looks as if there's more to it than that. Even you must agree.'

'Are you gloating, Ramond?'

'Yes, I suppose so. But you must be feeling more certain about things now?'

'As certain as one can be.'

'But?'

Nicola lifted a pile of letters off a chest and passed them to Ramond, sitting down and carefully spreading her skirts of cinnamon velvet over her feet. The time had come for some plain speaking, for some sharing of information. If she could not trust Ramond, then she could trust no one. 'You remember I told you that there was another reason why I'd accepted Fergus?'

'To do with Father, you said.'

'Yes, something I'd discovered about that promise to Fergus's father.'

'A recent discovery. Yes?'

'Well, it came as a bit of a shock, Ramond. You still want to know?'

He spoke quietly. 'I think I need to know. Does George know?'

'No, he doesn't. Although he may suspect.'

'Then tell me.'

'Father had an affair. There was a child, born while he was spending so much of his time at Bishops-gate. Remember?'

'Ah…yes, I do remember.' In his mind, pieces were falling into place.

'You're not shocked?'

'No. Why should I be?'

'Well, because the woman involved lived next door. The prioress, Ramond. The one whose funeral we attended the day before yesterday.'

This time, Ramond's 'Ah' was well drawn out, and

by the time he had let it go, one hand was resting over his pouch. 'How do you know this?' he said.

'She sent for me. Look here.' She delved into her embroidered pouch and lifted out the package she had received two days ago, unfolded it, and held it out for Ramond to see the delicate curl of baby hair. 'There, see. That's her. Our half-sister. And that's her birth date. Fourteen sixty.'

He leaned forward to look. 'Copper. And you are quite convinced of this?'

Nicola folded the package up and showed him the outside with their name on it. 'I'm quite convinced that a prioress would not admit to such a thing unless it were true, Ramond. But there's more. The child could not stay with the mother, and Father apparently couldn't admit to having a child born out of wedlock, so he told his long-time friend Sir Findlay Melrose about it. He and Lady Melrose agreed to adopt it since she could have no more children and dearly wanted a daughter. The prioress had no idea where her child had gone, only that it was to someone called Melrose in Scotland. So she pleaded with me to find her daughter before she herself died and to give her news of her safety. She'll be thirteen now, Ramond. But the crux of the matter is that this is the reason Father promised to wed me into the Melrose family. To thank them both for taking his bastard daughter.' She sat back, watching Ramond closely for his reaction. It was not quite what she had expected.

'And you would have been...how old?'

'In fourteen sixty, on that very same date, I was eleven years old.'

'I see. So take a look at this.' From his pouch he withdrew the folded copy of the letter to Sir Findlay Melrose. 'This was written by Father only two months before he died. I found it yesterday.' He rose to his feet and went to lean his back against the door. 'Listen,' he said. He read:

To Sir Findlay Melrose, my Dear Friend of Many Years, know that You and Your Lady Wife are much in My Thoughts, so long it is since We last met. I pray that You still prosper, and the Boys. It is on this last Matter that I write, having heard of your Younger Son's marriage last year, to recall the Matter of Our Agreement made in the Year 1460 when Nicola was but eleven years old. It is for This that I take the Liberty of urging You to speak favourably to your Eldest Son Fergus about the Matter, omitting what He need not Know concerning the reasons. At his age, we too had sown our Share of wild oats, though our Settling Down came rather earlier, but now my Daughter is also of an age to bear a family and is attracting quite some Attention in the Counties, and there will be little I can do if she wishes to make a choice soon, she being Headstrong and knowing her Mind regarding such Things. My dear Friend, I fear that I may not live to see this happen, and it would give me Great Ease of Heart to know that Our Intentions would be carried out. I am aware, of course, that You and Fer-

gus did not see all things man to man at one Time, as I and Patrick never did, but Trust that You are now Best of Friends and that You will do your best to bring about the Wishes of Your Most Grateful Bertrand Coldyngham on this 17th day of April in the Year 1472. I Trust that this will reach You before Your departure for the Gold Coast. I pray for Your Safe Return and for Lady Beth's health.
May God Bless You both.

'Well,' said Ramond, lowering the letter, 'it did reach him in time, I believe, but the prayer for his safety was not too effective, I fear. But does that tell you anything you didn't know before?'

'It simply confirms what the prioress told me, Ramond. As for what it is that Fergus doesn't need to know, well, that's obviously about Father's other daughter. What I want to know is where this daughter is now and why we have never heard a whisper of her until this. It's all very mysterious. I wonder if Father was ever given news of her and, if so, why he didn't pass it on to his mistress. He must have known how desperate she would be.'

'It certainly doesn't fit too neatly, does it? So there's something else here that we don't know about. Do you want to put it to Fergus?'

'No...no, Ramond. Absolutely not. Not until I have to. We shall be meeting Lady Beth before the week's out. She's the one with the answers. I shall confront her with what I know, and demand—'

'Hold on, love. I don't think demands are appropriate in this case. You may find that Father's prayers for Lady Beth's health were little more successful than those for her husband.'

'Why?' Her eyes widened in alarm. 'She's not—?'

'Oh, no, she's with the Scottish Queen at Whithorn, I believe, but Fergus told me—in confidence, I should add—that she's far from well. For pity's sake, don't let on that you know, love. He doesn't want you to be concerned.'

'Oh, dear, Ramond. This is so very sad. I had such a strong case, such good intentions. I was doing my charitable thing for the prioress, and I was doing my duty to both of our fathers. I was pleasing Fergus, at last. Now look at it.'

Brotherly, he took her in his arms and held her without speaking for a while. Then, like a lawyer, he advised, 'Hold things as they are for now, love, until we can discover what it's all about. Keep your happiness with Fergus. That can only improve matters. Learn to trust him. He's not devious, Nick. He'll look after you.'

'Yes,' she whispered. 'I think I do trust him, Ramond. I think I do.'

Chapter Ten

It was not the news she had wanted, now of all times, when she had thought herself to be well on the way to discovery. Nor was it only for the prioress's sake that she needed to know of her half-sister's whereabouts, but for her own sake too. The girl was her half-sister, the one relative she had most longed for and needed, the one whose company she would have enjoyed. Four brothers were all very well, but a sister would change so many things for the better.

In the face of the newest setback, she accepted Ramond's advice to build on her relationship with Fergus and to learn what mattered to him most, what he had kept hidden from her, or disguised, and most of all what she had misunderstood about his very high standards. She watched him with the crew and saw how their respect bordered on affection, for he tended to their needs as few other owners did. As Ramond had told her, he did not mince words with anyone, but the hard-edged manner she had once found so offensive was now seen in context and, because she loved him, she was able to accept it. What was more, his attempts to show her his compassionate side, his wonderful loving and his undisguised interest in her as a woman and free spirit had won over the heart around which she had erected a suit of armour where he was concerned. Piece by piece, he had removed it until now the only barrier she refused to relinquish concerned the core of the reason for this parental promise, which she was quite sure had influenced Fergus's choice of her as his marriage partner. Without that, he would certainly not have come to find her, duty or no duty. Conversely, without her extra incentive to find her half-sister somewhere in his family, she would probably not have accepted him either. Well, not for quite some time, anyway.

The voyage turned out to be the perfect way to spend the next few days in personal discovery, or with her maids reading, singing, sewing and watching the sea, or with Fergus's chaplain, Ramond, or Captain Ben Munro and his senior officers. There was no shortage of company, nor did the weather become so rough that they were put in danger. Their second port of call was the Island of Flatholme in the Bristol Channel, their third night was spent moored off the Isle of Anglesey, which Nicola had never heard of, and on the fourth night they berthed at the harbour of Peel on the Isle of Man, which she had heard of. Here she was told that the Bishop of Whithorn, where they were bound, actually owned land on Man and held the title of baron with his own manorial courts. He was also Fergus's uncle. The next day, Captain Munro told them, should see them in Whithorn, in Galloway.

'Tell-im-to-go-way!' shrieked the popinjay from his wicker cage, but then added some very nautical-sounding curses that, had the parrot but known it, put its future in some doubt as a suitable pet for a lady.

Their entry into the busy harbour on the Isle of Whithorn, actually a promontory linked to the mainland by a thread, was one of many that day, for the port thrived under the interest of pilgrims and other visitors to the shrine of Saint Ninian, increasing the trade in hospitality and, inevitably, the trade in goods. Traders' boats bobbed about like water-beetles in the shallows and, on the green and shingled shoreline, tents stood like a field of mushrooms in the sunshine, swarming with people and their animals. Over on the rocky peninsula that extended from the harbour, lines of people wended their way to and from the small stone chapel; the first thing travellers did on arrival was to give thanks for a safe journey.

They had all been given small pilgrim-badges to wear. 'For your safety,' Fergus told them. 'As long as you wear those and don't stay in Scotland for more than fifteen days, you have the royal protection. Oh, and you have to behave like pilgrims, too. No violence, Master Ramond, if you please.'

'No, sir,' said Ramond, soberly. 'No lewdness, either? No swearing or drunkenness?'

'Certainly not.' Fergus squeezed Nicola's hand, including her in the jest.

Like the three ladies, he had dressed elegantly for their disembarking. His long mantle of blue Cyprus cameline was decorated with narrow bands of gold and red, the immense dagged sleeves lined with red silk, though his arms bypassed these, emerging through slits in the sides. He wore a low-crowned red felt hat with a jewelled band, and around his shoulders was a gold collar studded with huge garnets.

Without planning it, Nicola had matched her colours to his, and her paler blue silk gown lined with gold fitted tightly to her figure, low-belted upon her hips, tight-sleeved, revealing her lovely shoulders. After the Burgundian fashion, her head-dress was tall and jewelled over which a veil floated in the breeze, though Rosemary and Lavender wore padded heart-shaped rolls in a less ostentatious style, and far less jewellery than their mistress. Heads turned as they entered the small chapel, boosting a surge of pride in Nicola's breast that she quickly and guiltily snubbed. Even so, she felt the stares, as much for Fergus as for herself.

Hiring horses to take them the three miles to the town of Whithorn proved not to be necessary, after all, for the highly efficient Master Ramond had sent a message to the royal court to say that they had arrived. Within the hour, harnessed animals had been sent for their use and so, with the ladies riding pillion behind their men, the party set off to meet their hosts at last, Nicola giving full rein to her excitement by a tight hug around Fergus's body.

She heard him suck in his breath and realised she had

hurt him. 'Sorry,' she whispered from behind. 'Another rib gone?'

'Almost,' he said over his shoulder. 'You excited, then?'

'Ooh, yes. Are they nice, the royals? Who shall we see first?'

'I'd like to find my mother first, but that will depend on who meets us. It may be some time before we get to see anybody. There must be thousands here.'

'Did you get all the cargo off the ship?'

'Only one waggonful. Just a sample. Look over there…the town…and over there in yon fields are the royal tents.'

'They're not living in tents, surely?'

'You should just see them. They're like palaces inside. Lined, heated, carpeted, hung with tapestries, all the furniture they need. It's not exactly a hardship to live in one of those for a while.' He pointed to the fluttering pennants and the bright flash of metal as armed men moved about, the size of the largest pavilions being bigger than some of the huts they were passing. No, it would be no hardship to stay in such luxury while so many ordinary pilgrims slept out in the open, summer and winter.

In droves, the pilgrims flocked towards the abbey up on the hilltop, some barefoot and limping, some on crutches or carried in litters, others festooned with badges like the ones they wore to show which other shrines they had visited in every part of Christendom. With utensils clanking on their backs, with bags and dogs and packhorses, the infirm and wretched joined shoulders with the professionals, some singing, some wailing prayers, others reciting merry tales or playing pipes and banging drums. It was impossible for Nicola not to compare the terrible plight of some of them with her own problems. What, after all, was the loss of a house when many of these people had never had one to lose?

She had not expected their arrival at the royal enclosure to prompt an immediate reaction of any sort, and she had been quite prepared to wait an hour or two before making brief contact with the recipient of Fergus's luxury goods. But men had been briefed to watch out for them, and suddenly there was a cacophony of Scottish words that to English ears was more like a foreign language than a dialect. Fergus and his Scottish sea captain were home at last, their deep voices wallowing in the guttural musical explosions of sound. The royal party, they learned, had been to the abbey that very morning to give thanks for their firstborn child and were now resting after their meal. If the party of Sir Fergus Melrose would care to wait in the anteroom, the chamberlain would see if they could be admitted to the royal presence.

'Queen first, my mother second,' Fergus murmured to Nicola.

She caught Ramond's eye. 'Won't your mother be with the Queen?' she said.

'I doubt it,' said Fergus. 'Ramond, would you go and make enquiries for me?'

'Certainly. I'll find her and tell her you're here. Leave it to me.'

'He's invaluable,' said Fergus to Nicola. 'And if the King wants you, you're not for sale. You hear me?'

'He has a seventeen-year-old wife. He's not likely to look at me twice.'

'I think you may find that he won't be able to take his eyes off you. I'm having the same trouble myself.'

Remembering their last night together moored in Peel harbour with the boat swaying gently beneath them, Nicola felt the sincerity of his compliment, for again she had woken to find him lying there just watching her sleep, feasting his eyes upon her nakedness. 'What's she like?' she whispered.

'Not my type,' he replied. 'Shh! We're to go in.'

By anybody's standards, the anteroom had been sumptuous enough, but the inner chamber of the royal pavilion was furnished and adorned with so great a display of ostentatious wealth that Nicola's first reaction was of claustrophobia, followed by a wonder that the royal couple's outward piety was so poorly reflected in their acquisitiveness. Every surface was cluttered with gold and silver plate, with textiles, rugs and cushions, glassware and boxes of jewellery as if both the King and his Queen were in the process of choosing what to wear or buy. As to Fergus's remark that the young Queen Margaret, formerly of Denmark, was not his type, Nicola could now see what he meant.

Sitting by the side of her twenty-year-old husband, King James III of Scotland, the Queen was dressed becomingly in a black silk full-skirted riding-gown with black velvet collar and sleeve trimmings, though its quality did little for her pallid complexion, her rather small eyes and double chin. Petite and childlike, her youthful figure had presented the king with a son in March of that year, and it was for that event, after almost four years of marriage, that they were here at Whithorn to give thanks. She beckoned to Sir Fergus and Lady Nicola to come forward without waiting for the King to do it, yet it was he who spoke for them both.

'Well, well. So you came by water, Sir Fergus? And was your hurry to bring our purchases,' he said, rolling his r's , 'or was it for your lady mother's sake? Eh? We took her to the abbey this morning for a wee while and I think it did her some guid. Shall ye show us what ye brought, man, and then be awa' to her? And who's the lady, then?'

The King's notoriously lavish spending was almost as great as his wife's, but Fergus knew that to be one of their few points of compatibility. 'Your Grace,' he said, bowing, 'may I have your leave to present the Lady Nicola Coldyngham, daughter of the late Lord Coldyngham? She and I are recently betrothed.'

The King's aesthetic dark-eyed face lit up with interest as he leaned forward to scrutinise Nicola from head to toe, though with lowered eyes she caught only a little of the lustful expression she could by now recognise so well in the eyes of men. 'So...are ye indeed?' said the King.

One of the ladies standing behind the Queen's chair

turned to whisper something to her companion, but the Queen stopped her with an imperious hand. 'Congratulations, Sir Fergus,' she said in an English as broken by Danish inflections as her husband's was by Scots. 'And to you, my lady.' There was an anxious look in her eyes, Nicola thought. 'Do you wed soon, Sir Fergus, while your mother is still with us?'

For once, Fergus chose to be indirect. 'Your Grace, I have not seen my mother yet. Is she…?'

'Not well, I'm afraid. In fact…' A glance at her husband must have told her to say no more on that subject. 'Let us see what you've brought, shall we? It was clever of you to bring it by sea. So much quicker. Now, where is it?' Nicola caught a glimpse of black satin shoes and an ankle's worth of black stocking. A pair of white ankle-socks were rolled up underneath her footstool.

With admirable patience, Fergus ordered his men to begin the unloading of the one waggon they had brought, explaining that the rest would follow. But here in advance of the rest were some of the rarest goods she had ordered: forty grey-squirrel skins, bolts of silk, satin, damask and brocade, ermine skins that only royalty might wear, gloves of soft Spanish leather and shoes with little cork heels, gold belts and chains, collars flashing with jewels, rarest unicorn-horn and a silver ball to fill with hot water to warm her hands, church lamps and embroidered cloths, hunting whips and books, velvet-covered saddles and stirrups. Yes, even they were covered with velvet too. Nicola had had no idea that the ship in which she had sailed held such treasures, and soon the chamber was piled so high with a dizzying rainbow of colour that she hoped the men had left them some means of escape.

But though the Queen and her ladies could not drag their eyes away from the ever-mounting pile of goods, the King's eyes hardly strayed from Nicola's fair form and face, and when the end came at last, she was so glad to make an exit with Fergus that she feared she had been less than correct in her manners. 'Come!' she cried, taking him by the hand outside the tent. 'Come away, for pity's sake. Let's go and find your mother. Where's Ramond?' She pulled at him like a mother with her child.

'What's up, lass?' he said, balking a little.

'What's up?' she flung over her shoulder. 'Did you not see him? Sat there, never saying a word…just gawping. What's the matter with the man? Where is Ramond? We must find your mother.'

Fergus held her back, stopping as suddenly as a mule. 'You know something, don't you?' he said, his face clouding with concern.

They were in danger of being overheard amongst so many people, so she came close to him and looked into his eyes. 'I know what the Queen was about to say before she stopped herself, dearest. Sadly, she thinks her needs are greater than yours, otherwise she'd have let you go to your mother immediately. Now come, we must—ah, there's Ramond. Look, over there!' She waved into the crowd.

Fergus held her again. 'What did you just call me?'

'Er...dearest, was it?'

'Am I?' he said. 'Your dearest?'

His boyish uncertainty pulled at her innards, and her free hand came up to brush lightly across his lips. 'Yes, my very dearest. You must know that you are, Fergus Melrose. And there was one of the Queen's ladies there who couldn't take her eyes off you. Did you not see?'

'Nah!' he scoffed, kissing her fingertips. 'But I'll tell you something, sweetheart, we're away from this place as soon as I've unloaded the ship and got my mother aboard it. What do you say to that?'

'I say yes to that, Fergus. The sooner the better.'

Ramond knew exactly where to lead them, and considering that Lady Beth Melrose was a senior lady-in-waiting to the Queen of Scotland, and very ailing, the place where she had been housed was hardly fit for a hound.

Apart from being very relieved and happy to see her, Fergus was dismayed by the poverty of her accommodation when he knew the royal couple to have wealth in abundance. 'God's truth!' he growled, entering the tent. 'Is this the best they can do for her?' Unlike the others, Lady Melrose's tent was pitched towards the back of the campus near the temporary forge where the sound of the royal farrier's hammer rang incessantly, and it was obvious to the visitors that, since she was not well enough to be on duty, she had better not take up any valuable space. The canvas tent was shabby and small with no covering over the earth floor and with barely enough room for a pallet-bed, an untidy pile of luggage, a stool, and a lantern on a chest with its candle burnt to the wick.

In one stride, Fergus was by his mother's side, dropping to one knee to take her into his arms. 'Ah…mother mine…dear lady. They told me ye were poorly but I never thought to see ye like this. Is it much worse then, love?'

Lady Melrose lifted her arms and clung to him, her long slender fingers splaying out across the rich blue fabric, touching and patting the gold collar. She was fully dressed in grey velvet, her head swathed in an old-fashioned wimple of white linen that merged into the paleness of her skin. A light sweat lay upon her brow, and her large once-beautiful eyes were sunk deep into hollow sockets like topaz in sandstone. They glanced over Fergus's shoulder to the one who stood, shocked and disgusted, behind him. 'Ah,' she whispered, 'so you've brought her. Well done, my dear. Well done.' Her eyes smiled, melting the last cold corner of Nicola's heart.

'Aye,' said Fergus, 'I've brought her as I said I would. And you'll not be staying here. Have ye had no one to tend ye?'

'One of the other ladies comes from time to time. They carried me up to the abbey this morning, to the shrine. I'm sure that will have helped. But come, introduce Lady Coldyngham to me, if you please.'

Fergus lifted her up to sit against the pillows, drawing Nicola forward to meet her at last. 'Mother,' he said, 'meet the lady I am to marry. Is she not a dream?'

Dropping to her knees, Nicola took the hand offered

to her and kissed the smooth cool knuckles, breathing in the aroma of some sweet perfume meant to mask an underlying smell of unwashed body. They had not done their best for her, those two royals. 'My lady,' she said, 'I have come for your blessing. Do you approve of this connection? Is it what you wanted?'

'More than I ever hoped for, my lady. This is a happy day for me. Of course you have my blessing on your union. Fergus didn't waste any time recruiting the Coldynghams, though, did he, my dear? Making your noble brother his secretary? That was a bit presumptuous from a minor Scottish laird, I think.' She smiled, and Nicola noted how her teeth were still good, her lovely mouth wide and laced with fine cobweb lines. She must have been an exceptionally lovely woman, she thought, and a gentle one, lovable and uncomplaining.

'Not so, my lady,' Nicola said. 'It was my brother who asked Fergus, not the other way round. But Fergus is right. This is no place for you.'

Already her son had taken matters into his own hands, telling Ramond to go and find the waggoner who had brought the part-cargo from the ship. 'Tell him to bring the wagon over here straight away,' he said. 'And the men too, Ramond. Here, offer him this.' He held up a bag of coins and threw it to him.

'Fergus,' Lady Melrose protested. 'I may not leave their Majesties like this. I need their permission.'

'Permission my foot,' he said. 'They'll not even know you've gone until tomorrow and then it'll be too late. We can have the rest of the cargo unloaded and sent here to keep them occupied, and we can be away on to-night's tide. I'll get Ramond to draft a letter explaining that you need urgent treatment. I'll apologise,' he said, taking note of her anxious expression, 'don't worry. They'll not do anything drastic. They need me too much.'

'What about the payment?' she said.

'That's settled with the King's agents in London. But getting you away is more important than that. Nicola agrees with me.'

Nicola was already folding and packing the scattered belongings into a large canvas bag and the small travelling chest, clearing up the mess that had been left since the arrival of the royal party. 'How long have you been like this, m'lady?' she said.

'I was unwell when we left Stirling Castle, but they thought I should try to ride. It looks better, you see. But I'm afraid I couldn't manage more than three days in the saddle, so they put me in one of the waggons. The stomach cramps, you know. They get so bad at times.'

'And did the Queen send food to you?'

'Yes, a little. But I could not eat it.'

'My simples-chest is on the ship. I have things that will help. Rosemary…Lavender…finish this packing, then help me prepare Lady Melrose's bedding. We shall need it for the waggon.'

But in only a few moments the cart had arrived, padded with a thick layer of straw that Ramond had begged from the royal field-stables next door, and the deed was executed by the best organised team of amateur abductors on that side of the English–Scottish border. In less than half an hour, the shoddy tent was empty and the Melrose party was on its way to the ship that lay at anchor three miles off, on the Isle of Whithorn, rocking on the swell like a cradle.

For Nicola to give up her cabin to Lady Melrose was no hardship when she had slept with Fergus each night. Three pairs of hands settled the patient into the clean bed, bathing her and then dressing her in the nightgown she had hardly bothered to use, so far. 'Heaven,' she murmured. 'This is heaven. I can scarce believe it. I had two maids of my own when I went to court, but the Queen has purloined them, I fear. Shall you ask Fergus to send a message to Muir? He should be home by now, and we shall be having a wee bairn any day, God willing.' Meekly, she sipped at the infusion of powdered marshmallow-root and meadowsweet to relieve her stomach cramps, having allowed Nicola to quiz her about the nature of the problem. Only the best of future daughters-in-law would have remembered to replenish her simples-chest before a voyage, she had said, approvingly.

'I should not say ought against my Queen,' she whispered to Nicola, 'but I doubt if she'd have given her bed up as willingly as you, my dear. She prefers to sleep alone, even now.'

'Until she's recovered from the birth, perhaps?' Nicola said, intrigued in spite of herself.

'Nay, 'twas the same before. She allowed the King to visit her at nights only till she became pregnant, but then no more. 'Twill be the same for always, I reckon. No wonder he seeks arms elsewhere for comfort. Not like you and Fergus, made for each other.' She smiled and sipped again. 'Anyone can see how it is with you. I'm so glad, Nicola. 'Twas what Sir Findlay wanted, too, but I expect you know as much from your father.'

'Yes, m'lady. Shall you rest now? Sleep, perhaps? I shall bring you some slippery-elm food soon. I know it doesn't taste of anything, so you may like it flavoured with cinnamon, or a sprinkling of fennel or peppermint?'

'Whatever is handy, my dear. You are an angel.'

Nicola returned to Fergus's cabin, opening the door with difficulty against the piles of baggage that now scattered the floor. She pushed the map aside that he held in his hands so that she could enter his embrace, silently needing to feel his strength and support. Things, she felt, were coming to a head. 'Hold me,' she whispered. 'Just hold me, Fergus.' It was the first time she had sought his loving.

Above the large hand that stroked her hair, she did not see his smile, but it sounded in his voice. 'Sweetheart,' he whispered. 'My ministering angel.'

'That's what your mother thinks I am too,' she said into his soft shirt-front. 'Two Melroses I have to minister to now. But we have to talk, Fergus.'

'Aye, lass. We do. You have things to tell me, do you not?'

She lifted her head away to look up at him. 'What things?'

He caressed the untidy strands of dark hair. 'You think I don't know what's been burning at you all this time? We agreed we have to set some things straight between us, and I knew you were waiting for my mother to give you more information. That's what you've needed all these last weeks, isn't it? Information. Well, I think it's time we talked, all three together. Is it best for us to wait a day or two till she's better, or is there a reason why we should talk sooner rather than later?'

She knew what he was asking. 'Lady Melrose needs at least one night's rest before we shall know. If she keeps some food down and the cramps lessen, she'll start to mend. We shall have to wait and see. We cannot press her to talk till tomorrow, I think. She's very poorly, Fergus.'

He sighed and was quiet for a while as the ship trembled beneath their feet and the crack of the wind in the big sails tilted them sideways on to the bunk. 'The wind's not in our favour,' he said, lifting her on to the furs. 'It's going to take us longer to get back home than it did to get here. But at least we have her safe at last, thanks to you.'

'No, it was your doing, Fergus. You might have insisted on waiting for a cargo to take back. No shipowner likes to sail an empty ship, does he?'

'We're not empty, sweetheart. Due to my competent secretary, we have a walk-on cargo in the hold.'

'A what?'

'Listen. You may be able to hear. Shh…' Above the rush of water and the crashing of waves on the bow could be heard the faint sound of singing. 'Pilgrims,' he said, rolling himself up beside her. 'He found droves of them waiting for a ship to take them down to Wessex. We've taken in thirty of them while you were tending my mother. Food and water too. They have instructions to be quiet. And you, sweet lass, have instructions to rest a while till supper.' He pulled her into his arms, nestling her head against his shoulder.

'Then I must obey, I suppose.' She yawned and snuggled closer. 'But I shall not only want you to get me pregnant, as she does,' she said. 'I shall want more than that. Much more.'

'Pardon?' he said.

'Tell you later. Just hold me, dearest one.'

The time for talking *did* present itself on the morrow, for Lady Melrose had slept well, tended in turns during the night by Nicola and Fergus, Rosemary and Lavender. They had berthed again at Peel, no great distance away on the Isle of Man, where the passengers were able to stretch their legs and attend to their needs, bringing fresh supplies of food aboard. The patient took some more slippery-elm with goat's milk, followed by a spoonful of pureed boiled nettles. It was for her blood, Nicola told her, promising a diet more suited to an elderly lady than the one she had been getting at court. After all that, it was Lady Melrose herself who decided that Nicola deserved to know the reason for this contentious promise made by their fathers, for she had already spoken to Fergus about it after her husband's untimely death earlier that year.

They had set off for Holyhead on Anglesey with a light squall keeping the sails full and the passengers in their cabins and, as the patient lay back upon her pillows in far more comfort than before, she listened to Nicola's hesitant and rather searching enquiries which were intended to give little away.

'When exactly?' said Lady Melrose. 'I believe you were but a child at the time, my dear. Do you remember Fergus visiting you then?'

'Yes, I remember. Can you take another mouthful?'

'No, thank you. That was delicious. There was a good reason for it, Nicola. Did you think it might have been a mere whim on their parts?' She watched Nicola replace the bowl on the table, then stretched out a hand to invite her to sit again on the stool by her side. 'You need to know, m'dear. Is that not so?'

'It is so, my lady. But…' She hesitated, sure that Fergus's mother was unaware of their earlier sad relationship, yet not wanting to pain her.

'It's all right. You can tell me. About Fergus, is it?'

'Yes. You see, I do remember his visits to Coldyngham Manor, and I remember how I felt about him then.'

'You disliked him?'

'I both disliked and adored him. He was like a god to me then, good at everything, handsome and full of vitality. But I was simply a child with four energetic brothers who looked forward to his visits and…well… you can imagine the rest, can't you?'

A frail hand covered Nicola's arm and squeezed, then slid down to hold her hand. 'I'm afraid I can imagine only too well. Fergus was a very angry young man then. An eleven-year-old girl would not interest him at sixteen, and nor did he particularly wish to please his father by pretending to be. You were in an unfortunate position, dear Nicola.'

'Looking back on it, though, I can understand how he felt about it. No young man of that age would find it easy to communicate with a child.'

'Fergus would, if he'd tried. He visited Coldyngham Manor at his father's request, but he made it quite plain to both of us that, while he didn't mind going there to be with the boys, he had no intention of fulfilling his father's wishes regarding a future marriage. He said he'd make his mind up for himself when the time came.'

'But that's what I cannot understand. How did his father persuade him to change his mind? I know it was something to do with his dying wishes, but—'

'But Sir Findlay told him there was more to it than that. He said that I would tell him the reason for the promise when he returned home. Which I did, after Sir Findlay's death.'

'I see. So Fergus knows. Then why has he not told me?'

'Perhaps because his part in the story does him no credit. Do you want to ask him to come in so that we can share our discussion with him?'

Nicola rose. It was what she had been waiting for.

Fergus returned with her a moment later, damp from the spray, his face shining and his eyes twinkling with amusement at Nicola's commands. 'I am ordered about on my own boat by two women,' he said. 'Lady mother, what is your will?'

Indulgently, she smiled at him and then at Nicola. 'Sit ye doon, dearie. Ye'll get a crick in your neck standing up in here. I'm telling Nicola what I told you after your father died because she needs to know, Fergus. And I cannot for the life of me find an easy way to say it.' She stared at him as if to gain some strength.

'I can help you out,' said Nicola, taking pity on her. 'My father took a mistress well before my mother died. They had a child, a daughter, and you and Sir Findlay agreed to adopt her as your own. Is that correct?' She kept hold of Fergus's hand, but now his arm came round her shoulders.

'You knew?' he said. 'How did you find that out?'

'You will discover,' she said. 'Lady Melrose, you were saying a moment ago that Fergus had a part in the story, other than the promise, I mean.'

'I think Fergus himself can best explain.'

He shifted on the stool, tightening his hold on Nicola. 'I was a cocky young stripling when this baby appeared in my father's arms. He and a nurse had brought it all the way from London. My mother had just lost a girl child, while I was away in Salisbury, and, when I returned home, there were my parents with one of almost exactly the same age. Well...' he cleared his throat of a sudden obstruction '...you can imagine what I believed, can't you? At sixteen, I thought I knew all there was to know about men and their mistresses, and I was convinced it was my father's bastard got on some woman or other while my mother was bearing his legitimate child. I was disgusted with him. Not only that he could bring it to my mother, but also because she loved him so much that she could take it. Willingly. I believed he'd made use of her grief to foist this babe on her, knowing that she'd not refuse it. My father assured me it was not his, that it was for a friend whose wife had died, but I didn't believe him because he couldn't give me any information about it. Naturally. He was probably not given any information either. Had I known it was your father's, Nicola my love, I might have been able to accept it. But their kindness depended on secrecy, and they were never told who the mother was, and I went on believing that it must be my father's. I had set him up on a pedestal, you see, and he came crashing down. I hated him for using my mother so, for foisting this girl upon our close family. I wanted nothing to do with her. That's when they sent me back down to Salisbury, and my world fell apart. I was being sent off, out of the way. I know it's usual, but that's how it felt.'

'You see,' said Lady Melrose, 'Fergus and Muir had become very close by that time. Very competitive they were. It would have been difficult enough for them to show an interest in a natural sister, but one brought so suddenly into the family in that fashion was even more so. Neither Sir Findlay nor I realised what a rift it would cause. Muir was less concerned. He's more easygoing. But Fergus didn't respond well to the swing of my affection from him and his brother to this little intruder. She howled a lot, although we had good nurses, and she claimed the attention Fergus and Muir had always had.'

'In short, Mother, I was as jealous as hell and unbelievably spoilt. I felt until then that the world revolved around me, and that a mewling girl-brat in my mother's arms, my father's by-blow, was too much to understand. I came to hate the child. I hated my father. I despised you for what I saw as weakness, and girls in general were to be treated with contempt. I make no excuses. I was intolerable. Perhaps I should have been given a good thrashing.'

'Your father knew the problem, love, but I suppose he thought that you'd get over it, eventually. Lord Coldyngham's kindness was the most wonderful, generous gesture at that time.'

'But you were not pleased, Fergus,' said Nicola. 'And that was when you came over to Coldyngham Manor to see what you'd been promised to. And you didn't want me.'

'I didn't want any female, sweetheart. It was nothing to do with you personally. I had to show my father how I was refusing to co-operate with his plan because it was my way of hurting him back, and I didn't want him telling me who I should marry, even one of the great Coldyngham family. I had to show them I didn't need the connection, that I was good enough without it. And you, scruffy little tomboy—' he kissed her forehead and the tip of her nose '—were like a shadow I couldn't shake off, falling into this and that, following us everywhere. And then I saw you at Bishops-gate, and I couldn't believe what I was seeing, even dressed in lad's clothes, as you used to be whenever I called. The most outrageously lovely thing I'd ever beheld. I fell in love with you on the spot, Nicola Coldyngham. All my plans ruined in one quick glance.' He smiled at his mother's astonishment. 'Remind me to tell you, love, what a hellish time I've had getting her to accept me.'

'Well, dear, I'm not in the least surprised if you were as nasty to little Nicola as you had been to the rest of us. You were obedient, but only just.'

'You fell in love?' said Nicola. 'No, you didn't. You were extremely bad-mannered, uncivil, and just as you'd always been.' She felt the vibrations of his laugh upon the back of her hand as he kissed it. 'Horrid man.' The memory of where his kisses had been since those early days made her feel giddy.

Lady Melrose's hand moved towards her, bringing her back to the subject. 'You discovered some of this for yourself, Nicola. May I ask how?'

'By living next door to the priory,' she said, 'where my father had stayed so much when he should have been at home with his family. The prioress sent for me.'

Then she told them, in full detail, about what the prioress had asked of her, giving them the dates, and eventually producing the tiny lock of hair that made Fergus's mother weep with sweet memories of Kitty's infancy. 'A copper-haired little mite, she was. A tiny, bonny wee lass.' She folded the envelope of paper, holding it close to her heart. 'And now she's a bonny lassie of thirteen, and you'll love her, Nicola. She's heard of you, you know.'

'Where is she now, my lady?'

'She's staying with Muir and his wife to help with

the new bairn. She has no idea, of course, that she's actually a Coldyngham instead of a Melrose. When I told Fergus about the babe, that it was not Sir Findlay's but Lord Coldyngham's, it was enough to make him go down to London and to see for himself whether he could pick up the pieces and marry the woman of his father's choice.' She turned her head upon the pillow to smile at her handsome son.

'It was not only for my father's sake,' he said, 'but for yours too, love. You so much wanted daughters, didn't you? Coldyngham daughters.'

'No, being a noblewoman has less to do with it than you think, Fergus. I saw Nicola but once when she was a wee babe in her mother's arms, at her christening, and I knew she'd be a beauty, even then. Beautiful mother, handsome father. How could she not be? And I was not wrong, either. Lovely nature, too. I guess you were only just in time, my lad.'

'I think my timing was just about perfect, Mother,' he said.

The two women's eyes met in mutual amusement, accompanied by the flick of one grey fading eyebrow. She knew her son's ways as well as anyone. And though Nicola was tempted to tell her how that fateful meeting had come about, she decided that her patient could do without the inevitable shock it would cause. Sons did not, on the whole, set about wounding the women they intended to marry.

But no one, not even Fergus or Ramond, could experience Nicola's jubilation at the certainty of having a sister after all the years of being a forlorn girl in a family of boys. Transformed with happiness, she glowed with a new and radiant light at the gifts that had suddenly come her way; the husband of her dreams, the longed-for sister, and now a very dear but frail mother. Suddenly, her family had grown in all directions. It was a miracle how everything had fallen into place so perfectly.

The emotion and the sharing of stories had exhausted Lady Melrose and soon, in the small cabin, she gave herself over to sleep and the peace that lay upon her. Lavender and Ramond sat over on the other side, whispering and holding hands, relieved that the last barriers had been lifted. It was time, they said.

In Fergus's cabin, however, there was a confrontation of sorts that any outsider watching might have misinterpreted as a clear case of the scolding woman. 'Perfect timing!' the woman was saying, scathingly. 'Your timing was quite disgraceful! You walked into my house…uninvited…unannounced, and then… Get off me! No, Fergus! Listen to me.'

She was lifted high into the air, almost thrown on to the bunk-bed and then held down with a hand over her wrists while the other began to undo the set of tiny buttons at the top of her bodice. 'I'm listening,' he said. 'Go on. You were saying?'

'I was saying, you great brute, that your arrogance is…no…you must not, Fergus. I've changed my mind after hearing all that…please!'

'After all what?' he said. In one move, he was over her, bending his head to her breasts, taking her mind off the subject. Teasing her with his lips, he gave especial attention to a newly healed wound, stirring her as he had done from the beginning in his various ways, at first unwittingly, then by every means at his disposal. 'I'd rather you didn't change your mind now,' he whispered. 'If I told you I was in love with you, would it make any difference?' His mouth continued to taste her skin, sending shivers into her thighs.

'How can I believe that, Fergus Melrose? Have you reformed?'

'No,' he said. 'Not much. But I am in love with you.'

'And your arrogance? Is that going to improve?'

'No,' he said, kissing her. When she began to soften, which did not take long, he went into more detail. 'My lovemaking might improve though, with enough practice. Could you love me a little, if it did?'

Cradling his head in her arms, she nibbled at his earlobe, the one with the gold earring in it. 'I'm past that stage,' she whispered. 'I'm loving you already. Tomorrow it will be more, and then more. I've always loved you. You must know that I have and, yes, before you ask, it was fear that put me off. You scared me half to death, Fergus.'

'Forgive me, sweetheart. I'm sorry, truly I am. I was scared too, of having to share my mother's love and of losing all respect for my father. I should have known better. Is it true that you've always loved me, sweetheart? I don't deserve it.'

'Deserving doesn't have a lot to do with it, beloved. And I wouldn't call broken ribs nothing, either. I've never felt safer than when I'm with you, saving that first dreadful meeting of ours at Bishops-gate.'

His lips were already travelling along the soft peaks and troughs of her neck and shoulders, his hands setting her alight as they helped her out of her kirtle, baring her completely. 'This is how I saw you then, Nicola Coldyngham. On your bed, helpless under me, waiting for my loving. I could have taken you then, right there, as you were, wounded and angry.' His eyes were dark with desire as she had seen them on that occasion, searching her, ready to dominate.

'Then take me now,' she said, 'as you wanted to. Come, take me.'

The light closed in upon them and the ship bounded ahead like a powerful horse through the surf, setting the stage yet again where they came together like duellists, both bent on conquest, but one of them knowing that to be vanquished was inevitable. But now there was the music of the water and the distant singing of pilgrims and their own cries of rapture. And the newest sound of all. 'I love you, Fergus. Beloved. I love you, more than I ever thought possible.'

They had five days of sailing in which to repeat their intimate and housebound loving which, after all, seemed to be the very best way of sharing the secrets of each other's heart and body. One would have thought that two such proud characters would get on each other's nerves, after a while, but that did not happen. Not once. There was far too much for them to do, to discover and enjoy. Lady Melrose needed their attention, for one, and although she made good progress, Nicola had to tell Fergus that they must marry quite soon while she was still with them to take part. That was a sobering thought. But the news on their return gave her some joy, for Muir was now the proud father of a son, his wife was well and wanted her mother-in-law to choose a name for him. Bertrand, she had said, after a friend of theirs.

There was a sadness, though, to balance the joys, one being that the two fathers would never see their offspring united, nor would Nicola be able to tell Prioress Sophie what she had so longed to hear from her lips and no one else's. To counter this, Nicola and Fergus sent a message to Kitty at Muir's home in Melrose to say that they were looking forward to seeing them all at the wedding. And what a wedding that would be.

If new relationships were about to be cemented, new partnerships were also forming at an alarming rate. Rosemary and Captain Ben Munro had decided on a life together up in Scotland and, if Sir Fergus would release him, he had a mind to set up as a merchant there, for there was money to be had in the pilgrim trade, and not half so much hard work. A wife would be a boon in that kind of living, with a wee cott on land for the winter months, and a blasphemous parrot to keep them amused until a brood of children should appear.

Ramond and Lavender, as gentle a couple as you

could find, wished to stay on as part of Nicola and Fergus's family in exactly the same capacities, just as Lady Charlotte had predicted. Ramond was indeed in his element and had never been happier, especially when Fergus offered him a house up on Moorgate.

Lotti did not like to say I-told-you-so, but her prediction regarding the miscreant Patrick came remarkably close to the truth and, on his return from Flanders, the difference was unbelievable. 'I'm hooked,' he told them, beaming and full of himself. 'I'm going to stay on the ship.'

'If Fergus doesn't mind,' said Fergus, sternly.

'Oh, yes, if you don't mind, Fergus.'

'What as, may I ask?'

'As navigator. Your captain says I'm a natural.'

'What, across to Flanders and back? Who needs a navigator?'

'No, we're going to go further afield. The captain says—'

Fergus beckoned and took him aside for a good talking-to, but his face afterwards was unreadable, and Nicola could get no more out of him.

As for the rabbit Melrose, there had been a gap in George's garden wall through which the white creature in the blue harness had hopped when no one was looking, with the result that the children reported seeing a litter of brown and white baby rabbits in the adjoining orchard. 'They must have been seeing things, George dear,' Lotti said.

'No, they haven't. I've seen them too. Melrose was

never a girl's name. He should never have been given aquamarines to wear, either.'

George's opinion about Fergus's other gift to Nicola was perhaps less critical, even a little on the envious side, for on the day of their wedding, Fergus had laid around her throat the most amazing necklace of rubies any of them had ever seen. And, like the first time, there were a few tears, though now he stayed to mop them.

'I have something for you too,' she said, laughing a little.

'Where?' he said, placing a hand over her beautiful gown of violet brocade, low down. 'There?'

'Yes,' she said. 'Down there. A brand new Fergus Melrose, I think.'

'Wonderful woman. Start choosing some genuine girl's names, my love. You know how men sometimes get these things wrong.'

So they called her Beth, after Lady Melrose, which would have pleased her.

* * * * *

**Four sisters.
A family legacy.
And someone is out to destroy it.**

**A captivating new limited
continuity, launching June 2006**

The most beautiful hotel in New Orleans,
and someone is out to destroy it. But mystery,
danger and some surprising family revelations
and discoveries won't stop the Marchand sisters
from protecting their birthright…
and finding love along the way.

**Hidden in the secrets of antiquity,
lies the unimagined truth...**

Introducing

a brand-new line filled with mystery
and suspense, action and adventure,
and a fascinating look into history.

And it all begins with DESTINY.

In a sealed crypt in
France, where the
terrifying legend of
the beast of Gevaudan
begins to unravel,
Annja Creed discovers
a stunning artifact
that will seal her destiny.

*Available every other
month starting
July 2006, wherever
you buy books.*

Paying the Playboy's Price

(Silhouette Desire #1732)

by

EMILIE ROSE

Juliana Alden is determined to have her last—
her only—fling before settling down. And she's
found the perfect candidate: bachelor Rex Tanner.
He's pure playboy charm…but can she afford
his price?

Trust Fund Affairs: They've just spent a fortune—
the bachelors had better be worth it.

Don't miss the other titles in this series:

EXPOSING THE EXECUTIVE'S SECRETS (July)
BENDING TO THE BACHELOR'S WILL (August)

On sale this June from Silhouette Desire.

*Available wherever books are sold, including most
bookstores, supermarkets, discount stores and drugstores.*

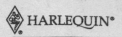

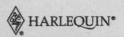